OPERATION
COUNTERPUNCH

OPERATION COUNTERPUNCH

Marc Marlow

Fresh Ink Group
Guntersville

Operation Counterpunch

Fresh Ink Group
An Imprint of:
The Fresh Ink Group, LLC
1021 Blount Avenue, #931
Guntersville, AL 35976
Email: info@FreshInkGroup.com
FreshInkGroup.com

Edition 1.0   2020

Book design by Amit Dey / FIG
Cover design by Stephen Geez / FIG
Cover art by Anik / FIG
Associate publisher Lauren A. Smith / FIG

Cataloging-in-Publication Recommendations:
FIC031050 FICTION / Thrillers / Military
FIC031060 FICTION / Thrillers / Political
FIC032000 FICTION / War & Military

Library of Congress Control Number: 2020904520

ISBN-13: 978-1-947867-78-9 Papercover
ISBN-13: 978-1-947867-77-2 Hardcover
ISBN-13: 978-1-947867-79-6 Ebooks

For
Maxwell

Acknowledgements

Thanks to **Greg Koewler** for his support and assistance with some of the details.

Thanks to my publishing crew at **Fresh Ink Group**: Cover artist **Anik**, associate publisher **Lauren A. Smith,** book designer **Amit Dey**, and my publisher/editor **Stephen Geez**. Thanks also to the video crew: **Geez** and **Beem Weeks**.

Table of Contents

Foreword

All people given the choice, a true choice, no intimidation; will choose to be free. History is replete with examples of peoples being subjugated under varying degrees of tyranny, by both foreign or domestic tyrants and their collaborators, then eventually rising up and challenging their oppressors in pursuit of freedom.

At the beginning of World War II, the Allied Forces (except Russia at that point) saw their own freedom threatened by the violent aggressive behavior of Hitler's Germany and the other Axis powers. They met the challenge and defeated Hitler's doctrine of hate, fear, intimidation, and death. However, as history has sometimes indicated the true freedom loving people, in the case of World War II the original members of the Allied Forces, find they must align themselves with a less than ideal partner, in this case Stalin's Russia, in order to finally defeat the enemy at the gate, in this case Germany and Japan.

One of the results of this seemingly necessary alliance, and the backdrop to this story, is the division of the Korean peninsula. The people of Korea have a long history. Like many older civilizations, up until the late 19th century, government on the Korean peninsula was one monarchy or another. Often the Korean monarchs would find themselves under the sway of China or Japan depending upon which neighbor had the upper hand during a particular period in history. In 1895 Japan had the upper hand with the defeat of China in the First Sino-Japanese War. Seeing an opening, Russia sought to expand its influence in Manchuria and Korea, which led to war between the Empire of Japan and the Russian Empire. The Empire of Japan won the war in 1905 setting up the complete Japanese occupation of Korea in 1910, which lasted until 1945.

In May of 1945 the Allied Forces, at that point including Russia, defeated Germany followed by the defeat of Japan in September 1945. After experiencing the deaths of perhaps sixty million souls the world was ready for the war to be over. But just as the original Allied Forces eventually found they needed to include Russia in the alliance, a less than best partner, less than best decisions had to be made at the end of the war to mollify Russia, such as the division of Germany and other parts of Europe, and the division of the Korean Peninsula.

The end of World War II was a good thing. Many people of the world since the end of World War II have enjoyed a relatively peaceful and prosperous existence, free to pursue their happiness. However, since the end of World War II many other people in the world have had to endure tyranny, and in some instances crushing tyranny. One of the worst examples of tyranny ever imposed on a people is the so-called Democratic People's Republic of Korea also known as North Korea. A country formed in the crucible of the end of World War II.

This is a story of one boy's pursuit of happiness who was born in 1997 but had the misfortune of being born north of the 38th Parallel on the Korean Peninsula.

Chapter One

Escape

D ew fell heavy on his exposed leg. His feet were cold. Gun-ho used his index finger to tenderly move her hair from his mother's cold face as morning finally arrived.

He kept running over in his mind Jae-sun's instruction: *Gun-ho, you must be strong. You must lie still beside your mother's body all the way to the pit. You must not make a sound!*

He didn't want to be strong! He wanted to cry out, to succumb to the anguish he felt over losing her, losing her so violently. But, so far, somehow, he summoned the discipline to lie still and be silent.

A mixture of blood and dew dripped from the fatal wound of the man lying mostly over him, dripping into his left eye. He closed it tight, while leaving his right eye open so he could see his mother. He resisted lifting his hand to wipe away the drip as it rolled down the side of his nose and into the corner of his mouth.

He froze!

Two soldiers were approaching the truck, Gun-ho's heart pounding in his throat! One of them laughed. The other cleared his throat and spit. Gun-ho clenched his teeth hard as one of them jumped up onto the back.

Cigarette smoke added to the stench of death all around him. The one on the back laughed wildly. "I will piss all over these bastards!"—a final effort to dehumanize and degrade.

The warm urine splattered on Gun-ho's exposed leg. Then a lit cigarette hit his leg, rolled back and stopped, trapped by the back of his leg and the corpse pressing from behind. As the butt cherry seared his skin, Gun-ho bit his lip and called on every sense of survival not to move.

The man jumped off the truck.

Both doors opened and closed.

Then the engine started. As the truck moved, Gun-ho bent his left knee forward, allowing the butt to fall off his leg.

The truck stopped. Someone said, "Destination?"

"Burn pit."

"How many bodies do you have?"

"Look, man, what does it matter? We are just going to dump them!"

"Hey, I must fill out this form, so don't be a prick. Let us see, date? M-A-Y 20th, 2009. Okay, how many bodies?"

"Twenty-four. Can we go now?"

The screech of the opening prison-camp gate landed hard on Gun-ho's ears. The truck began to move forward.

Jae-sun's escape plan might work! It just might work!

Gun-ho's fellow passengers shifted with each pothole during the ten-minute drive to the pit. The corpse lying mostly over him ended up rolling past him and came to rest against the siderail on the driver's side of the truck.

Gun-ho was grateful for the reprieve from the dripping. He allowed himself the luxury of pulling the collar of his shirt forward and using it to wipe his eye and the left side of his face.

The driver slowed, turned sharply to the left, and stopped. He engaged the clutch and ground the stick into reverse. When he got it in, the truck lurched and died. The driver restarted the engine and this time got the truck into reverse more smoothly.

Jae-sun's instruction came to mind. *Be aware of your surroundings, and once they begin to back the truck up to the edge of the pit, look to see if you have an opportunity to slip off the back so they won't be able to see you in the side mirrors.*

Gun-ho lifted his head and turned to his left to see out the back. The pit was still ten meters away. He was about to extract himself from the pile of bodies when the truck came to a stop, short of the pit.

He quickly lay back down.

Both truck doors opened.

The passenger shouted, "What is the matter with the damn thing?"

"I don't know. The power switch for the hydraulic pump must be broken; the bed won't go up!"

"I don't want to unload these bastards by hand!"

"Do you want to take them back to camp? If we do that, we might be joining them!"

Uh oh!

Chapter Two

Tears of Joy

Jae-sun stood beside his mama, holding her hand. His daddy hailed a cab from the curb of Union Station.

"Embassy, Republic of Korea, please, sir. I have address for you."

"I know the place, buddy. I'll have ya there in a jiffy."

As the cab pulled into traffic, heading to his daddy's new assignment in America, Jae-sun got comfortable sitting up on his knees on the back seat between his parents; now he could see out the windows. After such a long trip he could hardly contain his excitement. He wanted to see the embassy. He wanted to see everything.

"Mama, what smells so good?"

"It's the cherry blossoms, Jae-sun. Aren't they beautiful?"

Jae-sun breathed deep; he even liked the way America smelled.

"You folks moving to Washington?"

"Excuse my English, please. Yes, I am new secretary for Ambassador Republic of Korea."

"I guess you folks like ole Harry S. He and MacArthur really took it to the Japs, eh?"

"Yes, sir, very thankful. We have a country again."

Jae-sun's daddy nudged him and pointed as the embassy came into view. His mother's tears fell onto the back of his hand. Jae-sun sensed his mother's complete happiness. He turned and hugged her tight while enjoying his father's approving pat on his back.

*   *   *

Jae-sun marveled at the bedroom in the embassy, his very own bedroom. He stood just inside the door, giddy with delight. He took in the aroma of new paint, light blue with horses galloping on a wallpaper strip around the room. His bed even had a horse themed bed spread.

"Do you like it, Jae-sun?"

"Oh, Mama, I love it!"

"Let's put your things away, Jae-sun. No time to lose. Tomorrow we will go tour a school for you. It's called the Randall Hyland School. I want you to learn to speak English like an American boy. That will be very helpful to you as you get older."

The following Monday Jae-sun woke early and dressed quickly, anxious for his first day of school. On most days his father's driver from the embassy would take him, but on this first day, his mother and father brought him and introduced him to the headmaster, Mr. Hodges. Jae-sun patiently listened to them discuss his curriculum. As his parents prepared to leave, he bit on his lip, determined to be brave.

As they walked from the office down the hall to his classroom, Mr. Hodges held out his hand for Jae-sun. Mr. Hodges seemed like he was ten feet tall, but a good man.

Mr. Hodges led him to Room 4 and motioned for him to wait in the hall—message understood. He returned a few moments later with Jae-sun's very pretty teacher, Mrs. Price.

She easily squatted down to make eye contact, welcoming him with a smile. He looked into her eyes, confident a beautiful person, inside and out, had just entered his life. She stood back up, took him by the hand, and walked into the classroom—into the gaze of ten students checking Jae-sun out. The tops of his ears burned, but he resisted the urge to reach up and touch them. He counted six boys and four girls.

One of the girls smiled at him from her desk in the back of the room next to the windows. She looked cute in her powder blue jumper over a plain white blouse with yellow ribbons tied on the ends of beautiful long braids. Her bright blue eyes held his gaze.

Ms. Price began to speak, and all refocused on their teacher. Jae-sun did not know exactly what she said, but the blue-eyed girl's hand shot up so aggressively that Jae-sun recoiled slightly and his eyebrows shot up.

"Thank you, Rebecca!" She motioned toward the desk next to her.

Jae-sun quickly got the idea that he was supposed to sit next to Rebecca; concealing the smile forming on his face was difficult; school was going to be fun.

*   *   *

Time passed quickly. Within eight weeks Jae-sun understood everything Ms. Price said during lecture or when giving instruction to the class. Rebecca and Jae-sun were becoming great friends. She came from Oklahoma. Her father served in the Army and worked at the Pentagon. Rebecca's bright mind impressed Jae-sun; many English idioms and little sayings from the South were added to his vocabulary through their friendship.

During evenings Jae-sun tagged along behind Earl, custodian for the public areas of the Korean Embassy. A black gentleman and deacon at the Baptist church, Earl taught Jae-sun many English words and the fundamentals of Christian faith. Jae-sun liked Earl, his stories and his accent. He eagerly absorbed the concepts of right and wrong from a Western Christian perspective.

As fourth grade began at the Randall Hyland School, Jae-sun felt like an upper classman. The Korean War broke out in the summer of 1950, so the family stayed in the United States throughout the war. First, second, and third grades went very well for Jae-sun; and as fourth grade began, he felt appreciated by his teachers. They marveled over his exceptional command of mathematics and language.

On the first day of fourth grade, Jae-sun stopped at the office to determine this year's room assignment, Room 12—Mr. Clarke, a new room and a new teacher. Mr. Clarke stood by the door waiting for each of his students. He introduced himself to Jae-sun and gave him a seat assignment. Mr. Clarke meant business.

Delighted at seeing Rebecca in the class, Jae-sun smiled and waved enroute to his assigned seat. No doubt the war extended her father's assignment, too.

Jae-sun approached the desk. His desk mate had already arrived, so he extended his hand. "Hi. My name is Jae-sun."

Jae-sun looked up, and up even more as the boy stood to an impressive five feet and extended a hand back to Jae-sun. "My name is Billy. Are you a Jap?"

He smiled as he looked up at Billy, which seemed to soften his demeanor. "No, I am Korean."

Mr. Clarke's stern but subdued voice interjected from behind.

Speaking quietly so as not to embarrass Billy, the teacher said, "Mr. Johnson, even though many people use the word *Jap,* I do not want you to use that word. We defeated the Japanese; they are our allies now. Using such a term diminishes you, not them."

Three weeks into the school year, Jae-sun could tell that Billy was struggling with their math lessons. It bothered Billy; he just couldn't quite grasp the concepts. Billy lived for competition; he tried his hardest at everything. He wanted to grow up and be a naval officer just like his father. Jae-sun wondered how he might help him.

Mr. Clarke's schedule had the math lesson just before the noon recess and lunch period. One day, just before Halloween, Billy was having an especially hard time with the lesson, frustrated almost to tears. Already finished, Jae-sun used the time to read a Korean story book. He stole side glances, trying to assess Billy's frustration level.

"Hey, Billy, let's stay in at lunch. I'll help you."

"You'd be willing to do that?"

"Yessum!" Rebecca had taught Jae-sun that word.

For the rest of fourth grade and through the fifth, Jae-sun eagerly stayed in at least two days a week to help Billy.

School came easy for Jae-sun, but he also enjoyed a challenge; extra reading became the solution of choice. Jae-sun and Billy's friendship had blossomed during fourth grade, and now they happily discovered they shared the same home room in sixth grade. It didn't matter that Billy was still the biggest kid in their class, and Jae-sun one of the smallest; they were the *best* of friends.

Billy's mother had decided he could begin walking the ten blocks to school, but Jae-sun lived seven miles away, so when he arrived home after the first day he walked into his father's office and said, "Dad, six blocks from school my friend's route intersects with mine near a park. May I ask our chauffeur to begin dropping me there?"

"Yes, you may."

"Keen!"

"Keen? What is keen?"

"It's an English word, Dad. It means *That's Great!*"

His father looked over the top of his glasses and smiled.

One day Jae-sun arrived at the park to meet Billy as usual. They always left themselves plenty of time, but Billy was running a bit late. Jae-sun sat on a bench and enjoyed all the daffodils planted around the trees; they were just beginning to bloom.

Moments later three older boys he didn't recognize walked up to Jae-sun and began poking and taunting. This sort of thing had never happened to Jae-sun before, but his bright mind could not control his sharp tongue. Even though remaining silent may have been a better response, his cutting remarks belittling their cumulative intelligence seemed to provoke them further.

When the ringleader jerked him up by his coat collar, Jae-sun implied that the kid's mother must be a moron to have produced such a child.

The kid responded by throwing Jae-sun to the ground.

Jae-sun wished he hadn't heard what the ringleader said next. "Hold his arms, boys! I'm gonna teach you a lesson!"

"Hey!" shouted Billy, trotting up from behind.

Jae-sun and the kid reacted together.

Billy let his best fastball fly with a green apple. The apple caught the kid square on the nose.

Jae-sun winced at the blood, pushing the kid off, hands still over his face and screaming.

The other two boys rushed Billy, the one on his left two steps ahead.

Jae-sun cringed—two on one! His anxiety turned to pride as Billy calmly kept his guard down, as if to encourage their charge.

At the last moment Billy popped the kid coming on his left square in the jaw with a right hook—one down.

Jae-sun couldn't believe how fast Billy moved. He took a half step back with his right leg and landed a left precisely onto the side of the other kid's temple.

As Jae-sun drew his knees up to stand, Billy reached down and pulled him up. "Let's go to school."

"Okay! Thanks for getting me outta that jam."

"You bet." Billy reached down and picked up his apple. "I'm sure glad Mom made me bring this." He tossed it in the air once and put it back in his pocket.

They arrived at school to Rebecca waiting for them on the front steps, waving wildly.

Jae-sun and Billy returned her greeting, but never said a word, like it never happened.

Chapter Three

Somebody's Savior

Art Jackson marked his nineteenth birthday with the whole family all around their yellow-top kitchen table. His seven-year-old sister helped blow out the candles. Life had already toughened Art; his dad had been killed in a trucking accident five years earlier. Since then, he'd been the man of the house, oldest of seven. His was one of the poorest families in St. Paul, so being very resourceful, Art made sure that his mother never had to let her children go hungry. Over the years, one way or another, Art had contact with almost every police officer on the St. Paul force, and he'd appeared in front of Judge Murray at least three times. Now Art found himself standing in front of Judge Murray again. Art read the Judge's body language—he definitely looked pissed.

The trouble began when Art peeked in the Dumpster behind Safeway. Inside lay six good heads of lettuce, right on top and unsoiled. He found a new-looking box on the dock and started loading them. Cigarette smoke invaded the cool night air. Art stood and turned toward the back of the store.

"Hey! What are you doing over there?"

In the doorway stood a doughy twenty-something with a cigarette in his hand. Art recognized him from freshman year—George Phelps. Back then, Art had to eat a lot to tip the scale at 140 pounds, all 5' 6" of him. As a senior, George use to taunt and pick on him.

"I'm just salvaging some lettuce."

George threw his cigarette down in a shower of sparks and grabbed a broom. He jumped down off the loading dock and shouted back to a co-worker. "Thief!"

He evaded the first swing of the broom handle.

He easily avoided contact on the next swing, then disarmed George and tossed the broom back to him as he retreated.

A police cruiser rounded the corner just as George fell backwards and hit his head on the edge of the loading dock.

Art ran to help George, but the police saw an aggressive movement, and by the time they jumped out of their squad car Art's hands were covered with George's blood.

It looked bad, but really it was just a minor scrape. Being a diva, George played on the sympathies of the officers.

Art knew the charges were serious—theft and assault. Standing in front of Judge Murray now, he studied the tips of his shoes.

"Arthur Jackson."

"Yes, sir."

"You've been charged with assault and theft. You have your public defender here—how do you plead?"

"Not guilty, sir."

"Did you already know this guy?"

"Yes, sir, from school."

"Okay, go ahead and tell me your version events."

"Well, he fell because I took the broom away from him. I thought he was going to swing it again."

"You didn't attack him?"

"No, sir. I rushed over to help him up."

"Mr. Phelps, what do you say? Did you see him take the lettuce out of the store?"

George shook his head.

"Mr. Phelps, I can't hear your head waggle; you have to speak."

"That all sounds about right, sir."

"Mr. Jackson here didn't attack you?"

"No, sir. He tried to help me up."

"Okay, I've heard enough of this. Mr. Jackson, I don't ever want to see you in my courtroom again, so I'm going to give you a choice. Either you can go down tomorrow and join the service, or the next time I see you in here I'm going to put you in jail. What's it going to be?"

"Well, sir, I—I think I'll go join the service."

"Good! The Navy's a good choice. Son, you are going to be somebody's savior someday. Now go home. Bailiff, we are going to take a five-minute break."

Art walked out into the hallway.

Mom… What am I going to tell Mom?

*   *   *

On Thursday morning, April 4th, 1985, the sun shone brightly. Art lived on the west side of St. Paul. The Naval Recruiter's office was near County Road B2 W and Highway 51, about three miles away, so running seemed better than the bus.

Two years earlier, Art had saved his money and bought a car, but his little sister got sick. He sold the car to help cover her medical treatment. These days Art ran most places, which put him in great shape. Unlike many of his peers, Art held little regard for tobacco, which added to his well-being. He stopped at Mr. Carlson's barber shop and got a fresh haircut for the occasion. A handsome sort, anyway, but with a fresh haircut and his natural physique, he was a real standout.

Art walked into the recruiter's office at 11:00 a.m. There to greet him stood Petty Officer Pete Wilson.

"Good Morning, son."

His was a slow, mellow, deep voice, letting Art know that Minnesota wasn't home.

"Good morning, sir." A genuine, man's man—Art instantly liked the petty officer.

"Well, what can I do for you this morning, son?"

"I came to join the Navy."

"And why is that?"

Art thought about that question. He'd never been in any real trouble that could be tracked, but he was reluctant to share with the petty officer that the Judge told him to come join the Navy. "I'm just ready to get out of Minnesota."

"Well, first things first. Do you have a high-school diploma?"

"Yes, sir."

"Are you married?"

"No, sir—free as a bird."

"Okay then."

Art found himself scheduled over at the medical wing for an exam and an eye test that very afternoon. The nurse there introduced herself as Angela Beal.

"Okay, Mr. Jackson, we're going to create your medical chart, record your height and weight, and check your blood pressure."

"Yes, ma'am. You're not from Minnesota, are you, Nurse Beal?"

"No, no I'm not, Mr. Jackson. Where do you think I'm from?"

"I'd say Texas."

"You'd be right."

At just thirty years old and hard not to notice, she obviously enjoyed sparring with the recruits.

"Well, Mr. Jackson, I'll need you to dress down to your skivvies."

"Skivvies, ma'am?"

"Your underwear."

She turned her back, walking to the table to get her clipboard.

The medical intake area was a large room, about the size of a school gymnasium. It was a wide-open space, plenty of room for several young men to get checked in at the same time, but now it was just Art and the nurse. Art had run to the recruiting station wearing nothing but trunks, a jock strap, and a baggy hooded sweatshirt—no underwear.

As the oldest of three boys and four girls—plus his mom—all sharing one bathroom, he did not have the luxury of modesty growing up. He respected Nurse Beal's authority, so off went the sweatshirt and running trunks.

Nurse Beal flushed when she turned around from getting her clipboard, so he looked away.

"Are you all right, ma'am?"

"Yes, yes, I'm fine, Mr. Jackson."

As she wrote his vitals on the chart, she gripped her pen so tightly her fingertips turned white. "Six foot four and a half," she said quietly, pausing to take a deep breath. "Two hundred-twenty pounds." She looked back at him again, sighed quietly, and continued. "Twenty-twenty vision, b-p one-ten over seventy, hair blond, eyes blue…"

As he slipped his trucks back on, Nurse Beal call Dr. Mills on the intercom to come perform his part of the exam.

A man in white coat walked in from a side door. He nodded to Art and walked up to nurse Beal to receive the chart.

"Good luck, Mr. Jackson."

"Thank you, Nurse Beal."

After Dr. Mills finished his examination, he put his hand on Art's shoulder. "Son, you are as fit as a fiddle!"

Dr. Mills's instructions were to go back to the intake office, medical forms in hand. Art glanced at the clock and held his stomach—almost two o' clock. Walking back across the courtyard to the intake office, he encountered Nurse Beal sitting on the bench, eating her lunch.

"Well, Dr. Mills says I am fit as a fiddle."

"I would have put money on that. Are you hungry? I have extra here."

"Are you sure?"

He sat and gratefully accepted the half sandwich. They visited for about ten minutes. Art thanked her for the food and walked back into Petty Officer Wilson's office.

Wilson stood when Art entered and extended his hand. Art appreciated the gesture.

"Well, how'd you do, son?"

"Dr. Mills says I'm fit as a fiddle!" Art handed him the form from Dr. Mills with his left hand, his right still appropriately gripping Petty Officer Wilson's hand in greeting.

Wilson looked at the form for effect for a few seconds.

"Take a seat, son. First of all, the U. S. Navy would be proud to count you among its personnel. What we need to do is to figure out what role you would like to have in Uncle Sam's Navy. Do you have any expectations or predetermined goals in mind?"

"Sir, I expected you folks would tell me what you need, and then that is what I'd do. I didn't know I had a choice."

"Well, son, there are choices, but if you don't have a well-developed preference in mind, maybe we can figure out what you'd like. Do you get seasick?"

"No, and I know that because the year before my dad died, he took me up to Alaska to visit his brother. My uncle lives in a little village out on the Arctic Chain; he's a commercial fisherman. While my dad and I were there, my uncle took us halibut fishing three times. Each time we experienced rough water. It never bothered me; in fact, I thought it was fun."

"How about swimming? Do you like to swim? Are you fearful of the water?"

"No, sir, my brothers and I swim in the Mississippi all the time! After my dad died, we never had much money, so we just entertained ourselves in ways that didn't take money. On hot days the Mississippi does a pretty good job."

Petty Officer Wilson sat forward in his chair. "Son, step out for a moment, I need to make a call."

"Yes, sir." Art stepped out and closed the door. He breathed deeply and exhaled slowly.

Did I just screw up?

He spied a brochure rack across the room. He shook his hands at the wrists, rotated his shoulders, and walked directly to the rack, determined to come up with an answer to what he wanted to do in the Navy.

Art glanced over his shoulder to steal a glimpse of Petty Officer Wilson through the office window.

I wonder who he's calling.

*   *   *

Petty Officer Wilson waited for the click of the door latch to announce privacy, then picked up his phone and called Commander Jerry Peel at the Navy SEAL Training Facility in Coronado, California. Wilson had served under Commander Peel years earlier; they had a great relationship. Peel's secretary answered and told Wilson that the commander would be right on the line.

"Pete, how the hell are ya?"

"I'm fine, Commander, just fine."

After a few minutes of catching up, Wilson asked the commander when his next SEAL Training class would begin. The commander told him it started the following Tuesday and that all the men accepted to the class had to report by Monday evening.

"Do you have any open slots?"

"Well, I didn't until about an hour ago. I just got word that one of my incoming guys got into a car wreck, so he's gonna be out of commission for eight weeks. Whatta ya got?"

"Commander, I have a young man who would fit right in. He has a great attitude and he's built like Charles Atlas."

"Well, Pete, if you have a good one, send him down. I always need more grist for the mill."

"Okay, Commander. I'll call you later this afternoon and let you know if I am sending him your way."

*   *   *

Just as Art plucked one brochure from the information rack that held all the various Navy jobs a recruit could consider, Petty Officer Wilson rapped on the office window.

As Art walked in, before Petty Officer Wilson had a chance to say anything, Art held up a SEAL brochure. "Sir, this is what I'd like to do."

A big smile appeared on Petty Officer Wilson's face.

"Well, son, this is your lucky day."

Petty Officer Wilson finished all the paperwork and gave Art a travel voucher to fly from Minneapolis/St. Paul to San Diego. It all happened so fast, but Art was very excited. He had told his mother about joining the Navy when he left the house that morning, but he never expected to be flying out in three days. It was all right, though; he'd be able to send his mother most of his paycheck to help cover the family expenses.

At five o'clock Art walked out of the Navy Recruiting Center with his packet in hand. Taking the bus home seemed like a good option. He started walking toward bus stop, some 200 years to the west. A nice truck exiting the parking lot caught his eye. It stopped on the curb cut in front of him, and the tinted passenger window lowered.

Art smiled, recognizing Nurse Beal at the wheel.

"Need a ride, Sailor?"

"Yes, ma'am."

He climbed into the truck.

Being in the Navy is starting out pretty good.

Chapter Four

Finders Keepers

"**H**appy Birthday, Gus!"

The greeting from his grandmother startled him, not knowing anyone else was up.

"Thank you, Grandma. Thanks to FDR, I get to eat pumpkin pie *and* birthday cake!"

Gus Erickson turned eighteen on Thanksgiving Day, November 20th, in 1941. President Roosevelt opened a can of worms in '39 when he moved Thanksgiving up a week. Gus's family, Republicans all, just knew it had to be a big conspiracy. The truth: November 1939 had five Thursdays, and retailers petitioned the president to proclaim turkey-day a week earlier so they'd have more time between Thanksgiving and Christmas.

Since President Lincoln, the date was set each year by presidential proclamation, traditionally the last Thursday of the month. Gus knew that his folks, and a lot of other people, were pretty worked up about the whole thing; so in 1941 President Roosevelt acknowledged his mistake and Congress officially made Thanksgiving the fourth Thursday, but the legislation would take effect beginning in 1942. So, in 1941, Gus's birthday fell on Thanksgiving Day.

"I'm heading out to milk the cows, Grandma."

"Okay, Gus. I'll have your breakfast ready when you get done."

Gus entered the world on his great grandfather's homestead on the south bank of the Siuslaw River, downstream from Mapleton a bit. An only child, he grew up in a very rural three-generation household. His grandmother, a tough hardworking woman, never wasted anything. The family didn't have a lot of money, but they never wanted for anything. His father and grandfather would harvest a few logs each year from the homestead to sell to the mill. They always planted a big garden and raised cattle, sheep, hogs, and chickens. From the time he turned seven, Gus milked the cows every morning by himself. His mother, Grace, chilled the milk in the spring they used for water to the house; and his grandmother, Charlotte, made their butter and cheese.

The Morgans were invited over for Thanksgiving every year. There were eight in the Morgan family—in all, thirteen around the table for dinner. And coming up after dinner, all the deserts: pumpkin pie, blackberry pie, apple pie, and a birthday cake Gus's grandmother made from scratch.

The Morgan kids heard a rumor about ice cream, a rare treat. Gus loved his grandpa Henry, and Gus knew his grandfather adored him. Gus appreciated his grandpa making the ice cream that the Morgan kids were anxious to taste. He rigged the hand crank gear on top of the ice cream maker to a shaft and belt driven from a water wheel in the creek. Henry just kept the ice and salt fresh around the tub and let the creek do the work. He'd never gone to school, but Gus zealously held to the notion that no one alive could match his grandpa's intellect. He really could do anything with almost nothing.

Gus stood in awe of the Thanksgiving table overflowing with all kinds of good things: roasted venison, from a deer Gus killed the week before; roasted turkey from a bird Gus's mother raised from a chick, just for this occasion; mashed garlic potatoes that Grandma made with potatoes and garlic from their garden; steamed broccoli; sweet potatoes; lettuce salad with cucumber, peas, and water chestnuts—a real feast.

*   *   *

On Sunday morning, December 7th, Gus milked his usual three cows. He poured the milk through cheese cloth into a ten-gallon milk can and set the can into the spring to cool the milk. He walked back into his grandfather's shop. Grandpa sat by the wood stove, drinking a cup of black coffee. Gus grabbed a mug off the shelf above work bench, took a shop rag, and used it to insulate the metal handle of the coffee pot sitting on the edge of the stove. Gus didn't quite understand why, but black coffee sure tasted good. He set a piece of un-split alder on its end and sat down with his grandfather next to the stove.

Gus's dad, Joe, was in the pit under their Caterpillar dozer, draining the oil. He climbed the ladder from the pit, poured himself a cup of coffee, and leaned against the post, the three of them just visiting and enjoying the moment.

Shep, their collie, began to bark at the sound of a car coming up the driveway, which was kind of odd for a Sunday morning.

Gus stepped over to the window. "It's Mel."

Mel owned a little sawmill downstream from the Erickson home-stead. When the Ericksons had logs to sell, they always sold them to Mel. Mel lived next to Hwy 126 and had power from the co-op, and he had a radio. As he burst into the shop, Gus's dad turned toward the door.

"Hey ya, Mel. Is everything all right?"

"It's Japan! They just bombed the hell out of our fleet at Pearl Harbor!"

The Erickson boys were trying to process the news.

Henry scratched his head.

"Pearl Harbor—where the hell is that?"

"Hawai'i. It's an island way out in the Pacific Ocean where we have a naval base."

"What does it mean?"

"It means, sonny, there's gonna be a war."

Gus looked over at his grandfather—rail thin, always had been. Gus had seen him a million times, just like now, legs crossed, leaned back with his arms across his chest.

Henry rubbed the back of his neck.

"A war—I don't like the sound of that. My little brother died in the Spanish American War in '98."

Gus measured his dad's reaction—poking at a rock on the floor with the tip of his boot. Gus knew his dad fought in Europe during The Great War. He could read the worry on his face and knew his dad was concerned for his son.

Mel broke the silence. "I am going to spread the word. I'll come back when I have more news."

The Erickson boys just sat there in silence. The plans they'd just been talking about for spring would all be changing.

About six o'clock, Mel's car came up the driveway. He reported that the president was going to address Congress and the nation the next day at 9:30 a.m. Pacific Time. He invited them over to his place to listen to the speech on his radio.

Gus's grandparents opted to stay home, so Gus and his folks drove his dad's 1934 Ford truck over to Mel's place. Two weeks later, Gus was in the Army—four months later, on a troop ship heading for Hawai'i, and who knows where after that.

*   *   *

The war was brutal, but for whatever reason, Gus had a guardian angel on his shoulder the entire conflict. He left the Philippines with MacArthur in 1942, when they retreated, and remained with MacArthur until 1944, when they recaptured the islands. Gus fought in several combat situations; he'd seen all the horror of war, but somehow came through unscathed. In August of 1945, Gus's unit was stationed in China, attached to Lt. General Hodge. He received word that the Japanese surrendered. The mood in their camp—Euphoric!

The surrender ceremony was scheduled for September 2nd in Tokyo Harbor. Over the course of the war, Gus had been promoted to captain—no small feat. He left Oregon a very shy, cautious eighteen-year-old boy. The horrors of war turned him into a battle-hardened, still-cautious, about-to-turn-twenty-two-year-old man. He'd been in The Pacific Theater the entire war.

Lt. General Hodge briefed Gus and the other junior officers about their next move: their unit would go to Korea and be the military government there, south of the 38th Parallel.

Gus arrived at Inchon Harbor on September 8th and found chaos in Korea. The negotiations resulted in the Americans and Russians jointly administering the country. The agreement called for the Russian zone to be above the 38th Parallel, and the American zone, south of the 38th. When word spread that the Russians and their communist allies were going to be in charge in the North, 400,000 refugees flooded the South to avoid the tyranny they knew would follow.

Captain Erickson's orders were to create a safe perimeter around their operations center. They searched and secured the buildings around their administration building. The goal was to prevent snipers and other malcontents from causing trouble. The American military brass decided to utilize many of the Japanese bureaucrats, already in place, to help manage the American sector of Korea. That decision proved very unpopular with the local Koreans and their leaders. The Japanese had treated the Koreans horribly for the past 35 years, and the Koreans did not want the Japanese to remain in any way; but Gus had his orders: make a secure perimeter.

He got to work.

Gus and his men were on the fifth floor, the top floor, of a building south of the administration building. They'd already barricaded the entire first floor so the building would remain secure once they finished searching.

Gus ordered Private Scofield to lead a group to the north end of the floor. He watched apprehensively as his men carefully made their way up the hallway.

Scofield shouted, "Captain Erickson, we need your help!"

Gus approached the door Private Scofield shouted from. Frantic wailing came from inside—the distressed cries of a woman.

Gus carefully peeked around the doorjamb, then entered the room. Five of his men stood in a "ready for anything" position, rifles poised. He glanced around and saw no immediate danger, then assessed the woman wailing on her knees with her hands up, eyes cast down, obviously terrified. She wore a long shirt that came over her legs like a nightgown, no shoes—no hidden grenades or other weapons.

"Scofield, what is going on in here?"

"Captain, we were searching this area room by room, and we found her—" He pointed at the woman with the muzzle of his rifle. "In that closet."

Gus handed Scofield his rifle and walked over to the woman, who was still crying in terror. He knelt down to touch her on the shoulder.

She recoiled and gasped so hard she lost her air. Once she regained her breath, she began wailing again.

Gus reached across and gently held her shoulder, then began to rub her back. "Shhh, shhh, shhh."

Gus ordered Scofield to go find their interpreter, and the rest of his men to step back and guard the opening to the room.

He held the woman while gently rubbing her back.

After four or five minutes, she stopped crying, but continued to gasp and quiver like a small child winding down from a tantrum. Her lips pressing against the inside of his forearm felt chapped—she needed water.

Gus retrieved the canteen off his hip. He unscrewed the top with his thumb, then drew his left hand toward himself to pour a bit of water into his palm, wetting her cheek.

She tensed up when she felt the water.

He smiled with satisfaction as she eagerly cupped the back of his hand in hers and sipped the bit of water.

For the first time, she slightly relaxed.

He lifted her chin with his finger, then gently swept her hair from her face.

Their eyes met.

Gus read her mind—he was not Japanese; she wasn't going to die—not today, anyway.

Gus looked upon her face and saw a very beautiful young woman, then offered her more water.

She swallowed hard twice, then drew her hands up under her chin and collapsed into the crook of his elbow with her face buried in his chest. Her desperate cries of terror gave way to sobs of relief and grief all at the same time.

Down on both knees now, Gus cradled her in his arms and let her cry.

Ten minutes later Scofield returned with their interpreter, Myon, a Korean ex-pat serving his countrymen.

The woman stopped crying, still curled up in a fetal position cradled in Gus's arms.

He could feel all her ribs. He asked one of his men to find something to drape over the woman, then picked her up like a feather and sat her on an old couch. He covered her with the blanket and gave her a cracker and some peanut butter from a ration kit. He positioned two chairs in front of her, one for the interpreter and one for himself.

"Tell her my name is Gus," he told the interpreter, "and ask for her name."

"Kim Soo-ah," came the answer.

The interpreter explained to Gus that in Korea the last name comes first, then the given name, so one would call her Soo-ah.

"Why is she in this building?"

The interpreter repeated the woman's words in English. "I am from a village way up north near the sea. The Japanese came to our farm and killed my mother and father and took my sisters away. I was in the woods, picking mushrooms, or they would have taken me, too. There were five of them. My father tried to stop them. They forced him onto his knees and shot him in the back of his head. My mother hid in the woodshed, and when they shot my father, she ran out and buried an axe in the shooter's neck. The others shot her, and she fell next to my father. My father had been trying to keep us safe for the entire war; now my sisters are gone, and my folks are dead. My father has a sister here in Seoul, so I came to look for her. I don't know what else to do."

"Myon, tell her I'm sorry about her family, and tell her we will get her some help."

"Scofield, Stein, grab a litter and take her to the field hospital. Myon, you go help the docs talk to her. The rest of us will stay and finish clearing this building."

Three days later, Gus wondered how she might be doing. That afternoon, a note arrived from the hospital—the patient wanted to thank him for getting her to a safe place.

Lt. General Hodge called Gus into his office and informed him that he would be heading to Hawai'i to finish out his obligation to Uncle Sam. He'd be leaving on Saturday. Gus smiled at receiving the news, but also felt anxious after being in the war theater for nearly four years. Gus thanked the Lt. General, left the administration building, collected his interpreter, and headed toward the field hospital.

He introduced himself to the shift nurse, Deborah Campbell, explaining that the Korean woman, Soo-ah, had been found in an abandoned building by his unit, and he'd been asked to stop in.

"Captain Erickson, I was on duty when Privates Scofield and Stein brought Soo-ah to the hospital. We were very worried; I'm impressed with how well she has recovered in three days."

Nurse Campbell led Gus and his interpreter to Soo-ah. She was sitting in a chair, drinking hot tea. She wore a simple hospital gown tied tightly and high on her waist, her hair pulled into a half pony tail. The color in her cheeks almost glowed, like an aura—stunning.

She stood slowly and approached Gus with her hands out.

Gus stepped forward and extended his hand, which she grasped and held in a way that communicated sincere appreciation.

"Mister Gus, thank you for saving my life."

Gus never really thought about the entire incident in terms of saving her life; it just seemed the right thing to do, to get her some help. However, Gus could see that from her perspective he'd saved her life.

"You are welcome, ma'am. Did you find your aunt?

"Sadly, I found out she died three months ago. We didn't know."

Gus felt sorry for Soo-ah. It seemed her entire family, as far as she knew, was either dead or missing—not much hope that her sisters would ever be found alive. They visited for a few more minutes; then Gus excused himself and made his way to the front of the hospital, asking his interpreter as they walked what would happen to her.

Myon just shrugged.

At the entrance, Gus asked the shift nurse how much longer Soo-ah would be there. He learned that they needed to discharge Soo-ah no later than Saturday, the day he would head for Hawai'i.

That night, Gus slept fitfully. Despite all the carnage and human misery he'd survived the last four years, for some reason, he was concerned about what would happen to Soo-ah.

It still gnawed at the back of his mind the next morning. He finished his reports and continued preparing to fly to Hawai'i on Saturday afternoon. As an enlisted man, Gus had arrived in the South Pacific on a troop ship; now as an officer, he'd be flying back to Hawai'i to finish out his time in the Army.

Gus finally decided to ask Lt. General Hodge if it were possible for a person in Soo-ah's circumstances to get to the United States.

Hodge liked Captain Erickson because he worked hard and no one alive could be more dependable, so the Lt. General teased him a bit at the question.

"For Christ's sake, son, what do you think this is, finders keepers? She isn't a kitten you found on the side of the road!" He laughed at his own joke.

Gus smiled to give General Hodge credit for his one-liner.

"Seriously, sir, the Japs killed her folks and took her sisters *who knows where*. What is going to happen to her?"

"Well, son, it's a bitch. The best thing we can do for these people is to give them law and order. There is no way any of these folks are going to be allowed to the U.S. until those State Department stiffs get good and ready to roll out a procedure. Hell, that could be ten years. The only way any of these people are going to get to the States is if they're married to a GI. You've about got this mess in your rear-view mirror, son. Finish up your work and be ready for the plane on Saturday."

The conversation was over, so he stood and saluted.

"Yes, sir. Thank you, sir."

Lt. General Hodge waggled his head and waved Gus to the door.

Gus left the Lt. General's office, thinking about how Soo-ah could get to the United States. Well, hell—what if he married her? He'd never had a girlfriend. He'd always been shy and kind of gangly. What would his mom and dad think?—and his grandparents? Hell, they wouldn't care; based on their letters they'll be thrilled if he just made it back alive. If they only knew what he'd seen and how many times he'd cheated death . . .

He walked into the chaplain's office and waited in the reception area. After a few minutes Chaplain Ross walked through the door.

The chaplain pulled up short, surprised to see Gus there. "Hello, Captain Erickson, how are you doing?"

"I'm fine, Padre, but I have a question—do you have a minute?"

"Sure, come on in."

Chaplain Ross was a good, good man—the troops loved him. He'd been attached to Gus's unit for about a year now.

Gus sat at the table Chaplain Ross used as a desk, telling him the whole story about Soo-ah and the gnawing question in his mind. He confessed to the chaplain what he was contemplating, and asked the chaplain what he thought.

"Gus, the love of a good woman and a good lifelong marriage are more valuable than anything else you can imagine. Happiness will be the result. Children will likely come, and if you invest yourself in them, they will do right and add to your fulfillment. With these things, you will die a very happy man. Everything else that comes along will be gravy."

He paused, but Gus kept silent, hoping he would continue.

"Now, you've asked me about marrying this woman. I think it depends on you. Most women just want a man who will love them, be faithful to them, be kind and fair, and be responsible. Sure, it takes two to tango, but most failed marriages could be salvaged if the man would be a biblical husband. Many are not. If you marry this woman, you'll have a leg up because of the Korean culture, but you'd be wise not to take advantage by withholding the respect and nurture she and your marriage deserve. If she agrees to marry you, even if her sense of survival subconsciously influences her decision, you will both be in love before you know it. Follow through and work to keep faith with these principles, and you'll both remain in love for the rest of your lives."

After a few silent moments, Gus looked up and shook the chaplain's hand.

"Thank you, sir."

Gus went back to the officers' quarters and lay on his bunk, running through his mind everything the chaplain said. He knew enough about himself that he could and would do what the chaplain had laid out for a love-filled marriage. Gus could imagine he and Soo-ah building their house on the homestead and having a good life. Somehow, he'd made it through this war; and somehow, she'd survived such a horrible experience and made it to Seoul. He made his decision:

He would go back to the hospital in the morning and ask Kim Soo-ah if she would be his wife!

Gus rose early, confident in the decision he'd made, but deciding not to tell Lt. General Hodge until after he proposed. At 10:00 o'clock, he walked down to Soo-ah's section. Turning the corner in anticipation, all he saw was a made bed in a very tidy area. His heart started pounding as he imagined all the reasons she might be gone. How would he find her?—where would she go? Gus stood there, frozen in a moment of woe, hearing Nurse Campbell from behind.

"Sir, are you looking for Soo-ah?"

"Yes, yes. Was she discharged?"

"No, sir. She is out in the courtyard planting a flower garden."

"Oh."

He was about to ask her directions when she simply pointed past all the canvas dividers with a smirk on her face.

Before walking to the hospital, Gus pulled Myon aside and asked him how to say, "Would you be my wife and come to America with me?" in Korean. Gus could see him putting two and two together as a broad smile formed on his face.

Gus blushed, just a little. "Myon, not a word to anyone."

Myon smiled agreement, then drilled Gus on the phrase.

Gus pulled the canvas back and looked outside until he saw Soo-ah, there in the courtyard between all the sections of the field hospital, on her knees with her feet tucked under her bottom, preparing the planter under the cherry tree for flowers.

The sunlight reflected off her jet-black hair as it fell softly down to the small of her back.

As Gus stepped into the courtyard, the ring holding the top of the canvas clanked slightly on the rod, which held the canvas door.

Soo-ah turned her head to the left, responding to the noise. Seeing Gus, she quickly stood and faced him. Glad to see him again, she blushed slightly. She took one step forward to grasp his outstretched hand with both of hers.

"Hello, Gus. Hello."

Wanting to sit so he could look into her eyes, he motioned toward two lawn chairs in the courtyard. They positioned them in front of each other and sat knee to knee. Over and over in his mind, he repeated the phrase Myon taught him.

Gus drew a steadying breath and began slowly. "Soo-ah, would you—?"

Gus imagined she had absolutely no idea what he was about to say, but the two Korean words that rolled off his tongue captured her attention, and she looked directly into his eyes.

She was beautiful, so beautiful Gus began to lose his composure. He drew another steadying breath and looked at her hands, which were side-by-each on her knees. He held her left hand between both of his, looked back into her eyes, and in Korean said . . .

"Soo-ah, would you be my wife and come to America with me?"

*   *   *

She had just heard, in Korean, the last words she ever expected to hear. Conflicting emotions raced through her mind as she processed the words. She didn't want to send confused signals to Gus. She simply set her right hand onto his and gently squeezed. She looked deep into his kind brown eyes and thought of her father. He was gone, gone in a terrible way. In her culture he would have chosen her husband and given her away. Since she could remember and especially since the war began, she knew that her father endeavored every day to protect her and her sisters from the Japanese. Given the choice, would her father have chosen this man for her? She was sure he would have.

Tears welled in her eyes as all these thoughts poured through her mind. Then Soo-ah slowly nodded. The tears gave way and rolled down her cheeks as they stood together. Soo-ah welcomed his embrace; and thus, feeling it appropriate, wrapped her arms around his lean frame and buried her face in his chest.

Chapter Five

Survival, an Elusive Friend

Gun-ho listened as the guards bickered over whether to unload by hand, or to go back and try to fix the hydraulic lift. In that moment he held contempt for these men; they didn't deserve his fear!

If this escape plan worked—then great! If he died trying—fine! But from here on out, fear would be replaced by strategy.

"Let's try it one more time, or how about this? I'll lay on the floor-board and bypass the switch with a jump wire. We'll see if that works."

"Fine! What do we have to lose?"

Gun-ho's pulse throbbed soundlessly in his ear.

Finally the bed jerked up, then stopped.

Loud cheers spilled from the cab, and the truck began to inch back.

Gun-ho quickly sat up, scooched to the edge of the truck bed, then slid off and down the face of the pit into the burnt remains at the bottom. He worked his way to the back and hid himself with debris.

The bodies began sliding off and into the pit like ragdolls.

The passenger stepped around and looked into the raised bed. He seemed to purposely avoid looking into the pit—*Coward!*

The truck moved from the edge, then stopped.

The driver emerged from the front of the truck with a jerrycan.

"What are you doing, Hyuk? We're only supposed to burn on Saturdays!"

"I'm doing it now!"

"Then you'll have to explain to the sergeant why the fuel can is empty!"

"Fine! I'm burning these bastards!"

The driver opened the can and walked along the top edge of the pit, soaking the bottom with fuel.

As the driver made his way along the back, Gun-ho kept still.

Fuel seeped through the debris, soaking his shoulders and head.

Gun-ho tasted the liquid running onto his cheek—*gasoline! Not diesel! Damn!—this hole will explode into a ball of fire.*

"Give me a match. . . ."

Chapter Six

It Is Your Responsibility

What a memorable weekend for Jae-sun—Fourth of July. Billy invited him to stay at his house for the weekend, the first time Jae-sun had ever been away from his parents overnight; twelve felt old enough to him. The Johnsons took Jae-sun to a picnic with gunny sack races, watermelon-eating contests, softball games, and all the food you could eat. Jae-sun was becoming very aware of civics, and he enjoyed all the tradition and festivities of America's Independence Day.

Jae-sun took special interest in what happened in Korea, but he also wanted to understand the history and the Constitution of the United States so he could better appreciate why his host country was so special, and hopefully be able to help heal his own country. All of this was going to become even more important because his father told him earlier that week they would be going back to Korea soon.

During that weekend, Jae-sun told Billy he'd be going back to Korea. They vowed to stay in touch via letters—someday they'd see each other again.

*　　　*　　　*

The day of departure came too quickly. Billy didn't want to think about Jae-sun leaving. His grandmother suggested that he give Jae-sun a keepsake. Billy thought about that and decided to give Jae-sun a cruci-fix. Billy's father took him to a jeweler, and they had "Jae-sun and Billy" inscribed on the horizontal bar, and "Brothers for Life" inscribed on the vertical bar.

*   *   *

Jae-sun's heart quickened at receiving the gift. From his evening talks with Earl Jenkins, he understood the significance of the symbol and the words.

He'd wear it always.

Jae-sun tearfully said his good-byes. For a boy barely six years old when his family left Korea, it seemed like the years in America slipped right by. But he spoke English like a natural speaker now, so his mother's goal had been accomplished.

Jae-sun truly possessed remarkable intellect and an outstanding work ethic, he was becoming an exceptional young man. Jae-sun read everything available about the Korean War and its effect on his people. His heart filled with sorrow upon learning perhaps three million of his countrymen perished during the war. The population in Washington, D.C., was around 700,000; it made him sick to think more than three times that many died. Kim Il-sung was to blame for this misery, he and his Russian collaborators. Jae-sun vowed to expose the evil of Kim Il-sung.

Jae-sun and his family arrived back at Inchon Harbor on September 4th, 1955. They were driven from the harbor to the ministry building, about twenty miles. All his reading had not prepared him for seeing the destruction himself. Nearly every building obliterated, the rubble piled up everywhere with just the lanes cleared enough for vehicles to pass through.

Jae-sun's father told him an aggressive rebuilding program would begin soon; the Americans were helping his country recover from the war. In Washington, D.C., everything had been neat and clean, the parks with ball fields and rose gardens, neighborhoods with homes—real homes with families. Here, all around he found despair, families torn apart, brutally killed or maimed. What a lot of work to do.

Jae-sun felt himself becoming anxious, but was comforted by his father's arm over his shoulders.

"There is much to rebuild in our country. It is your responsibility—the responsibility of us all who survive. We are the lucky ones."

The ministry set up an apartment for Jae-sun and his folks near his father's office. His father's assistant in Washington, D.C., told Jae-sun that even basic things they took for granted in the U. S. were not available in Korea, so bleak were the circumstances. Jae-sun brought stationery from the U.S. He wrote his first letter to Billy as soon as they settled in.

Over the next three years, Jae-sun and Billy would exchange twenty-one letters. The correspondence kept their friendship sharp and fresh. They shared their hopes and dreams, their fears and toils. Jae-sun would encourage Billy with mathematic tips that really helped Billy thrive in his classes.

In February of 1958, Jae-sun's father received orders back to the United States.

Jae-sun would be heading back to Washington, D.C. again, in June.

Chapter Seven

A Bright Future

The DC-4 carrying Gus and Soo-ah prepared for landing at Pearl Harbor Airfield. It was a sunny Sunday morning at about 10:00 o'clock. They'd departed Seoul Saturday evening, then landed at Midway Island to refuel before leaving early the next morning.

Chaplin Ross performed a ceremony for Gus and Soo-ah Saturday afternoon at the field hospital. The nurses organized a small reception, then the newlyweds left for the airfield.

Lt. General Hodges cabled ahead to Hawai'i and arranged for Gus and Soo-ah to enjoy three days of leave, also arranging for a car to meet them at the airfield to take them directly to the hotel. Gus was a true American hero, with many battlefield commendations, also credited with saving the lives of nine of his brothers in arms. He received battlefield promotions to captain—the Lt. General liked Gus. He wanted to make sure that Gus and Soo-ah were treated special for their honeymoon.

A young ensign met Gus and Soo-ah at the airplane. He saluted as Gus stepped onto the tarmac. The ensign motioned Gus and Soo-ah to the car and whisked them off for a surprise weekend at the luxurious Royal Hawai'ian.

*   *   *

Soo-ah deliberately exhaled to slow her heartbeat. She'd never been in a plane, she'd never been in a car, she'd never seen such a big city like Honolulu, and she'd never been the center of attention. As the car pulled under the porte cochere in front of the hotel, the bellman, the concierge, and the front desk manager greeted them. The welcoming committee took them up to their third-floor room facing the beach with a view of Diamond Head—perfect! The trio arranged for room service to bring lunch simultaneous to their arrival—a beautiful four-star cart service. The concierge shooed his fawning colleagues out the door. The latch clicked as they departed.

For the first time, Gus and Soo-ah were all alone.

Despite the language barrier, communication was clear. It was nice just to be with each other. At 18 and 21, both had experienced more life than most people ever will, but neither had ever been alone in the company of the opposite sex.

A sweet girl, but also wise, Soo-ah had been part of the wedding plans for a family friend. She listened intently as the women coached the girl about her wedding night.

Now she took Gus by the hand and led him into the bathroom, large compared to most and appointed very nicely with a two-sink vanity, a toilet, a bidet, a walk-in shower, and a bathtub.

Soo-ah turned the shower on, then faced her husband, hugged him tightly, stepped back, slipped her dress off her shoulders, and let it slide to the floor.

His pupils expanded and his neck flushed.

Soo-ah stepped toward Gus and unbuttoned his shirt.

Gus slid the shirt off and pulled his t-shirt over his head.

Soo-ah unbuckled his belt and trousers and let them fall to the floor. She slid her hands under the band of his underwear and slid them down.

Gus stepped out as Soo-ah took his hand and led him into the shower.

The warm water felt so good, and the French milled soap smelled divine.

As Soo-ah finished rinsing her hair, she faced Gus and gently stroked his cheeks. Their lips met for the first time since the wedding.

He cupped her exquisite breasts and followed the smooth curve of her back to her bottom.

Tumescence inevitably complete, Soo-ah gently explored with her right hand as she turned off the shower with her left.

Barely toweled off, they slipped onto the bed while a gentle tropical breeze from the lanai wafted over them.

*   *   *

The leave ended all too soon, but Gus and Soo-ah were grateful for the respite and the chance to become fully acquainted. Gus decided he'd better write to his folks and grandparents and let them in on the news. March would be coming very soon, and they needed to know that the family had grown, but most certainly before arriving back at the homestead. Gus knew his parents and grandparents well. They followed the war daily since Gus left.

They were painfully aware of all the young men who would never return home.

Chapter Eight

Coming of Age

The first time Jae-sun and his parents travelled to America, they took a ship to San Francisco and a train to Washington, D.C. This time they flew from Seoul to Washington, D.C., on a de Havilland Comet jetliner. What a trip! Jae-sun fell in love with flying.

Jae-sun penned a letter to Billy, which included travel plans. Billy's father agreed to take him to the Washington National Airport to meet Jae-sun's plane.

Twelve years old when his family left Washington, now Jae-sun was fifteen and going through puberty. His culture and his own intellect kept him grounded, even during his teen years. The past three years Jae-sun read much about the war and the politics behind the division of Korea. He'd also formed very strong opinions about the folly of civilizations pursuing Marxist and socialist philosophies. His time in the United States and his observations of what was going on in North Korea gave a stark comparison between a socialist path and the path of a democracy delivered through a representative republic. Jae-sun fully embraced the latter and could expertly articulate the successes of a society that holds the rights and liberties of individuals dear, versus the utter failure and crushing tyranny of societies that promote the collective.

*　　*　　*

During the past three years, Billy redoubled his goal of going to the Naval Academy and becoming a naval officer. Now at fifteen, Billy had grown to 5' 11" and begun to take the shape of an athletic man. Billy missed Jae-sun during the last three years and was very excited about his return.

From where Billy and his father stood, they could see Jae-sun and his family going through the customs line. The crucifix was dangling around his friend's neck. Billy was pleased Jae-sun valued his gift. They began to wave wildly at the same time.

Soon enough, Jae-sun hurried through the gate.

Billy ran over and grabbed Jae-sun's hand in his, then stepped around, arms over each other's shoulders for a Polaroid.

They took up right where they left off.

*   *   *

During the next three years, Jae-sun and Billy relied on each to push the other toward their goals. They studied hard, they played hard. They were the best of friends—lifelong friends. Jae-sun began his freshman year at Princeton University.

They were on their way.

Chapter Nine

Homecoming

Gus would be discharged from the Army in San Francisco. He prepared to leave Hawai'i via passenger ship on March 3th for the eight-day run to the mainland. Their time in Hawai'i could be described as idyllic; Gus and Soo-ah were able to spend the six months enjoying each other in their new roles as husband and wife. Many evenings were spent walking on the beach, hand-in-hand, practicing English.

At 9:30 Sunday morning, March 3rd, Gus and Soo-ah walked up the gangplank of the SS *Lurline* to head for San Francisco. Technically still in the Army, Gus donned his uniform. In her fifth month, Soo-ah looked beautiful in a lovely silk maternity dress.

All could see they were a handsome, happy couple as they boarded the ship for California.

*   *   *

Tugboats guided the SS *Lurline* to the dock at the San Francisco pier on Sunday morning, the 10th of March. Blessed with smooth sailing and wonderful weather, Soo-ah and Gus enjoyed walking on the promenade, reading on the upper deck, and spending evenings enjoying dinner and music with the other passengers.

Gus and Soo-ah took a cab to the Palace Hotel. Wednesday morning they would board a train for Eugene, Oregon, then Thursday another train toward Cushman, just two miles from the Erickson homestead.

*   *   *

The train slowed to stop at Cushman.

Gus stepped onto the platform and turned to help Soo-ah step down. He looked up into her bright eyes and sweet smile. His heart swelled. Gus and Soo-ah were truly in love—Chaplin Ross was right.

In San Francisco Gus had bought a new suit for himself and a pleated wool dress with a white jacket and hat for Soo-ah. Now as the handsome couple turned, Gus could see his parents and grandparents through the train steam. Before they saw Gus and Soo-ah, Gus whispered into her ear—his family was there, there at the end of the platform.

Gus and Soo-ah walked toward them hand-in-hand.

A gentle breeze danced through, clearing the steam.

*   *   *

Through thinning steam, Joe and Grace and Henry and Charlotte beheld the answer to their prayers: Gus returned to them—intact—and with a wife, a beautiful wife, a beautiful pregnant wife. They all stepped forward, tears misting their eyes.

They embraced Gus and Soo-ah, not speaking, just weeping softly with joy.

*   *   *

Joe and Henry decided they needed to build Gus and Soo-ah a cabin of their own. The family home where Gus grew up had only two bed-rooms and the loft where Gus slept—clearly not enough room for expecting newlyweds.

They had a bridge that Gus's great-grandfather built across the river, tying their driveway to Hwy 126, a well-built bridge with massive stone bulwarks on each shore and a stone caisson in the middle of the river.

The homestead house sat on the right side of the driveway, up a gentle slope on the south side of the river. The driveway continued beyond the house, past a three-bay shop and the barn on the left side. The drive ended at a gate beyond the barn, which led to a pasture that continued south and east. On the right just beyond the house sat the woodshed and a green knoll this side of a fence that ran up the hill from the right end of the gate down at the barn.

Joe and Henry built Gus and Soo-ah's home on the knoll facing the driveway, turned slightly toward the original farmhouse . . .

A beautiful gesture not lost on Gus and Soo-ah.

Chapter Ten

A Good Choice

Art had only been on an airplane one time before, when his father took him to Alaska to visit his uncle. Now nineteen, he still enjoyed flying like when he was thirteen years old. Riding the bus from the airport to the SEAL training facility, Art looked forward to many new experiences.

Always competitive, and being the oldest in his fatherless family, Art also blossomed into a natural leader. Because of his family's circumstances, he always looked out for the welfare of his siblings.

These traits would earn him the love and admiration of his classmates. To a man, as they went through the training, they knew that Art Jackson had their back and that they could count on him.

Art thrived in SEAL Basic Conditioning. Throughout a program designed to weed out those not up to the challenge, Art seemed to rise further to meet each test and trial. His commanders were confounded by his performance. Moreover, Art's inspirational presence motivated at least two members of the class to gather the guts to stick with the training.

Hell Week behind them, training over, the graduates were assigned to SEAL teams and started into the routine of training and preparing for the day they were needed.

For Art and his team, the first call came in March of 1986. A Marxist group funded and supported by Castro's Cuba pulled off a military coup on a small island nation. In and of itself, this would not necessarily compel the United States to take direct military action unless an aspect of national security was clear. However, in this case 140 American tourists were being held hostage in their resort hotel, and the situation seemed to be deteriorating to the point that their lives were in peril.

The team's mission called for them to land on the island, perform special reconnaissance, and gather covert intelligence. Moreover, if the opportunity developed, their mission allowed for rescuing the hostages, delivering them to a remote beach east of the resort where other Navy assets would extract the group from the beach to the safety of Navy ships waiting offshore.

Under the cover of darkness and weather, the eight-man team arrived just off the coast two miles east of the resort. The team submerged two inflatable boats off the beach and emerged from the surf under the cover of darkness. They accessed the resort using an old jeep road, the only beach access in the area. By dawn the team positioned themselves in the jungle fringe around the resort. The jeep trail passed the resort and led another mile, albeit much more improved, west to the main town on the island, the place where the coup occurred.

The team determined that seven members of the insurgent group guarded the resort. The main insurgent force remained in the town. From the resort's beach, rocky cliffs and a surf-guarded shoreline prevented access to the extraction beach. An overland pursuit of the rescue effort would be futile apart from the jeep trail, as the jungle vegetation provided an impenetrable barrier.

The team decided that once the sun set and darkness returned, they would overwhelm the guards, then move the guests two miles to the extraction beach. The Navy would bring a landing craft forward and extract the tourists and the SEALS from the beach. Art and two other team members would remain behind and protect the rear of the rescue effort from an otherwise unabated pursuit that would likely come. They would break to the beach once the tourists were safely away and extract themselves to the naval assets offshore.

Positioned in the jungle fringe, Art anticipated the moment of synchronized attack.

His heart began to pound as adrenaline heightened his senses.

The game was one-on-one. Art's target—the insurgent posted at the corner of the resort nearest the road.

Art moved silently along the road to a point fifteen yards from his target.

A dim light from the resort walkway gave up the insurgent's position. His feet just off the ground, the target sat on an electrical transformer atop a concrete pedestal surrounded by grass.

With ghostly silence, Art erased the gap.

He plunged his combat knife through the insurgent's neck, the only sounds a blood-soaked gurgle from severed windpipe and a quiet crunch as the blade collided with bone.

Art laid the body quietly behind the transformer, then moved cautiously around the end of the resort, looking to help his teammates finish the first phase.

The one-on-one tactic succeeded; all of the unsuspecting insurgents died in a manner of moments without a shot fired.

The commander ordered Art and his teammates Kenny Creighton and George Kendall to set up watch on the road coming from town. He ordered the others to gather the guests in the lobby so they could organize the departure.

The commander planned to arrive at the beach just as a glint of morning light peeked over the horizon. He wanted to load the landing craft in natural light to avoid creating a target with artificial light.

With everyone accounted for, at 4 a.m. the group headed for the beach.

Art, Kenny, and George remained behind to cover the main group.

*   *   *

At the insurgents' headquarters in town, the commander waited anxiously for the hourly check-in call due at 4 a.m.

At 4:05 . . . still no call.

Another five minutes passed.

The commander grew tired of drumming his fingers.

At 4:15 he ordered ten men in two jeeps to run up to the resort.

*   *   *

At 4:30 a.m. Art saw the headlights of two jeeps approaching.

They slowed as they approached the porte cochere of the hotel. Art and his men saw no benefit in allowing the insurgents to disembark.

As the resort lighting exposed the jeeps and their occupants, the SEALS saturated the insurgents with automatic weapons fire.

Within moments, all the insurgents lay dead.

*   *   *

Distant gunfire disturbed the otherwise tranquil early morning at the insurgents' headquarters.

Their commander, with no regard for the men he'd just sent to the scene, ordered an artillery volley on the resort.

*   *   *

Hearing shells in the air, the SEALS dove for cover. Two shells found their target, unleashing fire and devastating damage on the resort.

Art found cover under one of the jeeps and survived unscathed.

Kenny and George were not so lucky. Art found Kenny with a head wound. He was unconscious, but still alive. George was conscious, but with a badly injured left leg.

One of the jeeps had a litter attached to the hood, plus a fifty-caliber machine gun mounted on the deck behind and between the seats. Art lay George on the litter, applying a tourniquet to the wound high on George's thigh. He grabbed a roll of duct tape from the concierge's counter and taped George to the litter.

Running back to pick up Kenny, Art imagined the enemy loading up the artillery to let another volley fly. Art applied a bandage to Kenny's head wound and held it on with gauze and duct tape. He hoped Kenny wouldn't lose his left eye.

Art pulled the dead insurgents out of the jeep, placed Kenny in the passenger seat, hopped behind the wheel, and backed the jeep out of the resort circle drive, just as the second volley hit.

At the head of the trail, Art stopped the jeep and ran back to the resort garage adjacent to the main building. He found the keys above the resort van's visor and pulled the large vehicle out, parking it across the roadway just west of the resort. Running back toward the jeep, he tossed a grenade into the van.

Art jumped back into the jeep just as the van exploded, providing a temporary barrier to those who were sure to follow.

*   *   *

Central Command in Washington, D.C., monitored the events via satellite imagery in real time. Commander Johnson, who developed the plan, sat with President Reagan and the national security staff. Johnson felt enormous pressure, as the entire nation had focused on the hostage situation. Many were pressing the administration on what would be done.

Just as Art exploded the van and headed the jeep toward the extraction beach, they could see the landing craft pulling away with all aboard. Everyone breathed a collective sigh of relief.

Now all eyes focused on the three remaining SEALS trying to evade pursuing insurgents. Commander Johnson knew the names of the SEALS that were on the mission, but he had no way of knowing in the moment which of the SEALS remained behind. Time would tell, but for now he was very impressed with his SEAL's courage and tenacity.

President Reagan turned to Commander Johnson. "Bill, who is that man?"

$*$ $*$ $*$

Having bought a bit of time, Art headed toward the beach, smelling fuel as he bumped along the rough road, trying to balance speed with getting his teammates out alive.

The fumes still a mystery, he decided to press on.

The east horizon brightened, providing plenty of light. A mile from the beach, Art could see the first of the vehicles pursuing him in the rearview mirror.

He raced around a turn in the trail, which blocked his view of the pursuers.

Three hundred yards up, Art stopped the jeep just before another turn. He stepped behind the fifty-cal, jacked the first shell in the into the barrel, and waited.

$*$ $*$ $*$

Johnson and the others watched anxiously as the SEAL on the screen stopped his jeep and stepped behind the gun.

Just about to make the second turn, the pursuers would come into the SEAL's view in seconds.

$*$ $*$ $*$

Art waited until three jeeps made the turn, the first now just eighty yards from the end of his barrel.

He strafed the front of the jeep, totally destroying the radiator and engine, careering it into the edge of the jungle.

Art peppered the second and third jeeps, creating another temporary barrier for his pursuers to overcome—a barrier of death and mayhem thanks to a barrage of fifty-cal bullets.

Art jumped back into the driver's seat, slammed the jeep into first gear, and raced for the beach.

As he emerged from the jungle, the jeep died, starved of fuel.

Art could hear the enemy in the distance trying to make their way past the cluster. Still 150 yards to the water and with two wounded comrades, Art decided he needed to create another barrier. Having gotten this far, he was in no mood to be shot on the beach trying to get himself and his men to the safety of the surf.

Art cut George loose from the litter and laid him on the beach, then picked up Kenny and laid him beside George, both with their heads pointed toward the surf, still more than a hundred yards away. He placed a piece of rope over each of their chests, under each arm, and tied the ends behind each of their heads.

He grabbed a bag of grenades and two guns, then ran back toward the resort.

Two hundred yards up the trail, Art stopped to listen.

Two more jeeps were coming.

He stepped into the cover of dense jungle along a curve in the road, then listened again.

As the first jeep neared, it slowed, trying to avoid the same treatment as his predecessor.

Art tossed a grenade with 4-second fuse into the jeep. It glanced off the right shoulder of the driver and dropped to the floor.

The grenade exploded, killing all aboard.

The second jeep skidded to a stop, everybody stunned for a moment—turns out, a moment *too* long.

Art burst from the jungle, guns blasting the dazed quintet. All perished in their seats, and the second jeep rolled into the first.

Art surveyed the scene, then ran back to where he'd left Kenny and George. He grabbed the ropes, one in each hand, and dragged his comrades toward the safety of the water.

*   *   *

The tension in the White House was back to unbearable, relieved only temporarily when the tourists were whisked away to safety. The team was witnessing three armed insurgents running up behind their hero's broken-down jeep—painfully aware that he was in danger, yet unable to inform him!

No longer able to contain herself, one of the president's aides jumped out of her chair and screamed at the screen. "Look behind you! Please look behind!"

President Reagan leaned sideways to avoid her flailing hands as she bounded up and down on her toes. He didn't think any less of her—wished he could join her. The last thing he wanted to do was to call the parents of these men, ultimately under his command.

It was his decision that put them in harm's way.

*   *   *

Just thirty feet from the sea foam left by the last wave, Art heard gunfire and bullets whizzing through the air all around him.

He instinctively lowered his profile and turned to meet the assault just as a bullet whizzed by his head, nicking the edge of his ear.

Art trained his weapon and let a burst go, catching the two insurgents on his left.

The remaining man threw his weapon down and charged Art with a knife.

As Art raised his weapon to repel this desperate charge, he heard the disappointing click of an empty gun. About to be engaged in hand to hand combat, Art's training kicked in.

He kept his eye on the blade, stepped back and away just as the attacker reached him, and swung wildly.

The attacker's momentum worked against him. Art skillfully avoided the wild swing, tripped the assailant as he flew by, and simultaneously opened his abdomen.

Art glanced back toward the jeep for more danger. Seeing none, he dragged Kenny and George to safety, just as the landing craft returned.

The gate deployed. Six Marines emerged, two each to carry Kenny and George, two to cover the shore.

As soon as the wounded were secured, Art and the other two Marines raced up the ramp, and the boat backed out into the surf.

*   *   *

For the first time since the operation began, Bill Johnson took his eyes from the screen and turned to address President Reagan . . .

"I do not know, Mr. President, but I'll find out."

*   *   *

The plan had worked and worked well, thanks to the SEAL everyone just watched confound the enemy again, and again, and again. Art Jackson would receive the Congressional Medal of Honor for his heroic efforts; and like most with his depth of character, he humbly and quietly accepted the thanks of a grateful nation.

Chapter Eleven

Time to Move On

Art Jackson enjoyed a very successful experience while in service to the nation. However, now he needed to decide whether to remain in the military or move on. He very much enjoyed the brotherhood of military life, and the excitement associated with the missions; however, he'd received a letter from his uncle Milton "Milt" inviting him to come to Alaska and work in his commercial fishing business.

Art's father's older brother, Milt was born in 1926, then went on to serve in Alaska during WWII. After the war, he moved to Alaska, fell in love with Esther Ivanoff, started fishing, and never left.

Now Art would honor him by going to Alaska, so he arrived there in June of 1991. His aunt and uncle owned 360 acres on an island adjacent to a very small natural harbor about an hour east of Unalaska. They lived on their land near the harbor and operated their fishing business from this enchanted place.

Art met his uncle just one time. It was in 1978, the year before his dad passed. Art stepped off the plane at 10:00 a.m. on June 12th, timing his arrival because his uncle's letter indicated he'd be in Dutch Harbor that day. After landing at the airport, Art noticed a man struggling to load freight onto his truck—with his left arm in a sling.

"Hi there. Can I give you a hand?"

The man looked up and beheld a giant of a man looking down at him.

"Yes, indeed, son. Thank you."

Art easily picked up the items on the pallet and loaded them onto the back of the truck. The man extended his right hand.

"Thank you very kindly. My name is Harvey Smith."

"You're welcome, Mr. Smith. I'm Art Jackson."

"Art Jackson? You wouldn't be Milt's nephew, would you?"

"Yes, yes I am."

"Milt said you'd be coming in today. He's waiting for you up at the Harbor View Bar. Can I give you a lift?"

"That would be great."

Art threw his duffel bag into the back of Harvey's truck and hopped into the cab. On the way to town, Art barely said a word because Harvey had plenty to say. He told Art how he'd found his way to Alaska and how he'd met Art's uncle. Harvey also shared that his uncle was very proud of him and how Milt would always speak highly of his nephew. All the way to town, Art politely let Harvey ramble on about whatever he wanted. Soon enough, Harvey pulled up in front of the Harbor View Bar. He pointed to the door.

"Milt will be in there. So long, son. Nice talking to you."

"Thank you, Harvey."

Art grabbed his duffel and walked into the bar.

Art had not seen his uncle for fourteen years; but scanning the crowd, he knew exactly which patron to approach. Art's dad and Milton favored each other. At the end of the bar, on the corner, sat his uncle, visiting with a guy on each side.

Art walked up to the bar from Milt's left side. His head was turned, and he was listening to the guy on his right. Art waited for a pause in the conversation.

"Excuse me, gentlemen—would any of you happen to be Milt Jackson?"

Milt snapped his head around, looked Art up and down, and put on big smile.

"Jesus, Mary, and Joseph—boy, you made it!"

Milt stood up and shook Art's hand, then introduced him to the men on either side and waved Art toward one of the booths near the windows.

"Let's have lunch. I told Esther we'd be home around five, so we have lots of time."

"That's a great idea. I'm hungry."

As they ate lunch and drank coffee, Art and Milt visited about Art's dad, and Milt told him about his grandparents. Milt told Art stories about where he and his dad had grown up. They visited about Art's brothers and sisters and mother, about the military, and about life.

As it approached 3:15, Milt looked at his watch. "Art, I don't want to dictate your life, or in any way make you feel obligated to become a fisherman; but I'd like to give you a chance to see if you like the life, and if so, the opportunity to take over the operation in a few years. I am 65 years old, and Esther wants to spend more time down in Hawai'i. I'll teach you about the ocean, and about fishing, and about business. Esther and I have done well, and you will, too, if you end up liking what we do."

Milt and Art agreed that they'd spend the next year figuring things out and work out the details as time passed. Milt paid for their lunch, and they walked down to the docks. They boarded Milt's boat, crept out of the harbor, and turned east toward Esther Bay, an hour away.

For the first part of the trip, Art stood at the bow of the boat and took in the beauty of the Aleutian Islands, the pleasant smell of the ocean, and the vastness of it all.

Coming here was a good decision.

He walked back and stepped into the wheelhouse. His uncle smiled a smile that reminded Art of his dad, a smile that communicated pride and approval. Milt reached up and hugged Art around his shoulders with his left arm. Art felt good about the future, and he knew Milt did, too.

The lessons of the sea, navigation, radar, and radios began on that ride home. As the boat entered Esther Bay and moved to the dock, two men walked out to tie off the boat. Milt introduced Art to James and Bert, two of his crewmen.

As they walked up the dock ramp to the shore, Art could see Milt and Esther's home just up the hill across a gravel road that ran to the shop. Milt and Art walked into the house at precisely 5:00 p.m.

Milt's wife, Esther, greeted them warmly. "Welcome, Art. Welcome! It is so good to see you again, and look how you've grown up."

"Thank you, Aunt Esther. It is good to see you, too!"

"I fixed up a room for you; come, I want to show you."

"Yes, ma'am."

She hooked her arm through his as they walked down the hall. She stepped forward and showed him through the door. It was a spacious room, with a private bath off to the side and sliding glass door that stepped out onto a small deck with a view of Esther Bay and the Bering Sea beyond.

Beautiful, just beautiful.

"This is great, Aunt Esther. Perfect!"

Art set his duffel bag in the closet and walked back down the hall with his aunt. Esther had dinner ready—halibut, scalloped potatoes, and green salad. Art enjoyed dinner with family for the first time in a long time.

"How long have you folks been married now?"

Esther, an Alaska Native—an Aleut—met Milt the first week he arrived in Alaska. Both were smitten from the jump.

"I met your uncle in Dutch Harbor—in the diner—in June of 1951. I loved him the first time I saw him. We were married in September, so it's forty years this year."

Milt reached over and held her hand.

"Forty great years, Art—forty great years."

Art felt happy and proud just to be in their company.

Chapter Twelve

The Measure of the Woman

Still living in the glow of Gus and Soo-ah's arrival, the Ericksons began to get used to their new normal. Days turned off the calendar, and much evidence began to tumble out that Gus made a good decision in marrying Soo-ah. Despite being seven months pregnant, she was the hardest-working person the elder Ericksons ever saw; and at just nineteen, she had skills that amazed the entire family.

On Thursday morning, April 18th, 1946, Soo-ah stood beside Henry's chair. "Grandpa Henry, may I butcher a hog today?"

Henry looked up with an inquisitive smile on his face.

"Well sure, Sue. Why today?"

"Sunday is Easter; we'll have fresh ham for the feast."

"Why sure. You go right ahead."

Grandpa Henry did a good job of concealing his incredulity, no doubt thinking he'd have to step in and salvage the operation.

Among other things the elder Ericksons learned about Soo-ah, was that she embraced the Christian faith. Her grandfather had embraced the faith in the 1880s when missionary Horace Allen worked in Korea.

Soo-ah stepped out into a beautiful, sunny morning.

Grandpa Henry moved a chair out in front of the shop to watch.

Soo-ah emerged from the shop with a pair of sawhorses. She set them up in front of the barn, but a bit off to the right, placing four 2

X 12 planks across the sawhorses to make a temporary table. She went back inside and gathered a washtub, two knives, a stone, a meat saw, and a block and tackle.

Soo-ah stepped into the barn, then moments later popped open the loft doors and rolled out the hay trolley on the iron rail beyond the end of the barn. She lowered the rope on the trolley to the ground, then walked back out and hooked the block and tackle to the rope, pulling the trolley rope up so that the top pulley was about fourteen feet off the ground. She used a corral post next to the corner of the barn to anchor the end of the trolley rope.

Soo-ah walked back into the barn and moments later came through the corral gate with a nice hog, directing it with a stick. She tied a rope onto each of the back legs just above the hooves, kind of like a long hobble. At the right moment, Soo-ah caught the middle of the rope with the hook end of the block and tackle, stealing a glimpse of Grandpa Henry watching slack-jawed as she yarded up a 250-pound hog. She suspended the beast in the air with its head two feet off the ground. She set the washtub under the hog's head, and with a quick expert motion sliced the arteries in the hog's neck with her knife, catching every drop of blood in the tub.

As Soo-ah pulled the hide off the hog, she saw Grace hanging laundry at the house. Knife in hand, she greeted her mother-in-law with a good-morning wave; Soo-ah appreciated the approving smile. She loved her new family, and she felt loved by them.

She utilized every piece of the hog, even saving the material inside the hog's gut to fertilize the garden. Soo-ah cleaned the last of the tools and put them away in the shop, then picked Grandpa Henry's coffee cup off the bench and filled it with hot coffee. She exited the shop and handed Grandpa Henry the hot coffee on the way to the house.

"Well thank you, Sue. Nice work on the hog."

"You're welcome, Grandpa Henry."

Walking away, Soo-ah smiled, confident she'd measured up.

Easter was indeed a feast. They used both hams, as the Morgans accepted an invitation to dinner. Ham, potatoes, salad, and broccoli served to fourteen souls, an event Norman Rockwell could easily record.

*   *   *

As April yielded to May and May to June, Soo-ah knew the baby was close. On Tuesday morning, June 25th, while making Gus's coffee, she felt a dull-but-steady pain in her lower back. She held the kitchen counter until the pain ebbed, then finished making Gus's breakfast. At 5:50 a.m. she walked into the bedroom to wake her husband. Sitting on the edge of the bed, she stroked his forehead softly.

"Good Morning."

"Good Morning to you, my love. Your breakfast is ready, and you should know that today you will meet your child."

Gus rolled out of bed and pulled on his denim logging pants. He rolled one suspender over his left shoulder and followed her to the kitchen.

"Today?"

"Yes, today."

"Well, I better stick around the house today."

"I think that's a good idea."

Since arriving home, Gus filled his time logging timber up one of the draws on the homestead, but she wanted him close today.

Soo-ah read Gus's face as she paced the floor.

"I'm okay, honey. Eat your breakfast."

Gus walked back into the bedroom, put on his shirt, and grabbed a pair of socks.

She paced as he sat at the table and ate his breakfast. With each lap, she lovingly ran her fingers across his back.

Their cabin featured two rooms, with an outhouse out the back. The main room measured 20' x 20' with the kitchen along the back wall to the left, then a back door, and around to a sitting area, then around to the front door straight across from the back door, then around to the bedroom door on the left. The table sat six feet from the kitchen sink by the bedroom door. On her fourth lap, Soo-ah dabbed her brow with a dish towel.

"Gus, I need to walk outside; it is too warm in the house."

The morning sun was obscured by the clouds; the cool air felt refreshing. Gus followed as Soo-ah waddled down the path from their front door to the road in front of the shop and barn. She appreciated Gus lovingly massage her back as she stopped with each pain. Soo-ah turned at the gate and walked back toward the house. The kitchen light in the main house signaled that Grace was up, making her coffee.

Soo-ah could see her through the kitchen window.

Their eyes met. Grace was ready.

*   *   *

Grace walked into the living room and leaned into Charlotte and Henry's bedroom.

"Mother, you better get up. We're going to have a baby soon."

Charlotte swung her legs over the edge of the bed, instantly wide awake in anticipation of the duties soon to be undertaken. Charlotte walked into the kitchen, looked out the window, and watched as Gus stood beside Soo-ah, rubbing her back.

Grace was watching out of the dining room window.

"Mother, we did a good job with that boy."

Charlotte walked into the dining room and stood beside Grace. They looked on together.

"Yes, we sure did. Thanks be to God for getting him back here alive."

*   *   *

Soo-ah started to walk again after the last pain.

She stopped abruptly. "Gus, my water just broke. It is time." A small puddle was forming between her feet.

"I'll carry you up to the house." Gus gently picked her up.

They passed Joe and Henry, who had been shooed out and sent to the shop. Gus turned sideways to bring Soo-up through the door head first, and walked through the kitchen into the living room.

Three weeks earlier, Charlotte had prepared sort of an operating table in the living room, three feet off the ground, just 24" wide, with a two-inch cotton mattress. Per his mother's direction, Joe added stirrups on the end of the table that could be rolled down if not needed. Soo-ah situated herself as Gus gently placed her on the table.

Grace gently placed her hand on Gus's shoulder.

"Everything will be fine, Gus. Go down and keep Dad and Grandpa company."

Grace stood near Soo-ah's head, and Charlotte sat in a chair at the end of the table. Charlotte gently set Soo-ah's legs on the stirrups and tenderly checked on progress. Soo-ah's cervix was nearly 100% dilated.

"Honey, the baby is almost here. On the next pain, push just a bit and let's see what happens."

Grace held Soo-ah's hands as she bore down and pushed. The baby's head began to crown. Charlotte was massaging Soo-ah's perineum, hoping it would stretch; but she had her razor at the ready if needs be. Charlotte did not want Soo-ah to tear.

"Soo-ah, I can see the top of the baby's head; she has black hair."

Soo-ah clenched her teeth as the next pain started. "It's a girl?"

Soo-ah grabbed her legs behind her knees and pushed with the pain. The baby's head emerged, and Charlotte helped one shoulder out. Soo-ah pushed one more time, and a wonderful baby girl slid into her great-grandmother's capable hands.

"Yes, honey, you got a little girl, a sweet baby girl."

Charlotte cut the baby's umbilical cord with her razor and clamped it off. She placed the baby in Soo-ah's arms and began to gently rub Soo-ah's tummy to coax out the placenta.

Soo-ah was sitting up at 45 degrees, Grace behind her. Together they marveled at their little angel. Soo-ah looked between her legs at

Charlotte and back at Grace. She touched the baby's little chin with her index finger.

"Her name is Charlotte Grace, Charlotte Grace Erickson."

Hearing this news, Charlotte looked up at Soo-ah and smiled, then wiped a tear away with the back of her left wrist, just as the placenta fell into her right hand.

Grace gathered up the baby and walked into the kitchen. She filled the sink with warm water and gently bathed little Charlotte Grace. Soo-ah was sitting up when Grace returned with little Charlotte swaddled comfortably.

Soo-ah received the baby to her breast. "Thank you, Mother."

"You're welcome, honey. I'll go get the boys."

Little Charlotte yawned.

Chapter Thirteen

Princeton and Annapolis

Billy Johnson entered the Naval Academy, full of enthusiasm and drive that did not ebb. He excelled in his classes and absolutely loved the structure of military life. Billy was living out a dream, a dream he'd been following since before first grade. He wanted to be a Navy man, just like his dad.

Through the first two years at the Naval Academy, attendees have the option of leaving, with no further obligation to the military. However, any student who continues must commit to two more years, followed by five years of service in the Navy.

There was never a question in Billy's mind.

He'd be completing his academy education and choosing the Navy as a career.

*   *   *

For Jae-sun, being admitted to Princeton was a godsend. He majored in physics and pursued a minor in English. With such a prestigious education, Jae-sun could really contribute to the progress in his country. Much had been accomplished in South Korea since the armistice, but there was much more to do. Moreover, Jae-sun held strong feelings about the atrocities that happened every day in North Korea.

He planned to tell the world someday, somehow, some way.

Just 170 miles separated Princeton and Annapolis. During the four years Billy attended the Academy and Jae-sun was at Princeton, they'd ride the train to see each other when the opportunity arose, which was not too often.

During the summer between third and fourth year, Billy and Jae-sun planned a trip to hike the forty-one miles of the Appalachian Trial in Maryland, then drive through Pennsylvania and hike the seventy-two miles of the trail through New Jersey.

Jae-sun was very excited about the trip; but, not having a great deal of experience with camping and hiking during his lifetime, he read everything he could. He learned about the flora and fauna along the trail—the wild animals, camping sites, insects, and outdoor food preparation. He had to catch up to Billy, who'd been a Boy Scout and had much experience with hiking and camping.

During his sophomore year, Jae-sun met a woman named Park Min-seo at a social event at Rutgers. She and Jae-sun had been spending quite a bit of time together, so she offered to drive he and Billy to the trailhead off US-40, then pick them up near the Pennsylvania border and drive them to the trail in New Jersey near the bridge over the Delaware River on I-80.

Billy's folks still lived in the house where he grew up in Washington, D.C., so Jae-sun and Min-seo drove down to Washington to meet Billy. They organized their gear and prepared for the hike there.

Jae-sun really enjoyed Min-seo's company and was very proud of her. Like Jae-sun, as a child she lived some in the United States and some in Korea. When she was admitted to Rutgers University, she insisted on getting her driver's license and getting a car. She owned a 1949 Oldsmobile 76 station wagon. It was a real boat, but it was in great condition—and it was hers.

On the day of departure, the trio headed west out of Washington to Greenbrier in Maryland. They got an early start on the two-hour drive. Jae-sun encouraged Min-seo to hike with them from the trailhead up to Annapolis Rock Overlook, bid them adieu from there, and return to the trailhead. The plan called for her to drive to the other end of the trail on the Maryland/Pennsylvania border to pick them up in three days.

From the trailhead off I-40, it is a mile hike up to the short cutoff to Annapolis Rock. Jae-sun convinced Min-seo to go that far.

As the trio approached, plaintive cries for help pierced the stillness of the forest. They listened hard and heard the plea again, but closer.

About the time they turned to walk down the cutoff, a young woman came running up the trail, crying for help.

The trio hastened their pace to close the distance.

"It's my brother! Please help me!"

Jae-sun put his hand on her shoulder.

"What about your brother? What's happened?"

"He fell. I was taking his picture, and the loose gravel on the edge of the trail gave way. He slid down the mountain and disappeared out of sight."

Billy was ready. "Show us."

He led the group down the cutoff toward the Overlook. The young woman showed them where her brother stood and where she was standing to take his picture. The scree on the edge had given way and pulled him down the steep incline in a slide. It looked to Jae-sun like the incline ended with a cliff.

Billy breathed deeply and exhaled as he analyzed the situation.

"Jae-sun, this is what I think we should do: Let's you and I hike south until we find a way down, then double back until we find her brother. We'll rig up a gurney and carry him west to the Eisenhower Highway. We'll try to come out as close to the park entrance as possible. What do you think?"

"Sounds good! Min-seo would you please take—uh, what's your name?"

"Jennifer, Jennifer Blake."

"Min-seo, take Jennifer and ask the park ranger to call an ambulance, then meet Billy and me at the park entrance."

Jennifer wiped her tears and watched anxiously. After a few steps, Jae-sun turned.

"Jennifer, what is your brother's name?" He felt sorry for her.

She laced her fingers on the back of her head and exhaled. "John, his name is John."

Jae-sun and Billy picked their way south along the incline. It took them about a half mile to find a route to the forest floor. They walked along the base below the incline, back the direction they had come. The cliff was really beginning to rise above them. By the time they got below the Overlook, it was going to be quite a drop.

Jae-sun worried about what they'd find.

At the point where John should be, Billy and Jae-sun began to look around. Thick trees hugged the base of the cliff.

"Geez, Jae-sun, that looks like an eighty-foot drop."

"Sure does."

Jae-sun walked around a group of small pines to a large American beech tree. It was growing right at the base of the cliff, and its top was above the top of the cliff. At its base, Jae-sun found a tennis shoe. He picked it up and peered up into the tree.

"I see him, Billy!"

"Sure enough, we better get him down before he slips off that branch and falls."

"I'll climb up with the rope and tie him off; then you'll be able to lower him down slowly."

Billy nodded, and Jae-sun scampered up the tree with their rope tied to the belt loop on his pants.

Jae-sun climbed up to the limbs John was draped across, trying not to wobble the branches. Jae-sun leaned over and felt John's neck. He found a pulse and saw his chest rising and falling.

"He's alive!"

His right arm appeared to be broken badly, and he had quite a bleeding gash on his forehead that extended up into his hairline. Jae-sun threw the end of the rope over a six-inch branch directly above

John, then rigged a harness and secured it under John's arms, tying it behind his back. Jae-sun fashioned a sling from his t-shirt and secured John's arm across his chest so it would not flop during the descent.

"I'm ready!"

"How big is he?"

"He's just a little guy—a kid, maybe twelve years old. I'd say about eighty pounds."

Billy wrapped his end of the rope around a hickory tree and pulled the slack up tight.

Jae-sun lifted John's legs off the branch, which allowed them to dangle. The harness supported his body. Billy began slowly lowering John to the ground, while Jae-sun climbed down the tree and guided John through the branches.

On the ground, Jae-sun laid him on his left side to keep his broken right arm out of stress.

Billy said, "I think we should cut two poles and tie our backpack frames between them as a gurney." He grabbed their camp saw and set out to find the proper poles.

Jae-sun took some water from his canteen, wetted a t-shirt, and cleaned the blood from the wound on John's head. He dressed the wound with white athletic cloth tape.

Billy returned with two ten-foot poles. He tied their pack frames between them, end to end.

Jae-sun tenderly lifted John's arm to try to secure it better for the push out to the highway. As Jae-sun raised his elbow, John moaned. Jae-sun used the moist t-shirt to cool John's brow. "How you doing, little man?"

"Who—who are you? What happened? Where's Jennifer?"

"We're Jennifer's friends. You fell—she asked us to come get you."

Jae-sun resumed slowly moving John's arm to a better position for the hike.

"Ahhh!" Tears flowed down John's face, primed by the pain.

"You've gotta be tough, John. Your arm is broken. Billy and I— we're gonna get you outta here."

John's eyes moved from Jae-sun to Billy and back to Jae-sun. He nodded while biting his lip. Jae-sun reassured him with a pat on his knee.

They gently lifted John onto the gurney.

Billy stood up and took a bearing off the cliff, then pointed toward where the highway and park entrance should be.

Jae-sun nodded.

They picked up Jennifer's baby brother and headed toward the highway.

*   *   *

Min-seo and Jennifer hurried back to the trailhead when Jae-sun and Billy were out of sight. Going down at a quick pace took them about fifteen minutes. Jennifer and her family were at the campground near the trailhead. She decided it best to stop and tell her folks what happened.

Min-seo turned her Oldsmobile into the campground and parked near the family tent. Jennifer's youngest brother, James, was playing with grasshoppers; and her folks were sitting at the picnic table, playing cribbage.

Seeing Jennifer, her mother knew something was wrong.

Min-seo hung back a bit to give the family space.

Jennifer explained the situation to her folks.

Jennifer's mother covered her mouth with her hand and gasped.

Jennifer's father wiped his forehead with his arm, kicked the ground, and caught Min-seo's eye. He motioned her over. His voice quavering, he asked, "Your friends, can they find John?"

"They are very capable guys, sir; they will find him."

Min-seo felt bad for the man.

The boy's father said, "Let's go—let's get over to the park entrance."

A sheriff's deputy on his daily patrol pulled into the campground. Jennifer's dad explained the situation; Jennifer and Min-seo filled in the blanks. The deputy keyed his radio and arranged for an ambulance to meet them at the park entrance.

The deputy directed Min-seo, Jennifer, and her family to follow. They'd wait together and hope for the best.

*   *   *

When they emerged from the woods, Jae-sun could see the park entrance structure straight ahead, across a grassy area between the woods and the highway.

"Hey, Billy, your instincts were dead on; there's the park entrance!" Jennifer saw them first. "There, there they are."

The ambulance crew saw them, too, and lit out across the grassy area to meet Billy and Jae-sun.

Jae-sun kept a running conversation with John during the hike, which encouraged him.

They lowered their makeshift litter to the ground when the medics ran up.

"Good job, guys! Whatta we got here?"

Bolstered by Jae-sun's encouragement and humor, John answered. "I'll tell ya what we got here, a broken arm and thump on the melon."

As the crew foreman knelt down to assess John's condition, he continued the banter. "Sounds serious!"

"You should see the other guy!"

Satisfied John was stable, the crew foreman stood and instructed his men to finish redressing John's head wound and bring him on up to the road.

Jae-sun and Billy walked ahead with the foreman. When they reached the others, the foreman assured John's parents that he was fine, a bit banged up, but fine. "Ma'am, these young men did a great job caring for your son."

John's mother looked to Billy and Jae-sun. "Thank you so much, boys. Thank you so much."

Billy replied, "You are welcome, ma'am—glad to help."

Jae-sun added, "Yes, ma'am—glad to help."

The ambulance crew tucked John into the ambulance. His mother rode with John to the hospital in Frederick, Maryland.

Min-seo took Jennifer and her family back to their camp so they could drive to Frederick.

Jennifer and her family warmly thanked Min-seo, Billy, and Jae-sun.

As the trio watched Jennifer and her family drive away, Jae-sun felt his stomach. "I could really use a burger."

Chapter Fourteen

Fate Provides a Meeting

Three years skipped by since Art stepped off the plane in Dutch Harbor. Art and his uncle began implementing their continuity plan. Art jumped right in and learned quickly. He'd passed his test to become a skipper, and the crews respected him and his leadership.

Art received a letter from his SEAL team commander letting him know that Kenny Creighton, one of the men injured on Art's first mission, never really recovered due to a permanent brain injury. The doctors did save Kenny's eye, but after the head injury Kenny struggled. The injury had rendered Kenny child-like, simple, unable to make a decision, or to plan things out. The commander's letter indicated that as far as the commander knew, Kenny lived on the streets in Baltimore.

Art knew what had to be done. After receiving the letter, Art booked a flight to Maryland and planned to walk the alleys of Baltimore until he found Kenny. At 29 years old, Art prided himself for being in tip-top shape, and wasn't worried about being in the underbelly of Baltimore. Art booked a room in a seedy section of town and set out to find Kenny.

After three days of walking the trash-filled alleys—talking to winos, drug addicts, prostitutes, and pimps—Art found Kenny sitting on a five-gallon bucket, crying like a child, intermittently burying his face in his hands, distraught that a stray dog snatched an uneaten burrito he'd found in a Dumpster.

Kenny—*a vet, a SEAL*—here in an alley, all alone and hungry, in the country that sent him into battle—it wasn't right. In that instant Art felt frustrated; he knew he couldn't change the world, but he could sure change Kenny's circumstance. Art walked up to where Kenny sat on his bucket and stopped right in front of him.

Kenny looked up at Art with tears running down his face and snot mashed up in the whiskers above his lip. Kenny looked into Art's eyes for ten full seconds. "Hi, Art, I been trying to find something to eat."

Art was six-foot-four and very fit; Kenny was six-foot-six and lean. Art stuck out his hand, and Kenny's massive paw swallowed it.

Kenny was glad to see him.

"Come on, Kenny, let's get something to eat."

Art led the way to a deli he'd passed up by his hotel. Art could tell Kenny's mental capacity would not allow him to make life decisions, so Art took charge. "Kenny, I want you to come back to Alaska and work with me."

Kenny looked up with half-eaten French fries hanging from his lips. "Okay, Art."

Kenny had been in Alaska with Art for about a year. He could understand and accomplish a job that was laid out for him; he just couldn't figure the next move, but he was strong as an ox and was a good hand. Art always kept him on his boat so he could look after him.

*   *   *

In September of 1994, Art and his crew were out in the Bering Sea fishing for pollack. They had a full hold and were getting ready to make the three-day run back to Dutch Harbor.

Bert piloted the boat while Art looked on. "Bert, I am not feeling so good. Run the boat for a bit while I lay down, okay?"

"Sure, boss."

A storm blew up, producing ten-foot rollers, with the wind knocking the tops off the waves. It was a snotty ocean, but it didn't worry Bert; he was worrying about Art, who rarely left the bridge when they were underway. He'd been below for three hours.

Finally, Bert called Gary on the radio. "Hey, Gary, go down and check on Art."

"Roger that."

Bert waited anxiously for what seemed too long.

The radio crackled and Gary came on. "Hey, Bert."

"Yeah!"

"I think we got a problem. Art is burning with fever and is doubled up in pain. I mean, Art would have to be dying before he'd let on like this."

"Okay, I'll radio Dutch and see what we should do." Bert knew most of the Coast Guard guys in Unalaska. "Unalaska Station, this is Bert Parks of the *Esther* calling."

"Go ahead, *Esther*."

"Yeah. Al, is that you?"

"Yes, Bert. Go ahead."

"Yeah, Al, we're two days out in a snotty ocean. We got a man down sick, real bad—fever, serious pain."

"Okay, *Esther*, stand by—*Esther*, what are your coordinates?"

"N59 41.0 – W169 18.2."

"Okay, *Esther*. Stand by."

*   *   *

Seaman Al Biggs had a flight crew getting ready to leave the Bethel hospital with their HH-3 Pelican helicopter. They had dropped off two men who were stranded at sea. Seaman Biggs called his flight officer, Lt. Commander Nelson.

"Unalaska Station to *Pelican 1*, come in."

"Unalaska Base, *Pelican 1* here."

"*Pelican 1*, we have a sick man—sounds like an appendix about to burst." He gave him the coordinates.

"Okay, Base, we are fueled up and ready to go, but we have no medical officer. Jones broke his leg while we were picking up these last guys off their boat. I'll have to go see if I can recruit someone, or you'll have to call Kodiak and get a full crew out there."

"Okay, see what you can do. Keep me informed. You are just an hour from their location, so you'd be ideal."

"Roger that, Unalaska Station, stand by."

*   *   *

Lt. Commander Nelson jumped out of his bird and ran back into the Bethel hospital where his med tech was being treated for a broken leg. Lt. Commander Nelson let the ER supervisor know that he had an emergency at sea. With no med tech, he needed a volunteer to go into the Bering Sea to pick up a very sick man and get him back to Bethel.

ER Supervisor Jan Henderson stepped out of her office and called her nurses around, a group of seven. She told them of Lt. Commander Nelson's request and looked out at her group.

As Lt. Commander Nelson looked on, he didn't see much enthusiasm for the daunting request. He glanced at his watch—10:30 p.m. Late September and raining sideways—he really didn't blame them. Jan was about to turn back to the commander when a hand rose up from the back.

"I'll go."

Leetia Kashevarof's hand was raised—a great nurse. Two years out of school and doing really good work, Leetia was one of Jan's all-stars. As an Alutiiq from Southwest Alaska, she respected—but was unafraid of—the weather.

"Good deal!"

*   *   *

Three minutes later, Leetia stepped onto the Pelican and prayed she'd made the right decision.

Lt. Commander Nelson informed the Coast Guard station they were on the way.

Leetia had never been in a helicopter before. She enjoyed the ride, despite the weather.

Nelson keyed his radio and called the *Esther*. The conversation came through the headset built into Leetia's flight helmet.

"*Esther*, this is *Pelican 1*. We are five minutes from your location."

"Thanks, *Pelican*."

"Hey, Bert. Who's sick down there?"

"Our skipper, Art Jackson."

"Art Jackson! *The* Art Jackson, Medal of Honor recipient?"

"That's the one. He is really bad sick. I hope you guys can get him some help."

"We'll get him—don't you worry."

Leetia didn't know an Art Jackson.

Lt. Commander Nelson had a hard job. His duty—to hover a helicopter over a moving boat all while being buffeted by twenty-knot winds at night.

Ensign Hernandez hooked himself and Leetia to the cable, then rode the cable down to assist Leetia to the deck of the *Esther*.

Just before they descended, Nelson shouted through the radio. "Nurse Leetia, we don't have time to dawdle. Get him prepped and get him outta there."

"Got it."

Ensign Hernandez gave the signal, and the cable spool lowered him and Leetia to the deck.

Gary waited topside, braced against the doorframe leading down to the living quarters.

As Ensign Hernandez's feet touched the deck, he released the cable, and Leetia followed Gary down the steps. Hernandez sent the cable back up, and the flight crew lowered their enclosed litter to the deck.

Hernandez helped John Dean, a member of the *Esther's* crew, secure the litter, then rode the cable back to the helicopter.

Leetia followed Gary to Art's bunk. When she pulled her helmet off, long black hair fell in front of her shoulders and framed her face. She leaned in to check Art's temperature.

Leetia's cool hand on his torso opened Art's eyes. Then they closed, and he lost consciousness.

"We gotta get him out of here."

It wasn't going to be easy to lift all 230 pounds of him—230 pounds of solid muscle—and get him topside. A small man, Gary positioned himself at Art's head and began to scoot him sideways to the edge of the bunk to try to carry his upper body from under his arm pits. Leetia scooted his feet and legs toward the edge of the bunk at the same time. She and Gary were going to have a tough time.

"We need a blanket to lay him on so we can drag him out of this room."

Gary stepped by Leetia to get to the closet in the hall.

Kenny was pacing, clearly agitated by the fact that Art was sick. Kenny was in front of the closet door when Gary emerged.

"Move aside, Kenny! She wants a blanket to slide Art out so we can get him topside."

"*I'll* get him topside."

Kenny stepped into the room.

Art lay on the edge of his bunk, looking rough.

Kenny nodded at Leetia, then leaned over and easily picked up Art, laid him over his own right shoulder, and walked out of the room.

Leetia grabbed her radio helmet and followed Kenny up the stairs. She motioned to Gary. "Get me a bucket of ice."

Bracing against the wind, Leetia opened the litter, and Kenny laid Art into the cage.

Leetia secured the top. She radioed Lt. Commander Nelson and asked that the cable be deployed back to the deck.

Nelson deftly hovered the helicopter over the deck, and the flight crew deployed the cable.

Leetia secured the cable onto the litter, straddled the cage, and grabbed the bucket of ice from Gary as she keyed the mike. "Take us up."

The flight crew began to spool the cable back in. Nelson swung the basket over the rail of the boat and moved the helicopter away so the ascending basket would not swing into the bridge or boom.

When the basket was at the door of the helicopter, the flight crew swung the basket through the door.

Leetia gracefully hopped off, then opened the top of the man-basket as the flight crew closed the helicopter door. They set Art onto a pad on the helicopter deck and stowed the man-basket.

Leetia quickly assessed Art's condition and asked the commander to radio ahead to the hospital and inform them so a surgery suite could be prepped and ready.

Leetia prepared an ice pack for Art's forehead, then removed Art's shirt and began using the ice to cool his torso. Art's fever had to come down; she prayed silently that his appendix would not burst. They were making good time, as the wind gave them a push back to Bethel.

At 12:30 a.m. the helicopter set down adjacent to the hospital. The entire staff were kept updated on progress because on this mission they had one of their own—Nurse Leetia Kashevarof.

The surgery team pushed the gurney to the edge of the helicopter and wheeled Art right into surgery.

After the last two-and-a-half hours of action, the pace slowed abruptly. The flight crew headed back to Unalaska, and the surgery crew was likely performing an appendectomy.

Leetia was off the next day, so she decided to go home and take a shower, then come back to see how Art's surgery went. During her time on the boat, Leetia had focused on getting Art stabilized and back to Bethel; but now, stepping into the shower, she began to appreciate Art Jackson being so handsome, even sick—what a hunk. Twenty-six, two years out of nursing school and single, Leetia smiled to herself at the notion of dating a man like Art Jackson. She whispered a prayer for his recovery.

When Leetia returned, Art had just come out of surgery. He indeed suffered with an infected appendix, which they removed successfully.

They moved Art into a room to recover from the anesthesia. Art had no one in Bethel, so Leetia appointed herself his support group. She pulled a chair up beside his hospital bed and gently slipped his hand into hers, palm to palm, with her fingers tenderly gripping his thumb. Leetia kept a moist cloth on Art's forehead and kept an eye on his vitals, which were flashing on the monitor every minute or so.

Leetia felt Art's hand squeeze hers. She opened her eyes and looked up at Art's, which were still closed. She gently squeezed his hand in return.

Twenty minutes later Art stirred ever so slightly.

Leetia sat up and remoistened the cloth on Art's forehead.

As she leaned over, gently positioning the cloth, Art Jackson opened his eyes. "Are you my—my Angel? I think I've seen you before."

"No, Mr. Jackson, I am your nurse. Your Angels are Kenny Creighton and your crew. They saved your life. They got the Coast Guard out to your boat. The Coast Guard brought you here to Bethel."

"I am in Bethel? What smells so good?"

*   *   *

Art waved his hand from his elbow, searching for the hand that had been holding his.

Leetia slipped her hand back into his.

As Art's eyes closed, he knew what smelled so good. He gently squeezed the hand holding his as sleep returned.

Chapter Fifteen

Reflections

At 1:15 a.m. on Saturday morning, June 16, 1969, Soo-ah sat in her study, reflecting on life, counting her blessings. Gus had long since gone to bed. Later this day, Soo-ah's oldest child, Charlotte, her only daughter, would be married. Soo-ah had much to be happy about.

She replayed Charlotte's sweet life in her mind, happy for Charlotte, but maudlin for a chapter closing in her own—her little girl all grown up. Soo-ah thought about her mom and dad, and her poor sisters. She wished they could be here for this event.

Soo-ah's little Charlotte was just nine days from her 23rd birthday. Her fiancé was a young man she had met at Oregon State University named Jacob "Jake" Flynn. The entire family loved him. After finishing his undergraduate degree, now he was studying to be a certified public account.

In 1948, Charlotte's first brother, Gus Jr., was born. In 1951, the twins, Henry and Joe, were born. And in 1955, Charlotte's little brother, Sam, was born. All the boys were in the wedding, helping one way or the other.

Charlotte's great-grandfather, Henry, died three years earlier at 89; but Charlotte's namesake and great-grandmother was still going strong at 88 and would be witnessing her great-granddaughter's nuptials.

At 2:00 p.m., the families and friends gathered at the Baptist Church in Florence, Oregon. It was foggy that morning, but by 2:00 p.m. the sun was shining, filling the sanctuary with dazzling light through the large stained-glass window.

The ceremony was beautiful and came off with just one hitch—the one that was *supposed to* happen.

*   *   *

Almost two years later, in February of 1971; Soo-ah, Gus, Grace, and Joe were all in the maternity waiting area of the Florence hospital. Everyone was anxious as the minutes ticked by.

A nurse came through the doors leading back to the birthing area. She announced a new boy in the family, then invited them back one at a time to visit the baby.

Soo-ah went first. The nurse asked her to slip on a hospital gown over her clothes, then left to get the baby from the nursery. She came through the door into Charlotte's hospital room with a bassinette on a roller table.

Charlotte and Jake watched with glee as the nurse placed the baby into Soo-ah's arms.

"Mother, his name is Jacob Gil-su Flynn."

A tear fell off Soo-ah's cheek as she heard her father's name. Soo-ah decided then and there she'd teach little Jake the language of his Korean great-grandfather.

Chapter Sixteen

Leetia on the Mind

Art was in Bethel Hospital for three days. Art and Leetia ate every lunch and dinner together. The other nurses told Art about Leetia going out with the Coast Guard to retrieve him. Moreover, when Lt. Commander Nelson came back to Bethel to pick up his med tech, he stopped in to meet Art, and told him of Leetia riding the man-basket up to the helicopter and working to keep his fever down. For the three days after Art's surgery, Leetia and Art nurtured the beginning of a relationship.

The doctor popped into Art's hospital room to check on his progress.

"Well, Mr. Jackson, you are looking good, but you really need to give yourself four weeks to fully recover."

The phone rang.

"Hello."

"Art, it's Milt. The guys called down and told us. How you doing?"

"I'm fine, Uncle Milt. The doctor is here. He says I need four weeks."

"Well, come down here, damnit; your old aunt will get you healed up."

"That sounds pretty good. I'll call in a bit and work things out."

"Sounds good, buddy. Bye-bye."

Milt and Esther had a nice home in Hawai'i, on the Big Island, a spacious place on a small farm up the hill with a view to the ocean.

Two days later, Art was discharged. Leetia wheeled Art out to the front of the hospital to the cab stand. He planned to catch a plane to Anchorage, then on to Hawai'i.

A cab pulled up to the curb, and Art knew it was time to go, but he did not want to leave. He turned to Leetia and opened his arms, inviting a hug. Leetia stepped between his arms as he enveloped her.

"Nurse Kashevarof, I do not want to leave you."

"And I don't want you to go."

"Come to Hawai'i with me and oversee my recovery."

"Is there room? Where would I stay?"

"There is lots of room. It is a four-bedroom house. You'd have your own room, and we'll spend the days together, seeing if we have something here."

"I want to come, but it will take me a week to arrange the time off and get ready. Will you pick me up at the airport next Sunday?"

"It's a date—a real date!"

Art arrived on Hawai'i late in the evening. Rather than bother his Aunt and Uncle, he took a cab to the house.

The next morning, Art remembered why Milt's and Esther's home was so wonderful. He walked out onto the veranda and took in the spectacular view to the ocean, three miles in the distance—the 1200-foot elevation was just enough. The privacy the five-acre parcel provided gave any visitor a sense of sanctuary.

He walked back into the house, found his aunt in the kitchen, and greeted her with a hug.

"Sit down, Art. I'll make you some breakfast. Coffee?"

The glass doors to the veranda were open, and a warm tropical breeze was coming up the hill from the ocean, freshening everywhere in its path. Art sipped his coffee and enjoyed the moment.

Art ate his breakfast while regaling Esther with all the details of his illness, getting flown off the boat, and waking up in Bethel.

"I met a nice girl while I was in Bethel—a nurse."

"Ohhh?"

"What would you think about her joining us down here for a few weeks? I thought it might be a good time to try to get to know her a bit better."

"I think that's great. We'll move you over to the front bedroom on this side and we'll fix her up in the back bedroom on that side so she can see the ocean."

"She'll like that."

It seemed to Art like the first week took forever to march off the calendar, but soon enough Sunday arrived. He arrived at the Kona International airport early, wanting to be at the gate when Leetia's flight arrived, trying to contain his anxiousness.

*   *   *

The plane stopped abruptly, and the seat belt sign went off.

Leetia's heart started to pound. Anxious to see Art, she felt apprehensive, with butterflies all at the same time. She'd never felt like this before.

Waiting for the other passengers to exit, she used the time to slow her heart rate and not seem too anxious.

Finally she emerged from the jetway and saw Art before he saw her. A little girl had fallen next to him, and he was helping her back to her feet and comforting her while handing her off to her daddy.

In that moment, Leetia understood her feelings.

She loved this man.

*   *   *

As Art turned his attention back to the jetway door, he beheld the object of his anticipation—beautiful, sweet Leetia. Her jet-black hair looked radiant against her white top. Her blue slacks framed her delicate waist and led his eyes down her legs to the tips of her toes.

He smiled and waved.

Leetia calmly walked over and set down her bag.

Art hugged her and breathed in the aroma of her person.

"Hi, Art."

"Hi, Leetia. I've missed you."

"I've missed you, too. How are we doing down here—may I see?"

"Sure." He lifted his shirt.

"It looks good."

Art picked up Leetia's handbag and put it over his right shoulder, then held his left hand out, inviting her to hold his as they strolled to the baggage-claim area. Leetia took his hand and confidently walked out of the airport with her man.

They were married three months later at La'aloa Bay.

Chapter Seventeen

A Life Well Lived
(But just getting started)

Geon Jae-sun waited in the lobby of his condominium building in Seoul for his sixteen-year-old daughter; she was finishing just one more curl in her hair. Jae-sun dropped his youngest daughter off at school each morning on the way to the Korean Institute of Science and Technology. A professor, Jae-sun had been teaching physics at the Institute since finishing his graduate degree at MIT in 1969.

Married since 1973, Jae-sun and Park Min-seo were blessed with two daughters, one at Princeton—now that women were allowed—and one in high school.

Jae-sun's peers respected the remarkable contributions he made to South Korea through physics and the education of the next generation—they loved Geon Jae-sun.

Jae-sun also enjoyed some fame, but not for his work in physics—for his words. In 1975, Jae-sun accomplished a dream come true—being given a weekly column in the *Chosun Ilbo* newspaper in Seoul. Through that platform Jae-sun spent the last twenty-one years laying bare the lies put forward by the North Korean government and exposing the atrocities that the North Koreans continually used to brutalize the people of the North. At least fifteen-million people in South Korea—and at least one in North Korea—followed Jae-sun's column.

Sitting in the lobby of his building in May of 1996, Geon Jae-sun enjoyed notoriety in the South Korean market equivalent to the notoriety Paul Harvey enjoyed in the American market.

*   *   *

The North Korean government of Kim Jong-il hated Geon Jae-sun with a zealous passion, as did the previous regime of Kim Il-sung. The North Korean government knew that Geon Jae-sun's column and political commentary were very effective in checking the North's constant efforts to improve their standing in the world. Jae-sun fearlessly criticized Kim Jong-il, and Kim Il-sung before him—a slight that would not be tolerated in the North.

Now the North Korean government was apoplectic with news their intelligence network had delivered to Pyongyang. Rumors were circulating in South Korea that Geon Jae-sun would be given a syndicated radio talk show to be broadcast throughout Central Asia.

This could not be allowed to happen.

Kim Jong-il just could not allow the intellect, wit, and charm of Geon Jae-sun to influence key players in the region.

Something had to be done.

*   *   *

The magazine Jae-sun leafed through was interesting, but he was anxious to get going. They were not late, but Jae-sun had a meeting later that morning with a media firm to discuss the possibility of a radio talk show styled after the successful *The Rush Limbaugh Show* in the United States.

Jae-sun looked at his watch and decided to step through the glass doors onto the sidewalk to get a newspaper.

*   *   *

Mi-na stepped out of their flat on the sixteenth floor and punched the elevator call button. Mercifully, she caught the express elevator. She exited at the lobby level. Through the glass doors of their building, Mi-na saw the profile of her father, standing in front of the newspaper box, dropping coins in.

With a smile on her lips. she thought about how handsome he is.

She had begun to cover the thirty feet between the elevator and the outside doors, when a black van skidded to the curb next to her father.

She froze as two men emerged from the sliding door.

One of the men hit her father in the stomach, then pulled a black canvas bag over his head, down to his waist. They picked him up and threw him into the van, then pulled away from the curb.

The entire maneuver took less than ten seconds.

The doorman ran out onto the sidewalk with Mi-na a step behind.

The van turned right on the next block and disappeared behind the building.

Just like that, Geon Jae-sun was gone.

Chapter Eighteen

Life is Good

In the summer of 1995, Milt told Art and Leetia that he and Esther wanted to live full-time in Hawai'i, and that they wanted Art and Leetia to move into the house at Esther Bay and make it their own. Esther really needed to spend her time in a warmer climate because the cold made her arthritis painful.

Art and Leetia shipped all of Milt and Esther's personal items to Hawai'i then flew down to help put it all away and arrange things in their Hawai'i home.

The 1995 fishing season proved to be very good—no accidents, no major maintenance, lots of fish, a prosperous time for all.

Art and Leetia really enjoyed their first year of marriage. They redecorated the house in Esther Bay and bought some new furniture to go with the new décor. They spent September in Manokotak visiting Leetia's parents, Andrew and Lillian, and extended family. They spent October in Esther Bay fishing the Bering Sea, and November doing all the maintenance on the fishing fleet. They spent December and half of January in Hawai'i with Milt and Esther, and they spent part of January and February in the Philippines with Leetia's sister and her husband. In March, they headed back to Esther Bay to get ready for the 1996 fishing season.

The master bedroom of Art and Leetia's home in Esther Bay was on the east end of the house, and it had an elevated deck on the north side of the house, off the master bedroom, facing Esther Bay and the Bering Sea beyond.

At 6:30 Sunday morning, July 14, 1996, Leetia opened her eyes, then kissed her sleeping husband on the temple and slipped out of bed. She pulled on her bathrobe and let the belt dangle on the hoops, then stepped out onto the deck adjacent to her side of the bed and slid the door closed behind her.

She loved Alaska.

This morning was so clear it seemed like she could see all the way across Bristol Bay to her village, 500 miles northeast. Leetia breathed in the ocean-kissed wind and let the sun shine on her face.

Minutes later the door slid open, and she felt the loving arms of her husband cradle her in a welcome embrace. She turned and kissed Art on the bottom of his square jaw.

"It is beautiful here."

"Yes, it truly is."

"Art?"

"Yes, Leetia."

"What was your dad's name?"

"It was Andrew. Andrew Gunnar Jackson."

"Really! Andrew?—just like *my* dad?"

"Yep, he had the same first name."

She turned toward him inside of his embrace. "Well, you know what I think?" She knew what he thought—his eyes focused on the open front of her robe.

"No, what?"

"I think you should name your son Andrew Gunnar Jackson too."

"Oh, you do, do you? And when might he be arriving?"

Leetia kissed Art on the middle of his chest, then looked up into his eyes. "He'll be here in March."

Then she slipped under his left arm and walked back through the door, slid her bathrobe off, and dropped back into bed.

He knew she was serious.

She invited him to her side, and they enjoyed the news together.

Chapter Nineteen

Dreariness all Around

His right shin really hurt. Jae-sun pulled his right leg up and tucked his knee under the lip of the bag they'd put over him, rubbing his shin, trying to ease the pain from banging it on the door threshold when they threw him into the van.

Two guys were in the front seats talking about a transfer vehicle. Their dialect revealed them as being from the North.

Are they going to kill me?

The dread evaporated, convinced that if they were going to kill him, they would have done that already and they wouldn't be worried about a transfer vehicle. The dread of being separated from his family would not so easily leave his mind. And what of his family?—would they be targets, too? Jae-sun's hands were not bound under the bag, not yet, anyway.

Jae-sun instinctively reached up and grasped the crucifix around his neck. A true believer living faithfully, he did not fall into the category of a *sometimes* Christian. Truly practicing his faith, he felt calmed by the assurance it gave him. As he grasped the crucifix, he thought, *If Billy were here, that would even the odds.*

Jae-sun smiled at the thought.

At some point he'd be questioned—and maybe worse. Knowing if they saw his crucifix they'd take it, he slipped it off, cupped it in his hand, and with his thumbnail forced a tear in the band of his boxer underwear, poking the crucifix and chain into the hole.

The van slowed and turned sharply to the right, then stopped. The driver exited the vehicle. Jae-sun's heart pounded in anticipation.

The side door opened.

"We are taking you out here." Someone on either side directed him to the door.

He cooperated. To his mind, resisting offered no upside.

"We are transferring you to another vehicle. We'll be on the road two hours. Step forward five feet and piss, if you need. Keep the bag over your head."

Jae-sun thought that might be a good idea, so he complied. Then two people led him up a ramp into what seemed like a box truck. An overhead door rolled down. Someone directed him backwards to a hard chair. It seemed bolted to the floor because it would not slide or tip. They shackled his ankles to the chair legs and wrists to the arms. They replaced the big bag with a smaller one that just covered his head.

Just ten minutes in captivity, and in a different truck. The vehicle started and backed up, then pulled forward and over a curb cut and out onto a street. Despair crept into his mind, so it would be a good time to pray.

After about twenty minutes, the stops and starts vastly diminished, so they must be on a freeway or highway. They said about two hours. Jae-sun could bend down and hold the top of the bag with his left thumb and forefinger, sliding it up just enough to look around. Sunshine poured through three holes in the front of the box over the cab, so they must be heading east. Jae-sun leaned over and pulled the bag down, closed his eyes, and prayed.

The truck came to a stop.

The rolling door rose.

Someone unshackled his ankles, then his wrists. They stood him up and handcuffed his hands in front with chain cuffs. With help, he walked out onto a wooden floor. It sounded like water under the floor—a wharf warehouse or something like that maybe. They told Jae-sun to piss again if he needed to, then slipped his bag up to his nose, put a water bottle to his lips, and told him to drink. They picked him up, laid him inside a wooden box, and closed the lid above him. What sounded like a forklift moved the box.

He felt heat from the sun shining on his arm through the cracks in the box. The box lurched upward, swung, and descended. The sunshine rays warming his arm were gone. The box stopped abruptly. A hatch slammed shut.

All fell quiet.

Several minutes later, the distinctive sound of a marine diesel engine started behind him. The boat began to move. It crept forward, just above idle for a bit.

Jae-sun banged his head against the side of the box as the boat lurched forward, and the engine screamed behind him.

*   *   *

After several hours, the engine pulled back to idle. Jae-sun still had his watch on, so he raised the bag up to his eye and pushed the back-light button with his lower front teeth—2:00 p.m. They'd been underway about four hours.

The boat bobbed up and down on the open ocean. Waves lapping over the end of the pipe muffled the exhaust. The deck hatch opened, and someone walked toward the box. The lid opened, and two some-ones helped him to his feet and lifted him out of the box. They hung a wool blanket around his neck and walked him to a set of stairs, which led up to the deck of the boat. They walked him over to an obstruction, lifted him over whatever he had come up against, and sat him down on a bench. Someone climbed in behind him. A hydraulic spool started.

Whatever he was in moved. He felt a gentle rocking. Small waves splashed against the side. He was on a small boat.

A small outboard engine started, and the boat jerked forward as the motor clicked into gear. The little boat never got onto step because of rough water. The driver just cruised over the waves about 1/3 throttle for about five minutes. He throttled back to idle, then unchained Jae-sun's wrists and ankles.

"I'm going to idle up next to the boat we are coming up to. I'm going to pull the bag off. Do not look backward. When I say, 'stand up', do so and grab the ladder to your left and climb up to the deck. They will not tie your wrists or feet. They'll be looking for any excuse to simply shoot you, so you'd better follow instructions, and not try anything stupid. Nod if you understand."

Jae-sun nodded. The man behind him slid something into the breast pocket of his shirt.

"Give them these; they might go easier on you."

Jae-sun looked down into his shirt pocket at a nearly full pack of cigarettes and a butane lighter.

"Stand now and turn left."

Jae-sun obeyed. He reached out to grab the ladder hanging over the side of a larger boat. As he stepped onto the bottom rung, the boat he arrived in sped away.

Jae-sun climbed the ladder to the deck with his wool blanket still over his neck. Two very angry-looking North Korean soldiers greeted him with the barrels of their guns.

As Jae-sun stepped onto the deck, he held his hands out and up, trying not to be provocative.

One of the soldiers stepped back and toward the salon door.

The other stepped back and toward the stern. He pointed his rifle toward a wooden box lying against the far gunnel. "Sit there."

Jae-sun nodded, then opened his right hand wide and slowly brought it toward his breast pocket. He pulled the cigarettes and lighter out, and offered them to the soldiers. The soldier on his left reached out and took them. They didn't smile, but their scowls seemed to soften.

His hands still raised, he walked to the box and sat. Despite the sunshine, Jae-sun still felt cold out on the water. He draped the wool blanket over his shoulders and braced against the wind.

Four hours later, Jae-sun could see the shore in the distance. As they grew closer, a city with a port came into view.

The boat pulled up to a wooden dock in the boat basin. Jae-sun hadn't seen a place so stark since arriving back in Korea in 1955—like he'd gone back in time, gray, and dirty, and featureless. No slick yachts in the boat basin, or new concrete docks. No glass office buildings facing the waterfront, no landscaping—just dreariness all around.

One of the soldiers ordered Jae-sun to step off the boat. Jae-sun complied, stepping out onto the middle of the dock. They directed him toward the shore ramp and walked behind him. At the top of the ramp waited an old flatbed truck with racks around the perimeter, except for the back. Five pitiful-looking souls were sitting on bales of straw, two on one side, three on the other. Jae-sun felt the barrel of a rifle poke him in the back, directing him to the back of the truck. He climbed up onto the deck and sat on one of the straw bales. It smelled wet and moldy. The soldiers got into an open top jeep, which followed behind the truck.

Fifteen minutes later the truck stopped at a gate with a guard shack and an eight-foot fence running out on either side. From his position on the back of the truck, Jae-sun could see a compound about three-hundred yards up the road. The gate opened and the convoy rolled through. The truck approached the compound and parked parallel to the end of the building, farthest to the right.

The six passengers were ordered out and directed to line up abreast, facing a separate wooden building with a covered wooden porch. They were in a line twenty feet from the building. An officer emerged and walked to the edge of the porch.

"Remove your clothes and place them on the ground directly in front of where you are standing!"

Jae-sun and the others complied. Lowering his wool slacks and underwear, he pulled his crucifix from its hiding place and let it lie in the leg hole of his slacks. When the crucifix fell to the ground, he covered it with his foot. Jae-sun folded his slacks and placed them on his shoes and socks, then took off his shirt and placed it on the pile.

A soldier walked over and picked up Jae-sun's clothes and put them on the porch next to the officer. He gathered up the clothes of the rest of the group and put them in a common pile over by the truck.

A soldier came to Jae-sun and ordered him to remove his rings and his watch. The soldier placed these on Jae-sun's clothes up on the porch. The officer ordered the group to hold out their right arms one at a time. Two soldiers walked up to the man on the end and ordered him to hold out his arm. One held an ink pot, the other a needle. He started tattooing the man's arm.

The third man cried and winced at the needle, so he was beaten unconscious by the soldiers. Then they tattooed him.

When they came to Jae-sun, he stood stone-still and silent, even though it did hurt. They tattooed his arm with two numbers: *711* and *Block 1.*

A soldier brought a bundle and set one in front of each man. The officer ordered the men to put on their camp clothes.

In his bundle, Jae-sun found flip-flops, cotton trousers that tied at the waist, a shirt akin to a flour sack with arm holes, a coat that looked like something Mao would wear, and a wool cap. Jae-sun stepped into the leg hole of the trousers while they were bunched on the ground. Before he slid them up, he tucked his crucifix into his palm.

He looked down the line at the man they'd beaten. Frothy blood oozed from his mouth, and he did not seem to be breathing.

Jae-sun finished putting on his clothes, slipped his crucifix into the pocket of his coat, and stood back at attention.

Moments later, two soldiers dragged the beaten man over to the pile of clothes near the truck and dropped him.

Another soldier picked up the unused bundle and walked away.

Jae-sun stood at attention and waited.

Chapter Twenty

Leetia's Boy

I f ever a family had a favorite, it would be Leetia, the third of five children. Growing up, she always took care of her two younger brothers, and played peacemaker between her older sister and brother. Her mom worked at the school in the village and depended on Leetia to keep her siblings on task and on time. Her dad fished commercially in Bristol Bay in the summer and trapped in the winter. Leetia adored him. Never giving her folks any trouble—never using tobacco, drugs, or booze—she applied herself and got an education and a job.

Everyone loved Leetia.

In September, Leetia called her mother to share news of a coming baby. Lillian Kashevarof was over the moon, calling all her sisters and her mother. Soon enough, everyone from Manokotak to Naknek knew.

Art and Leetia's prenatal visits were in Dutch Harbor, but as March grew closer, they decided being closer to civilization was prudent so they wouldn't be stuck in Esther Bay by weather when the baby decided to come. One of Leetia's aunts, her dad's sister Nita, lived in Anchorage. On February 25th, Art packed things they needed, and they flew to Anchorage to stay with Nita and her husband until the baby arrived.

At 1:00 a.m. on the morning of March 9th, 1997, Leetia got out of bed to pee. Another labor pain reminded her the baby was nigh. She walked to the bed and whispered to her husband, "Sweetheart, it is time to go."

Art sat up and rubbed his face. "Are you okay?"

"Yeah, but I don't think this will take long."

Nita's home was just about one-half mile from the hospital. Art had his Nike pants and sweatshirt laid out and ready to go. He slipped on his clothes, brushed his teeth, grabbed Leetia's bag, and they were off.

On Sunday morning, March 9th, 1997, at 3:30 a.m., an OB nurse laid Art's son, Andrew Gunnar Jackson, in his mother's arms. The baby's head was supported by her left elbow.

She looked at her baby and then looked over at her husband, standing beside the bed.

Tears were flowing down Art's cheeks. His emotion touched Leetia, and she drew him close.

"I told you your son would be here in March."

"Yes, you did, and he is beautiful."

*   *   *

The next day Andrew and Lillian Kashevarof flew to Anchorage to meet their new grandson. After they got to meet little Andrew and hold him, the nurse took Andrew back to the nursery, which had a display window into a common hall. Andrew Kashevarof stepped out of Leetia's hospital room to use the restroom. Walking down the hall adjacent to the display window, he met his cousin, Carl, coming from the other direction.

"Hi ya, Andy. What brings you to Anchorage?"

Andrew put his arm around his cousin and turned to the window, looking into the nursery.

"That's Leetia's boy. She named him Andrew.

The two men stood at the window, arms over each other, misty eyed together.

Chapter Twenty-one

New Reality

The evening of Thursday, May 16th, 1996, Jae-sun arrived at Prison Camp 15, Section 9. He missed the 6:00 p.m. meal line, but learned the next day not much was missed. He was assigned to Block One, the name they'd tattooed on his forearm. Block One was on the end of the first building next to the fence. The section of the building named Block One was a long narrow room with one door in the middle of the long wall facing the courtyard. Thirty-five two-man bunks filled the far wall—one man up, one man down. Thirty-four more bunks filled the door-side wall, seventeen to the right of the door and seventeen to the left. In all, 138 berths crowded the room, forty-four women and ninety-four men. All prisoners were required to be inside their assigned buildings by 8:00 p.m.

The only berth not taken the night Jae-sun arrived was the last one on the bottom on the far right of the far wall. Nobody wanted the berths in the corners, because they had two outside walls for the cold to come through at night. The berths were simply a platform 75 centimeters wide, made of rough-sawn wood planks with no padding, nothing but hard wood for the prisoners to sleep on. Each had a piece of old canvas for a blanket, the only consideration for comfort. The sleeping berths were attached to the outside walls on one end and supported by posts on the other. Eighty centimeters separated each set of berths.

In the month since Jae-sun arrived, twenty-three people died in his block, four women and nineteen men, most starved to death. Each morning at 6:00 a.m. each inmate walked through the meal line and received 40 soya beans and a cup-and-a-half of cold cabbage soup. The same meal was served at noon and again at 6:00 p.m. Jae-sun figured his body needed 1200 calories just to survive, but was getting only about 450 calories, so he too was on a path to starvation. He'd lost about fifteen pounds since arriving, but he was in a lot better condition than most when they first arrived in this hell.

For twenty years, Jae-sun wrote about the horrors of the North Korean Marxist government; he had no doubt that is why he'd been abducted. He knew about the prison camps, but was very surprised to see just how inhumane conditions were. The guards treated the prisoners like animals—less than animals.

His second week in the camp, two men trapped a rat in the courtyard in a corner where two buildings meet. They were fighting over the rat, each willing to tear it apart and eat it raw.

A guard intervened and shot both men in the head with his sidearm. As they fell, the rat ran away, ignored by the guard. The men lay where they died for a week; inmates were not allowed to move the fallen until directed. The guards used the corpses as a warning to the living not to step out of line. The rat returned with others and ate the eyes of the men from their eye sockets, and ate their fingertips and toe tips—horrible.

The first morning after Jae-sun arrived, he stood in the meal line at 6:00 a.m. for the meager breakfast—his 45 soya beans and his cold cabbage soup. Later they marched Jae-sun to the far end of the courtyard to the latrine, a 4" diameter wooded rail elevated 16 inches above grade on posts, the wooden rail approximately thirty feet long. A trench dug into the ground just behind the rail served as the receptacle for human waste. The prisoners were required to use this latrine and five others like it to relieve themselves in full view of anyone in the area, both male and female—another tool to deny dignity to the prisoners.

Jae-sun received his assignment—to clean all five latrines. His tools, a wooden hoe attached to a four-foot wooden handle and a wooden stave bucket. At gunpoint, Jae-sun cleaned the human waste out of the trench at each latrine, then carried it in the bucket to a waste pit located approximately 200 yards from the building clusters.

Every day as Jae-sun toiled about the continual process of keeping the latrines empty, he noticed the commander watching him—watching him more than casually. Jae-sun endeavored not to make eye contact or to even let on that he knew of the surveillance.

Jae-sun developed a routine to help keep sane. He woke at 5:00 a.m. each day to pray; his prayer time helped him endure. He also kept a calendar of sorts on the ceiling of his bottom bunk, today beginning his 31st day in captivity. Jae-sun went through the morning meal line and received his meager allowance. Each prisoner had to bring his own soup tin. Jae-sun began asking that his beans be placed in the soup tin, so he didn't have to touch them. Prisoners were not allowed to wash their hands or bathe, and Jae-sun worried that his job might make him more likely to contract cholera or hepatitis.

That morning, Jae-sun retrieved his first load of waste from the latrines and made his way toward the pit. Two of the guards stopped him. The guard on his left ordered him to set his bucket and hoe down. They marched him to the administration building.

They marched him up to the edge of the covered porch and ordered him to stop. The guard behind him and to his right walked past and knocked on the door, then walked back and assumed his position.

They waited there for two full minutes. Then the door opened.

"That is all."

The guards immediately turned and left, leaving Jae-sun standing alone.

The commander held the door and motioned Jae-sun in. Jae-sun entered and stood in front of the commander's desk.

The commander sat and looked up at Jae-sun. "Geon Jae-sun, my name is Colonel Ji. Do you know why you are here?"

"I believe I do."

"Then tell me, why are you here?"

"Your superiors have stolen my liberty because I have often told the world of their sins and their shortcomings."

"Sins? Are you a religious man?"

"Yes I am."

"Why has your God allowed you to end up here?"

Jae-sun wondered if the colonel was curious or just toying with him. Aware that the North indoctrinates their people to believe the state is their god, Jae-sun decided to answer the colonel's question with a question of his own.

"Why has *your* god required *you* to be here?"

The colonel looked up at Jae-sun with an almost fearful look. He got up, walked past Jae-sun, and opened the door. "Resume your duties."

Jae-sun walked out, and the door closed gently behind him.

The next day the same two guards stopped Jae-sun and again marched him to the administration building. Again, one of the guards knocked on the door and again Colonel Ji dismissed the guards and ordered Jae-sun into his office. The Colonel sat down, exhaled, and looked at Jae-sun; but to Jae-sun's mind the Colonel looked through him, almost like he was arguing with himself how to proceed.

Colonel Ji finally spoke. "Yesterday you said you believe that your being here is because you've told the world of my superiors' sins and shortcomings. How have you done that?"

"Since 1973 I've written a weekly column in one of the newspapers in Seoul. The column is available all over the free world."

"So, anyone in the South can read your column?"

"Anyone in the South, anyone in the United States, Japan, and Europe—anywhere there is basic freedom of the press."

Jae-sun could read curiosity in the Colonel's face. In that moment Jae-sun realized Colonel Ji was essentially a prisoner, too—just with a longer leash.

"So, you believe people in the United States read your column?"

"Yes, I know they do. I sent it in Korean and in English. There is a large Korean community across the United States."

"So, you speak English? Have you been to the United States?"

"Yes, I lived there from 1949 until 1955, and again from 1958 to 1969."

"An evil place, is it not?"

"I think you've probably been told that all your life, but that is not true. The United States is a wonderful place, a place where individual liberty and freedom is encouraged and protected. This place, this entire country is the evil place."

The Colonel's body language seemed to say that he may be willing to consider Jae-sun's statement.

Jae-sun looked Colonel Ji in the eye. "Why would I lie to you? I did not come here voluntarily or infiltrate this camp as a spy. I was kidnapped and brought here to silence my pen. I have no reason to lie."

"If you are pious, why would your God allow you to be brought here?"

"Colonel Ji, God does not dictate the lives of his faithful. He does not impose his principles and mores onto people and treat them like puppets. God's way gives each man free agency to make a choice, to have freedom of thought and association. Even your superiors have free agency, which they exercised to kidnap me. They do not like me exposing the truth about them to the world. I am not required to worship my God. I do, because I want to. The salvation offered is for eternity—life after this life. There are no guarantees in following God's path that trouble will not cross the path."

The colonel sat and looked at Jae-sun, processing his words. After three minutes of silence, the colonel stood and dismissed Jae-sun as he had before.

On the third day after his initial meeting, they marched Jae-sun into Colonel Ji's office again.

"I am reassigning you to kitchen duty. You'll be helping to prepare and serve meals to my guards and officers. You will report to the kitchen immediately and receive further instruction. That is all."

Jae-sun counted his blessings, maybe an act of charity on Colonel Ji's part. Jae-sun saw no upside in thanking him and making a big deal of the re-assignment—these things are complicated.

"Yes, sir."

The guards escorted Jae-sun to the kitchen. Finding a middle-aged woman working there, he introduced himself and asked her name.

"I'm Lee Mi-sun. So, *you* are who they chose."

Confused, he asked, "Chosen—for what?"

"To replace me."

"How do you know this?"

"Because I told Colonel Ji yesterday that I am sick and that I will die soon."

Her matter-of-fact approach to her own death stunned Jae-sun. "How can you be sure?"

"I have breast cancer. There is no treatment here, except a bullet. Soon I'll be on that truck and dumped into the pit."

Jae-sun looked at her with no expression.

"You thought they take the people out of here on the truck to give them a respectable burial? They drive the bodies two kilos north of camp and dump them into a sand pit. Every week they soak the pit with diesel and burn the bodies."

"How do you know this to be true?"

"I've been preparing their meals and serving them for seven years. After a while you learn things."

"You've been here seven years! Why are you a prisoner here?"

"Seven years ago, my brother tried to escape to China. He was caught near the border without the proper paperwork. He was executed by firing squad, and my mother and I were snatched from our home and brought here to be punished for my brother's crime. My mother only lived six months after we arrived."

These are the kinds of things Jae-sun heard about the North Korean prison camps. He had written about the injustice of the North's system, but somehow living the injustice and seeing it first-hand was sobering.

Jae-sun prayed in the moment—if it be the Lord's will, someday, he would be allowed to escape this hell and redouble his efforts to end this horrid regime.

"Let's show you how things work here."

Jae-sun nodded and began helping Mi-sun prepare the prison guards' 6:00 p.m. meal.

Ten days later, Mi-sun ceased coming into work.

Chapter Twenty-two

A Calling

A sense of urgency quickened Jae-sun's steps. He finished preparing and serving the 6:00 p.m. meal, and hurried to be inside his Block before 8:00 p.m. Just before the horn announced curfew, Jae-sun stepped through the door.

A truck arrived at the gate.

Jae-sun walked inside to the end of the barracks to watch the truck through the cracks between the boards. The truck parked where it did when he'd arrived in this hell. The guards ordered the nine souls in the truck to disembark and line up in front of the administration building. Six men and three women complied. As they walked around the corner of the building toward the courtyard, Jae-sun walked back to the courtyard wall of his block near the door to get a better view. The six men and two of the women looked to be North Korean—all the North Koreans in the camp were five or six inches shorter that his South Korean countrymen. The entire North Korean population did not have access to the nutrition that people in the South did, so they were nearly all stunted. The third woman in the line was tall—Korean, but at a head taller than any of the others, she had to be from the South.

Jae-sun watched through the crack as these poor people were dealt the same treatment as anyone else who arrived here. They all received their tattoos bravely and dressed in their camp clothes. One at a time a guard pointed directions to the block they were to enter. The guard directed the tall woman to Block One, grabbing her shoulder and turning her toward the door. She was young, not much older than Mi-na, his youngest daughter. At the thought of Mi-na, Jae-sun's throat and chest tightened. He held back tears—tears that would do no good right now.

The woman walked slowly toward the Block One door, but the guard prodded her with the barrel of his rifle. The woman turned and swept the barrel aside with her forearm. "Bastard!"

The guard swung the butt of his rifle and hit the woman in the face, which knocked her to the ground. Jae-sun gasped as the thud of the rifle butt met her face. She began to rise, pushing herself up with her hands. The guard kicked her with the top of his booted foot. She went back down and did not move.

Stay down girl, stay down. Lord God, give her the wisdom to stay down!

The guard stood over her for a full minute. Satisfied she was down, he walked away, leaving her in the middle of the courtyard.

Jae-sun watched her intently and could see her breathing. He waited until dark, then waited until the guard in the tower above the back corner of the administration building faced west. Jae-sun figured he'd have about ten seconds to get to the girl and get her back to the door.

At the right moment Jae-sun stole out of the door and silently covered the distance to the girl. He picked her up, carried her back to the door, and ducked through, then met the closing door with his foot so it would not disturb the silence.

Jae-sun carried her to his berth and laid her down. He kept a small bottle of water hidden behind the board holding up his berth against the outside wall. He wet a small rag and dabbed the wounds on her face.

Recoiling slightly at the pain, she was starting to come to. The girl moaned and tried to rise.

Jae-sun tried to calm her, assuring her she was safe.

The girl lay back down and opened one eye, while the other remained swollen shut.

Jae-sun moved her hair away from her face with his index finger. "What is your name, sweet girl?"

"Ji-su." She closed her eye again, sighed, and slept.

Jae-sun lay on the dirt floor next to his berth. He was trying to work out what to do with Ji-su. She couldn't stay in the block; the guards would drag her out in the morning to give her a work assignment. If she couldn't perform—well, he didn't want to think about that.

Jae-sun decided that he had to take her to the kitchen with him in the morning, give her a job, and try to make a case to Colonel Ji that her help would be beneficial. In the thirty days since their first meeting, they'd had many short discussions. Jae-sun knew that the Colonel had many questions, that he was curious but very cautious. Jae-sun reasoned that the kitchen assignment was given to him either out of charity or so the colonel could more easily engage conversation. Either way, Jae-sun hoped he'd built some credit with the colonel.

Jae-sun had to be in the kitchen by 5:00 a.m. to accomplish his assigned duties, so he woke Ji-su early and put his hand on her forehead. She opened her good eye. Jae-sun still knew nothing of this girl's plight, only her name.

"Ji-su, we have to go. You cannot stay here today because they will kill you if you cannot accomplish whatever they assign you to do. I'm taking you with me to the kitchen. Maybe I can get the colonel who oversees this place to allow you to stay there."

"Let them kill me—I do not care."

"Ji-su, it is not time for you to die. Let's go."

Ji-su sighed, raised herself, and swung her legs onto the dirt floor. Jae-sun supported her as she stood.

"I am fine, I can walk."

"Okay, that's good. Stay right with me and walk confidently, with purpose. They probably won't stop us because they know I am supposed to be out and making my way to the kitchen at this time. If they stop us, let me speak."

Mercifully, they arrived at the kitchen unnoticed. Jae-sun set Ji-su up at a counter and had her begin cutting up vegetables for the stew he had planned for the guards' noon meal. Jae-sun started the rice for their breakfast and hoped the colonel would arrive early.

By 5:45, the breakfast was ready to serve. Hearing activity in the guard's dining room, Jae-sun stepped through the saloon-style doors and saw Colonel Ji talking to one of his officers. Jae-sun stood silently until he caught brief eye contact with Colonel Ji. Jae-sun backed into the kitchen.

Moments later Colonel Ji walked in. "Is the breakfast ready to serve?"

"Yes, the breakfast is ready. Colonel Ji, this prisoner arrived last night. She is beat up and cannot perform all tasks right now. Once she heals, she will be able to perform any duty, and could well be useful. Might I use her here, with your permission, for a few weeks until she regains her full potential?"

Colonel Ji simply nodded his approval toward Jae-sun and stepped back through the door. Jae-sun breathed a sigh of relief and served the morning meal.

The first day with Ji-su in the kitchen went well. With Ji-su on his heels, Jae-sun hurried again to get to his block before the curfew. Once inside, Jae-sun slowed his pace, making his way toward his berth. Ji-su touched his shoulder from behind. Jae-sun turned.

With tears in her eyes, Ji-su said, "Thank you for today, Jae-sun. I really do not want to die."

"Come, tell me how you came to be here."

The berth directly adjacent to Jae-sun's was empty, so he invited her to use it.

Once settled, Ji-su told Jae-sun the tale of how she ended up in Prison Camp 15 in North Korea. "My mom and I went shopping at the mall near our house in Seoul. I had to use the restroom, so I walked back to the center of the mall. There is a hallway there from the mall to the outside; the bathroom doors are in the middle of the hall between the mall and the outside door. I went into the restroom and saw one woman washing her hands. I walked around the corner to use the toilet. When I walked back to the sinks, she was gone. I washed my hands, then walked out into the hallway. The woman was on the floor with four men surrounding her. They were tying her hands, so I turned and ran to go to the outside door. Two more men were standing at the outside door, I tried to pass them, and one of them grabbed me. I screamed. He tried to cover my mouth, so I bit his finger. The other man hit me hard and knocked my wind out. They tied my hands and dragged me out the back door and threw me into a van. They threw the other woman in right behind me."

She continued, "After riding in the van for what seemed to be about an hour, the van stopped. They covered my head with a black bag, then pulled me out and put me in what seemed like a shipping container. I lost track of time, but when they took me out all I could see was water; I was on a ship. A small boat came alongside, and they lowered me into the boat. They took me to a small town up by the Russian border and put me in a house with other girls."

Jae-sun watched Ji-su sit up in the berth. She took a deep breath and her eyes welled up with tears.

"I didn't know what the place was," she explained. "One of the other girls told me what happened there—it was a brothel. I am just nineteen years old. I'd never been with a man, and I've never had a boyfriend. My father got sick when I was fifteen, so my mother and I took care of him until he died, just this past February. Our shopping trip was our first outing together to have fun since my dad passed away. Anyway, when I started to cry, the woman who ran the place pulled me aside and hit me. She threatened me and shouted at me to stop crying. I pulled myself together and stopped crying. A few minutes later we—four other girls and me—were led to the door of a large parlor with two Russian military officers seated inside. We were told to walk in and spin around, then walk back out one at a time. We did that, and a few minutes later I was led to a bedroom and told to wait. After three or four more minutes one of the Russian officers came into the bedroom."

Ji-su took in a big breath and blew it out slowly, like she was trying to work up courage.

"I was terrified; all I could do was quaver with fear. He was a huge man, over two meters tall. He had piercing blue eyes and very short blond hair. He seemed to enjoy the fact that I was scared. He walked over to me and grabbed the hair on the back of my head, then growled at me in Russian. He hit me with the back of his hand. He tore the sheer top off me that the woman had dressed me in. Then he threw me to the middle of the bed. I curled up, waiting for the next blow. He removed his uniform and hovered over me on the bed on his knees. He grabbed me and forced me onto my back. Then he spread my legs. I tried to curl up again, but he hit me again with the back of his hand. I relented and he hurt me, Jae-sun. He hurt me."

Jae-sun tried to comfort her, but except to listen, there wasn't much he could do. He burned with anger at the tyranny imposed on this poor girl, on all these people—on him!

"After he left, I couldn't stop crying. The next morning two men came into the room and carried me to a truck and brought me here. At least my mother doesn't have to know what happened to me."

Jae-sun nodded.

"One day, Ji-su, we will settle the score."

Jae-sun silently prayed himself to sleep. 4:30 would arrive soon enough.

*   *   *

Another month passed, and Ji-su was into the routine. One day when she and Jae-sun were preparing the noon meal for the guards, Jae-sun needed to go outside and use the latrine. He was walking back across the courtyard toward the kitchen when he heard blood-curdling screams. Emerging from the factory, two guards were dragging a woman by the arms toward the whipping pole in the middle of the courtyard.

They stripped the woman, bound her wrists, and hooked the bindings to a spike on the pole above her head so her toes barely touched the ground. With no clothes and hanging, the woman was obviously pregnant.

Jae-sun had been in the camp almost three months. He had seen every deplorable, inhumane treatment he'd thought possible, but this—this was just evil. Once the woman was stretched up, without warning or mercy, one of the guards sliced open her abdomen and spilled her fetus and her entrails onto the ground.

The guard kicked the fetus, then turned to the woman and cut her throat.

The guards walked away and left her hanging.

Jae-sun looked over and saw Ji-su among the many prisoners looking on in horror. Walking briskly back to the door of the kitchen, he took Ji-su back inside.

Ji-su was gasping for breath, obviously shaken by what she had just witnessed. Jae-sun stood in front of her, hands on her shoulders, trying to convince her that in the face of evil they must be strong, that they must survive to tell the world.

She caught her breath. "Jae-sun, it's not that. I know what you say is true."

She paused and looked into Jae-sun's eyes.

"I think I am pregnant."

Jae-sun backed against the counter, deflated and feeling hopeless.

Colonel Ji walked into the kitchen from the dining room. "Is your noon meal ready to serve?"

"Yes, sir. Sir, we just witnessed a horrible act of brutality. Could you tell us how that can be allowed to happen?"

"You are speaking of the pregnant woman?"

"Yes."

"Policy is from Pyongyang: unsanctioned sexual relationships are forbidden in the camp. It is the policy, and every guard here is drilled in policy before he arrives. It is the policy that pregnancies occurring from unsanctioned relationships shall be terminated, and the offending participant or participants be punished by death. I cannot change policy, or I will be the one on the pole."

"How is a relationship within the camp sanctioned?"

"Only I have that power."

"Colonel Ji, I request that you sanction Ji-su to be my camp wife. She is young and vulnerable to rape and abuse. Being my camp wife will afford her some protection from similar treatment and ensure her continued service in this camp."

Colonel Ji thought for a moment, looked at Ji-su, then back at Jae-sun. "So sanctioned. Now, serve the noon meal."

The colonel spun on his heel and left.

Alone again, Jae-sun turned to Ji-su. "Are you sure?"

"Not sure, but I'd say 90%. Ever since I've been fourteen, I've had my period like clockwork every month, but now I am late, two weeks late. I've never been late!"

Jae-sun's mind was racing through all the complications that could arise for Ji-su if she were pregnant. Not just the danger of being pregnant, but the effort it would take to keep Ji-su alive, much less a baby in this ghoulish place. Jae-sun was always thinking of survival. He tried to anticipate things that might threaten survival, and tried to memorize contingency plans to deal with each thing that might arise. Working in the kitchen was a huge benefit in trying to survive this place. In the kitchen he had access to more calories than anyone else in camp besides the guards. He knew better than to sneak food out, because being caught with stolen food was instant death. He would ingest a little bit here and a little bit there throughout the day. Never too much—his aim was to stay gaunt, but enough to keep his mind sharp, his organs functioning well, and his teeth healthy. Jae-sun had stressed the importance of moderation to Ji-su. Jae-sun's plan was to keep her in the kitchen, too, and he didn't think Colonel Ji would change the arrangement. He and his guards were very pleased with their meals and the service. If he could only keep things going smoothly . . .

Finally, Jae-sun looked up at Ji-su. "I cannot imagine having to deal with a baby in this place, but if you are pregnant, we'll deal with it. It will be our calling."

Jae-sun was trying to convince himself as much as he was trying to assure Ji-su.

Six weeks later—no question. Ji-su was pregnant by the Russian officer.

As the months went by, a routine developed—not a pleasant routine in this horrible place, but a routine nonetheless. Jae-sun endeavored every day to do a good job—rather, a great job—in his assigned duty, seeing this as key to survival. Jae-sun was actually a pretty good cook. He took gourmet classes with Min-seo while at MIT getting his graduate degree. Those classes had come in handy. The food he was given to prepare for the guards was simple, much better than the gruel the prisoners got, but simple nonetheless. Jae-sun did good job with what was available, and the spices Colonel Ji acquired over time allowed him to make the simple food into culinary delights, as far as his diners knew. Jae-sun had no sympathy for the guards—they were evil, but he regarded them as prisoners, too. No matter who the diners were, it was his duty to do a good job.

From the time Jae-sun and Ji-su accepted the fact that she was pregnant, Jae-sun determined that she would have a healthy pregnancy. He developed a nutrition plan for her so she would remain strong and the baby would be born healthy. Even though they had Colonel Ji's sanction, they took no chances. It was dark when they arrived in the kitchen each morning, and it was dark when they arrived back at Block One each evening, so the darkness gave them some cover. Jae-sun did all the table service so the guards wouldn't see Ji-su. They kept a low profile.

Jae-sun calculated that Ji-su was about twenty weeks along. The prisoners did not have access to calendars or clocks, but Jae-sun had kept a very accurate count of the days since he arrived on the ceiling of his berth. He calculated that today was October 30th, so that meant that the baby would arrive in early March.

Jae-sun decided a stethoscope would come in handy. He noticed that the pull on the closet door in the kitchen was a round metal pull about the size of a poker chip, with a concave face and a screw in the middle that attached it to the wood door—the perfect bell of a stethoscope! The pull also had a flat surface on its edge about the width of a small pea with a groove. Jae-sun took the pull off the closet door and replaced it with one of the plastic handles from his rice bags. One of the soft latex caps from his soy sauce bottle stretched over the metal door pull worked as a diaphragm. A wire fastener from the container his fish arrived in kept the latex diaphragm in place.

The hand-soap dispenser in the kitchen had two bags connected with a small plastic wye, with a soft tube directing the soap to the nozzle. The plastic wye and tube worked to attach the tube to the back of the screw hole on the door pull. More of the soft tube from the wye served as ear tubes.

Each of the two refrigerators in the kitchen had a hard plastic 7mm drain hose. The end of the hose was fashioned into a 90-degree angle. Jae-sun took a serrated knife from his prep area and carefully cut off each hard plastic 90-degree angle. He put one end of each 90-degree fitting into the ends of the soft plastic hose from the soap dispensers. The other end, he fitted into his ears.

Jae-sun walked over to Ji-su and set his stethoscope over her heart. Hearing her heart beating very well made him smile. Jae-sun cleaned the wooded prep table and asked Ji-su to lie down. His stethoscope would be a valuable tool in monitoring the progress of Ji-su's baby. Once she was lying prone, Jae-sun placed the end of the stethoscope on Ji-su's tummy and listened.

He closed his eyes, then frowned.

"What's the matter?"

Jae-sun did not answer. He simply moved the stethoscope over to the other side of Ji-su's tummy and listened some more. Again, with eyes closed, he frowned.

"What is wrong, Jae-sun?"

Jae-sun opened his eyes and looked at Ji-su with worry. "Ji-su, there are two hearts beating in your womb. They sound great, but there are two!"

Ji-su sat up and hung her legs over the end of the table. She looked at Jae-sun, drew a big breath, and let it out slowly.

"Jae-sun, I can see that you are worried for me carrying and birthing twins, and I know you are worried about how we will manage when they arrive. When I came to this place, I wanted to die, I really did. When I first learned I was pregnant, my first thought was how unfair for me. I wanted to rid myself of the parasite planted in me by that Russian bastard. Jae-sun, I don't wish to be here. I'd rather be at home with my mother, but for whatever reason I *am* here. In a way, you've saved my life—at least for eternity. If I ever achieve my freedom, my liberty again, I will be a better person for having known you. You've taught me about the love of Jesus Christ, which I was ignorant of before. You've taught me contentment—before, I was bitter and angry about my father. You've taught me patience and grace. I know because of you that these babies are not guilty. I will give them life, and I will cling to the hope that someday we'll all be away from here. This place is awful, but in some ways, I am happier for having met you. Jae-sun, don't worry. We will be fine."

With tears running down his face, Jae-sun hugged little Ji-su. She was wise beyond her years.

His own hope was restored because of her.

Chapter Twenty-three

Discreet Arrival

Breakfast had been served and the kitchen was clean. Jae-sun walked out into the courtyard to use the latrine. He noticed a shadow on the ground and looked up to see a partial eclipse of the sun. Jae-sun knew better than to look right at the sun, but the event was interesting nonetheless. He determined to calculate the date when he returned to Block One.

Jae-sun walked back inside to help Ji-su prepare the noon meal for the guards. As they were finishing cleaning up, Jae-sun noticed Ji-su walking with her hands on her back.

"Ji-su, are you having labor pains?"

"Yes."

Jae-sun had developed a contingency plan for this day, preparing a meal in advance that could be cooked and served on short notice. In fact, he had several meals prepared and frozen, ready to go. This way he could serve dinner and help Ji-su, and it appeared as if she'd need his help delivering these babies *today*.

Jae-sun hustled around to get the evening meal ready and watched Ji-su all the while. The kitchen for the preparation of the guards' meals was between the dining hall and a large receiving area, which was along an outside wall with a loading dock. The receiving area had an office that was not used. Jae-sun received the food on delivery days and put it away under lock. He was responsible for the supplies, so nothing was left in the receiving area—ever. It was all put away upon delivery.

Jae-sun fixed up the receiving office as a makeshift delivery room. After the noon meal, Jae-sun retrieved the frozen casseroles for the evening meal, needing the extra time. Ji-su seemed to be coping with the pains just fine. He finished cleaning up after the noon meal, then encouraged Ji-su to walk back to the receiving office so they could check progress.

Jae-sun helped Ji-su work her way up onto the table he built for the delivery. He checked progress and reported to Ji-su that, as far as he could tell, the babies were in the correct position and that their heartbeats were good. Ji-su was about halfway dilated and 50% effaced.

The babies were indeed coming.

Jae-sun encouraged her to get up and continue walking through the pains. He went back to the kitchen and began doing what he could to prepare the evening meal.

All that afternoon, Jae-sun watched as Ji-su walked through the pains. By the time the evening meal was finished, Ji-su thought she was ready.

"Jae-sun, it is time."

Jae-sun heated two water bottles and laid them in the bottom of an apple box. He had one of the ovens on *warming* and had warmed several dish towels. He placed the warm dish towels over the hot-water bottles and carried the box into the receiving-dock office, then returned to the kitchen to fill a deep pot with warm water.

In nine short months Jae-sun had come to love little Ji-su as a daughter. He was determined to do everything in his power to help her.

*　　*　　*

Ji-su looked around the room she and Jae-sun had prepared for this moment. It was stark and cool. The only source of light in the room were candles; they seemed to warm the room.

Ji-su slid her cotton camp pants off, unbuttoned her Mao coat, sat on the platform Jae-sun prepared, then spun her legs toward the end. For Ji-su, modesty had long since faded from her mind. This horrible camp, where one must relieve oneself in public, was humiliating enough; and now without a choice in the matter, she was giving birth in this awful place.

She had come to love and trust Jae-sun as a father, and she knew getting these babies born was paramount. She opened her legs and rested her feet on the posts Jae-sun fashioned at the end of the platform.

The hormones coursing through Ji-su's body had done their job in preparing her for birth. After checking, Jae-sun reported to Ji-su that she was 100% effaced and 90% dilated.

It was time to push.

As the next pain began building, Ji-su prepared to push.

"Ji-su, not a sound. It will hurt, but you must bear the pain in silence."

Ji-su nodded.

As Ji-su pushed, the first baby's head crowned at the entrance to this world. On the next push, the baby's head emerged.

Jae-sun turned the little head to the side and used a baster to suck the fluid from the baby's mouth.

"One more push, Ji-su."

He'd no more breathed the words and a little girl slipped into a harsh world. Jae-sun cut her umbilical cord and clamped off the ends with wire ties. He swaddled her in warm dish towels and laid her in the apple box.

"A baby girl."

Ji-su craned her neck forward to get a peek. She smiled.

Jae-sun looked back around, and a little hand clenched in a fist had presented itself. "Oh!—a little warrior. Okay, Ji-su, let's get her sister here."

Ji-su pushed again, and following the fist, came a head.

"One more push! Oh, Ji-su, not a sister—a brother! You have a girl *and* a boy."

Jae-sun swaddled him and placed one baby in each of Ji-su's arms. Any remaining animus held by Ji-su evaporated.

"So far so good, Ji-su. An uncomplicated discreet twin birth in a horrid place at a convenient time—how much better could be expected?"

The babies were full term, but mercifully small. Their size and Ji-su's youth and constitution helped her with the births. Ten minutes after the placentas expelled, Ji-su got up and slipped her pants back on. There wasn't really a choice.

"We'll stay here tonight. What will you call them?"

Ji-su looked at Jae-sun and smiled. "She is Mari; he is Gun-ho."

Chapter Twenty-four

Joy

Their plane landed in Dutch Harbor at 4:00 on Tuesday afternoon, March 11th, 1997. Art and Leetia were glad to be going home. They made it to the harbor by 5:00 p.m. Their small boat waited for them at the boat basin, fueled up and ready to go. Andrew Gunnar Jackson was going to go on his first boat ride, the same day as his first plane ride.

Art radioed ahead so the crew knew they were coming in. As they neared the end of Esther Bay, they could see Kenny, Bert, James—the whole gang—waiting on the dock. Art slipped the boat next to the dock, and the guys tied it off. Leetia handed little Andrew to his daddy, and Art placed little Andrew into the massive hands of Kenny Creighton.

All the guys huddled around Kenny, admiring the little prince.

Art had a two-step stool in the boat that Leetia used to climb to the top of the gunnel.

Bert offered a hand to Leetia as she stepped onto the dock.

"What do you think, guys?—pretty cute, isn't he?"

They all agreed in unison as Kenny handed little Andrew back to his mama.

She took Andrew into his nursery.

"This is your room, Andrew, but you'll sleep in mama and daddy's room for a few weeks first, okay?"

Like he was going to answer . . .

*   *   *

Andrew's first year went by quickly for Art and Leetia; they thoroughly enjoyed being parents.

Andrew walked early at ten months, and by his first birthday he was running all over the house. Art loved getting down on the floor and playing with him, blowing on his belly and listening to him squeal in delight.

Leetia nursed Andrew for the first sixteen months, and she could tell that he was a thoughtful and considerate soul. As he nursed, he would talk to his mother with his eyes, his big brown expressive eyes.

She loved her boy.

Every year Art and Leetia would go to Hawai'i and spend a month with Milt and Esther. Andrew celebrated his second birthday at his great aunt and great uncle's home on Hawai'i.

Art taught Andrew to swim in the swimming pool. Andrew loved the water, and they thought it best that he learn to swim early.

Art and Leetia were very considerate in making sure Art's mom and Leetia's folks got to see their little grandson. Leetia visited her village five or six times during Andrew's first two years, and Art's mom and Leetia's folks came to Esther Bay a few times each. By the time Andrew was 2½, he was talking well. Leetia's sense that he was a thoughtful and considerate soul proved out. As Andrew grew and his vocabulary increased, all who encountered him loved him. He was a well-behaved child with a quick smile and free hugs.

For Andrew's fourth birthday, he got some Carhart overalls. He was so proud to be dressed like his daddy.

One morning in early May of 2001, Leetia brought Andrew down to the shop so Andrew could see his dad. Art was busy getting one of the boats ready to go out fishing. Andrew was dressed in his Carhart overalls, his Extra Tuf rubber boots, and his red-and-black Mackinaw—strutting around the shop, emulating his dad's every move.

Leetia was standing in the shop, talking to Kenny; and Art was on a ladder, retrieving a buoy stored on the shelves that ran along the side of the shop. The forklift was sitting just inside the door with a heavy wire cage on the forks being loaded with supplies for the boat. The forks were up about forty inches. The deck of the wire cage was supported by 1¼" X ¾" angle iron. The ends of the angle iron protruded three inches beyond the edge of the cage.

Andrew was standing near the bottom of the ladder.

Leetia watched him from the shop door.

He saw his mama and ran toward her.

"Be careful, Andrew. You don't want to crash on this concrete floor."

Andrew ran past his mother, around the back of the forklift, and was about to turn the corner in front of the forks when his feet slid out from under him on a layer of pea gravel. His momentum sent his head toward the forks.

He tried to catch himself, but his face caught the outside angle iron sticking out from the end of the cage. The end collided with Andrew's face, right under the outside edge of his left eye.

Leetia heard Andrew's cry and knew instantly something was very wrong. She dashed over to her boy.

Art slid down the ladder and charged across the shop.

Andrew was sitting on his bottom, still crying, with blood running onto his shirt. Art picked him up and held him tightly so his mother could assess the extent of the laceration on his face.

Leetia held pressure on the wound with a tissue. After a few moments, she lifted the blood-soaked tissue to try to get a look at the cut. It was pretty deep, forming a perfect L shape.

Leetia's medical training kept her amazingly calm under the circumstances. "He is going to need stitches, so we have to go into the clinic."

"Kenny, please ready the small boat."

*　　*　　*

Kenny nodded to Art and ran down to the dock to make sure the small Boston Whaler was ready and waiting. Within a matter of moments, the Jacksons were heading for the entrance to Esther Bay. Art turned right at the mouth and headed for Dutch Harbor.

It was just about noon when Art guided his boat into the slip. It was raining, so he carried Andrew up to the parking lot under his poncho. They kept an old Suburban at Dutch Harbor. Leetia slid onto the back seat, and Art laid Andrew down with his head on his mother's lap.

The doctor put five stitches on the vertical part of the cut and three on the horizontal. He sat Andrew up and gave him a hand mirror to look at his injury.

Still numb to pain from the local anesthesia, the four-year-old looked at himself in the mirror, then handed the mirror back to the doctor. "Mama, it looks like and L, just like in your name!"

"Yes it does, sweet boy. Yes it does!"

Chapter Twenty-five

Guard Encounter

The night the babies were born, Jae-sun and Ji-su slept in the receiving office. The next evening, they stayed in Block One. The guards had found and destroyed his calendar, so he couldn't determine their exact birthdate, but the day started with a partial eclipse; with such a reference, he could figure the date out later. They were prepared for this day. Jae-sun made several diapers from the older dish clothes, and fashioned safety pins with the stiff wire from the rice bags.

Ji-su fashioned tiny clothes and sewed them together with long synthetic fibers from the rice sacks and a curved poultry needle from the kitchen.

Ji-su nursed the babies, so their nutritional needs were being met. Jae-sun made sure that Ji-su had plenty of good nutrition and lots of clean water. They got into a pretty good routine. Jae-sun created a playpen in the kitchen so they could be near Ji-su.

Ji-su nursed the babies just before the guards' mealtime each day. That way there was the smallest chance that they would fuss when the guards were eating.

Within the first two or three weeks, Jae-sun and Ji-su started the babies' education, right there in the kitchen. They agreed that Jae-sun would speak to them in English and Ji-su would speak to them in Korean.

During the first year of the babies' lives, Jae-sun often thought of his own wonderful childhood. His anger flared at how these children were being denied their liberty, their happiness—their very life. The utter disregard for the natural rights due to all the prisoners in this horrible camp redoubled his resolve to escape this place and fight the regime.

As Mari and Gun-ho's first birthday approached, Jae-sun was pleased with how well they were doing, especially under the circumstances. During a light moment when Jae-sun was playing with the babies in the receiving area, he realized that these children were giving him renewed strength and stamina to carry on. His desire that they would someday have a chance to pursue their happiness drove him to implement an education that would help them survive in the camp and let them transition seamlessly into civil society—if they ever made it out.

Each morning before sunrise, Jae-sun would rouse Ji-su, Mari, and Gun-ho. They'd make their way to the kitchen and remain there until after dark. Colonel Ji and his staff knew of the children, but Jae-sun kept a very low profile, nonetheless.

Nurturing the babies kept both Jae-sun and Ji-su encouraged in a very difficult situation. Mari and Gun-ho were still too young to grasp that they were prisoners, and they did not know what they were missing. They didn't know about the joys of being bathed by loving parents or grandparents in gallons of warm bubbly water, being dried with a soft cotton towel, being dressed in soft flannel pajamas, and snuggled in a soft bed. They didn't know about ice cream—or cookies. About carnivals—or puppies. But they knew they were loved by Jae-sun and Ji-su.

That was enough for now.

The summer after the kids turned four, Jae-sun decided that part of their day should include some chores and responsibilities. Jae-sun could tell that both Mari and Gun-ho were very bright. They were speaking both English and Korean very well. They were becoming aware of their circumstances. Every night Jae-sun would tell them stories with facts about the world sprinkled in. This way he taught them orally about geography, zoology, botany, and basic science—and faith. Jae-sun also taught them to be wary of the guards.

During one of his oral lessons, Jae-sun was amused by Mari equating the guards to living with cobras.

She was indeed listening.

*   *   *

At the end of each day, the kitchen waste was piled into a canvas container with a rope handle, and the kids took it to the hog pen, which was 200 meters south of the administration building. They had to go down the steps adjacent to the receiving dock, through the courtyard, past the administration building, and out beyond the building cluster to the hog pen. Mari would carry one side and Gun-ho the other.

One day when the kids were heading back toward the buildings, about fifty meters from the loading dock, they were stopped by two guards between them and their destination. Mari was on the left side, holding the empty bag, and Gun-ho was on the right.

One guard snapped his crop. "Stop! Why are you dragging the bag?"

"Sir, we will not drag the bag anymore. We are sorry!"

"You are indeed sorry, boy!" He raised his crop to strike Mari.

"Run, Mari!"

Mari dodged the blow and ran toward the steps.

Gun-ho had to run around the guards, then make a dash for the door.

The guard on Gun-ho's right anticipated his maneuver and tripped him.

Gun-ho ended up on his hands and knees in the dust. He saw Mari duck inside just as the guard's boot caught him on the side of his face.

The blow spun Gun-ho around.

As he hit the ground, he remembered one of Jae-sun's lessons about the guards: "If the guards attack you, lie still-do not fight them or try to flee. Just lie still."

Gun-ho did lie stone-still.

The guards laughed and joked about him.

Gun-ho waited for what seemed like forever.

Finally, the guards walked around the corner of the administration building.

Gun-ho lifted his head and glanced that direction. He hopped to his feet, grabbed his bag, and ran toward the loading-dock door.

Seeing Jae-sun, he charged up the loading dock steps. Jae-sun closed the door behind him and squatted down to examine the wound on Gun-ho's cheek, right below his left eye. The outside of the boot had left a vertical cut about four centimeters long, and the heel left a horizontal cut about two centimeters.

"Gun-ho, you did a good job of lying still. There is no benefit in provoking them. This cut needs some stitches."

"Will it hurt?"

"Yes, it will, but it will heal much better."

Gun-ho lay on the prep table in the kitchen. Jae-sun prepared a garlic poultice, hoping the wound would not become infected.

"I am ready."

Jae-sun cleaned the wound with water, then applied the poultice paste into the cut. Gun-ho lay there without even twitching, just gripping the edged with one hand and bracing against the wall with the other.

Jae-sun sharpened the poultry needle and pulled several strands of fiber from an empty rice bag. He picked the smallest strands, then put three stitches across the horizontal portion and five along the vertical. Then he tied the ends of each strand to each other, closing the cut tightly along its path. Jae-sun packed the surface of the cut with more garlic poultice.

"Gun-ho, you are one tough cookie. We just gave you eight stitches without the benefit of anesthesia, and you never cried out once or shed a single tear."

"I'm not going to let that guard make me cry. I'll get him back someday!"

*   *   *

Jae-sun had an epiphany: Gun-ho would be the key to escaping this place. When the boy was old enough, somehow Jae-sun would smuggle him out to summon help.

He didn't know how or when, but he was certain Gun-ho would be the key.

Chapter Twenty-six

Heartache

As Andrew grew, he came to love and appreciate Esther Bay, a wonderful and enchanting place. The bay entrance was formed by a high rocky peak giving way to cliffs on the west and a low-lying sand spit on the east. The opening to the bay was barely fifty yards wide. The bay extended back about ¾ of a mile on the west side along the rocky cliffs. The dock that Andrew's great uncle built was at the back of the bay at the end of the cliff where the water was deepest. Even at low tide, the edge of the dock had thirty feet of water for the boats to safely be moored.

The ramp to the dock was built with steel I-beams supporting heavy timber decking. At the dock ends of the I-beams, Milt had attached large aluminum rollers, which traveled along the dock in an eight-inch wide shallow channel as the tide ebbed and flowed. The ramp was attached on the shore with a large concrete bulwark, with a ledge formed in the concrete to accept the end of the I-beams. A heavy steel embed was cast into the concrete on each side of the ledge, through which a three-inch steel pin ran from one side to the other so the ramp could hinge at the bulwark as the tide ebbed and flowed. The ramp was wide and heavy enough that the fishing crews could drive vehicles right down onto the dock and stock the boats.

The ramp led up to a gravel road which led to a shop building on the bay side fifty feet from the end of the ramp. The shop was built on piling, so the floor of the shop was level with the road. The road led up to a bench on which the Jacksons' home was built.

To the east of the shop the rocky shore gave way to beach, which extended almost a mile in a large curve to the east, then continued around to the north about another ¾ of a mile back to the east side of the entrance to the bay. Just before the sand spit, at the end of the beach, a creek emptied from the grassy lowlands into Esther Bay. About a mile upstream was a freshwater lake at the foothills of the island. The lake was fed by the mountains in the center of the island. Each summer, red salmon would run up the creek and spawn in the lake. This was Andrew's world. He loved the ocean and this place where he was blessed to be growing up.

By the time Andrew was eight, his dad allowed him to explore any corner of Esther Bay and the area around it. He would hike along the beach and cross the creek, up and over the sand spit to the beach facing the Bering Sea; or he would hike up the creek to the lake and watch the swans swimming gracefully and the brown bears gorging themselves during the salmon run. He would hike up the foothills to the mountains behind his house, then back down on trails he carved through the brush.

When Andrew was ten, his dad gave him a 12-foot inflatable Zodiac with a 20 hp Honda outboard motor. Andrew was thrilled. He could set out crab pots and shrimp pots. He could fish for halibut and rock fish, and on calm days he could go out into the Bering Sea and explore the coves and beaches on either side of the entrance to Esther Bay.

The summer after Andrew turned eleven, his cousin Peter came to visit. Peter was also eleven and savvy to the outdoors just like Andrew. Peter had the good fortune of growing up in Manokotak near their grandfather, so by age eleven Peter had killed a moose, had been on the trap line with his grandfather in winter, and was an accomplished angler.

One day was very calm, so Peter and Andrew decided to go halibut fishing. Leetia and Art were working in the shop as Peter and Andrew were putting on their life jackets and gathering their halibut rods and bait.

"Where are you boys going?"

"We're going out and fish just off the rocky point, Dad. There is a good hole there."

"Okay, have fun."

Andrew pointed his boat toward the entrance to Esther Bay and popped the craft up on step. The boys enjoyed the cool wind in their faces and the smooth ride. They made it out to the point just at slack tide, which was Andrew's goal. He didn't want their gear to be pulled by the tide. The bottom was rocky here and, at slack tide on a calm sea, they would have a rare opportunity to fish this hole.

Peter took the circle hook on his rod out of the bottom eye and carefully baited it with a piece of herring. Peter sent his hook to the bottom with a 16-ounce piece of lead one foot from his hook. He must have hit a halibut on the head because, no sooner than his line hit the bottom, the tip of his rod bowed hard to the sea, indicating an anxious halibut was on his hook. They were in seventy-five feet of water, so Peter began the arduous task of reeling the flat fish up from the deep. Peter would pull up two feet, reel as he let his tip down to the water's surface, then pull up two feet and reel again.

Soon enough Peter's fish breached the surface, revealing itself to be a nice 30-pound halibut about 40 inches long.

Art had built Andrew a six-inch PVC pipe tube to store his gaff so it would not accidentally puncture his boat. Art also built Andrew a 4-inch PVC pipe tube to store his 30/30 carbine in. It had a piece of foam at the bottom for the muzzle to rest on, and a bag of desiccant attached to the side to keep the gun dry. Each tube had a threaded PVC plug in the top.

Andrew expertly gaffed the fish and pulled it aboard. Peter took his hook out of the fish, set his rod aside, and thumped the prize on the noggin so they could go back to fishing. Andrew held his hand up to high-five his cousin.

They were pleased with themselves.

Andrew restowed the gaff and baited his hook. Peter did the same. They reached the bottom about the same time and, after a few minutes, Peter's rod bowed again to the sea. Andrew quickly reeled up his baited hook as he teased Peter about catching all the fish. Peter's second fish was as impressive as the first.

They sent their hooks down a third time and were enjoying the calm sea as they repeatedly bobbed their lead weights on the bottom.

This time Andrew's rod dipped—and hard, violently. Andrew set the hook and pulled against what felt like the bottom. If the tide had been moving, he would think he was hung up, but this was a fish, a big fish.

Peter quickly reeled up his line.

Andrew reeled the fish up about five feet, but it decided to head into the bay. The monster was large enough to pull the boat and the boys. After 100 yards or so the fish tired, and Andrew was able to start reeling again.

After more good progress, the fish was up about fifty feet when it decided to go back down. Andrew didn't dare set the drag any stiffer; the only thing to do was to give the fish line.

The fish stopped.

Andrew reeled again, slowly making progress, a few feet at a time. After an hour the flat fish appeared at the surface. The boys couldn't believe their eyes. A huge halibut was floating at the end of Andrew's line.

"Peter, that thing has to weigh 300 pounds!"

"Easy, 300 pounds!"

"We can't gaff this guy; he'll run back to the bottom and take the gaff with him. I'll have to shoot him."

"Okay. What you want me to do?"

"Here, you hold the rod while I get out the gun. I'll shoot him while he is tired, hopefully before he decides to head back down."

Andrew handed Peter the rod, then unscrewed the top of the 4-inch PVC tube and removed his 30/30 carbine. He jacked a cartridge into the chamber and took careful aim at the fish. He had to hit it in the head to kill it, but he couldn't hit his line in doing so; otherwise, they'd lose the fish.

Andrew took careful aim and fired.

The bullet found its mark. The fish tossed about for a few seconds, then calmed as blood stained the water around the fish's head. Andrew tucked his gun back in its scabbard and pulled his filet knife from its sheath. He poked a hole through the fish near its gill, then threaded a quarter-inch nylon rope through the hole, tied a bowline knot in the rope, and tied the fish off to the back of the boat. Andrew reached out and cut the line off his rod, leaving his hook in the fish for the time being.

"We'll never be able to get this guy in the boat—we'll have to *tow* him back."

"You're right about that, Andrew. Better go slow."

*   *   *

The boys had only been out about two hours, when Leetia saw that they were heading back in. She grabbed the binoculars from the wall peg and stepped around the corner to watch.

She called to Art. "Something is wrong with his engine; they are going very slow."

She handed the binoculars to Art. He could see the problem. Art handed the binoculars back to Leetia.

"Look behind the boat. Whatever they are towing, it is making its own wake. They probably got a big halibut or a skate. Let's go down to the dock and meet them."

*   *   *

About thirty feet from the dock, Peter stood up. "Andrew caught the biggest halibut in the ocean; it is huge."

Andrew eased the boat up to the dock where his folks were standing. Art tied off the bow. Leetia tied off the stern. "Andrew, that is the biggest halibut I've ever seen."

Andrew smiled wide at his mother's approval. They were moored stern to stern with one of the big fishing vessels.

"Son, let's untie him and drag him over to the back of the *Esther II.* I'll grab the scale from the shop, and we'll pick him up with the hydraulic boom and weigh him."

Art retrieved the scale from the shop, then hooked one end through Andrew's rope hoop and hooked the other end to the boom. He then pulled the lever, lifted the fish out of the water, and swung it over the dock. Hanging in the middle of the dock, seven feet nose-to-tail, the fish weighed 344 pounds. Leetia took several pictures of Peter and Andrew standing by their fish.

Kenny walked down to the dock and offered to help the boys filet and vacuum-pack their fish—an offer they both appreciated.

Peter would not be going back to Manokotak empty handed.

*   *   *

A week after Peter went home, Leetia noticed that Andrew was lethargic.

"Andrew, are you okay, honey?" She felt his forehead for fever.

"I'm okay, Mom—just tired."

Leetia didn't buy it because he was never tired. She checked him over and noticed bruising on his stomach.

"Andrew, what is this from?"

"It is from the end of my pole when I was reeling up that big halibut. My stomach is still kind of sore."

"Hmmm, I think we better go into Dutch Harbor tomorrow and get you checked out. You may have mononucleosis or something."

She tousled his hair just to lighten the moment.

The next morning, Art and Leetia took Andrew into Dutch Harbor. The Doctor checked Andrew from top to bottom. The way Leetia remembers it, is that the doctor concluded that he was okay, probably just growing pains. However, the doctor did order a blood draw and a complete panel of tests. The Jacksons headed back to Esther Bay with instructions to come back in ten days to receive the results.

The next ten days were filled with normal life. Andrew did seem to perk up a bit, and the bruises on his stomach did slowly dissipate. Art was out fishing the day Leetia and Andrew headed into Dutch Harbor in the Boston Whaler. They hopped in the Suburban, which was waiting up in the parking lot. They were early for their appointment, so Andrew suggested they get an ice-cream cone from the local fountain. Andrew and his mother enjoyed their ice-cream cones and each other's company, as they always did. Andrew's relationship with both of his folks was great, but he did enjoy a special bond with his mother, a bond that Art encouraged and cherished.

Andrew and Leetia were doing the crossword puzzle together in the waiting room at the clinic in Dutch Harbor when the nurse came to the door. "Andrew, honey, can you wait here? The doctor wants a few moments alone with your mama."

"Sure." But his smile never faded.

The nurse took Leetia to the doctor's private office rather than an exam room. The doctor invited Leetia to sit. "There is no need to beat around the bush, Leetia—the results are preliminary, but Andrew may have leukemia."

"Leukemia—blood cancer."

"Yes, that is correct."

"Wow, I didn't see that one coming."

"We should take him to Anchorage for more tests, and if confirmed, nail down the exact type of disease so we can begin a treatment regimen ASAP."

"We've gotta tell Andrew."

"Do you think that is a good idea?"

"Oh yes. There is no other choice. Andrew is very, very perceptive, and he is an only child. He is wise to the world, so he'd know something was up. We have got to be straight with him."

"Okay." She asked the nurse to bring Andrew in.

Leetia thought Andrew took the news like a trouper. He asked lots of good questions and was very rational and logical. The doctor was very impressed, especially coming from a person who was just going on twelve.

Andrew asked, "When will we go to Anchorage?"

"I'll set it up for Tuesday. That way you guys can come in Monday morning and take the afternoon flight to town."

Not much was said on the way back to the boat basin. Leetia and Andrew walked without talking down the ramp to their boat. Leetia stopped at the fuel dock and had the boat topped off, then crept out toward the harbor entrance.

While the boat was just idling, Andrew said, "Mom, I want you to promise me something." Andrew looked her dead in the eye. "Mom, if this leukemia ends up kill—"

His mother interrupted him to protest about such a prospect, but Andrew was insistent.

He put his finger on his mother's lips. "If this leukemia ends up killing me, I want you to promise to bury me at sea."

Leetia looked at Andrew, and the first tears began to flow. "I promise, baby. I promise."

She pushed the throttles forward and bumped the boat onto step.

Chapter Twenty-seven

Heartbreak

Somehow over the years Jae-sun and Ji-su endured the horrid conditions at the camp. The extent of their world was Block One from 8:00 each night to 4:30 each morning, then the kitchen, receiving area, and the guards' dining room all day. Many people died at the camp each week, but it seemed there was a never-ending supply to replace them. Jae-sun and Ji-su survived each year under the oversight of Colonel Ji and their access to more calories than the typical prisoner. It became kind of a host-and-parasite relationship. Colonel Ji and his officers and guards enjoyed the superior food service that Jae-sun and Ji-su provided.

And they survived—existed, really.

With Mari and Gun-ho's help, Jae-sun and Ji-su had the kitchen detail down pat and operating very efficiently. This gave all of them more time to rest during the day, which helped, because sleeping conditions in Block One were awful—cold in the winter, hot in the summer, and completely uncomfortable all the time. Any effort to improve personal conditions would be destroyed by the guards or stolen by the other prisoners. Jae-sun and Ji-su were left pretty much alone in their kitchen realm, which allowed them to take naps in shifts during the day, one resting while the other watched.

The efficiency also allowed Jae-sun to really focus on the education of Mari and Gun-ho. He was allowed pens to write supply orders for Colonel Ji, but he had to use the panels from food boxes for paper. Mari and Gun-ho practiced their English alphabet, their Korean script, mathematics, penmanship, and writing. Jae-sun was impressed at how exceptionally bright the kids were. If only he had them in Seoul, directing their education and future, rather than here in this hell on earth, hoping his efforts would at least prove useful.

After Mari and Gun-ho were attacked by the guards, Jae-sun began developing the notion in the minds of Mari and Gun-ho that someday, at just the right time, Gun-ho would be smuggled out of the camp to try and get help. Jae-sun's goal was to impart enough information about the world that Gun-ho could make his way to the South and somehow, some way, get word to Bill Johnson in the United States.

Jae-sun wasn't exactly sure what Bill could do, but he'd think of something.

*   *   *

Time marched on while Jae-sun was captive. The kids had just turned twelve a few months earlier, and it was time for something to give.

They had to make a move.

One fateful day, the evening meal just about over, Gun-ho and Ji-su were clearing dishes and serving tea. The door from the kitchen was in the back corner of one of the long walls of the rectangular dining room. The room was approximately 16 by 28 feet. In the middle of the room, a single long table seated 14 guards and officers at a meal. Ji-su worked her way up the long wall opposite the kitchen door, clearing plates and pouring tea.

After taking a load into the kitchen, Gun-ho turned the corner of the table, heading toward his mother to relieve her of the dishes.

The guard who had kicked Gun-ho years earlier, Major Lee Dae-du, was talking loudly to the guard on his right as Ji-su poured tea on his left. Major Lee laughed loudly and made a wild gesture with his left arm. He knocked the teapot out of Ji-su's hand, which splashed hot tea onto his leg. He pushed his chair back and stood up, which knocked the plates and flatware in Ji-su's other hand to the floor.

"You stupid bitch!"

She knew it was the major's fault, but she quickly knelt to pick up the mess.

"So sorry, sir. So sorry!"

Gun-ho moved quickly to help her pick up the mess.

Major Lee's hand went up.

Gun-ho recoiled, expecting to be hit.

"Get back, boy, or I'll scar the other side of your face!"

Ji-su's maternal instincts kicked in. She picked up a fork and stabbed Major Lee in the back of the leg. "You leave him alone!"

On her knees, Ji-su looked around the legs of the Major and made eye contact with Gun-ho. She frantically motioned him into the kitchen. He heeded his mother's directive.

Infuriated, the Major spun around, lifted his sidearm from his holster, and shot Ji-su in the chest, hitting her just above her left breast. The bullet pierced Ji-su's heart.

Collapsing against the dining room wall, she died instantly.

*　　*　　*

Hearing the commotion, Jae-sun arrived at the kitchen door just in time to witness the evil.

By now all the guards were on their feet.

Colonel Ji ordered everyone out of the dining hall. He ordered the last two guards to take Ji-su's body to the truck.

Jae-sun retreated to the kitchen, followed by Colonel Ji.

"This is unfortunate. Clean this mess up quickly." He turned on his heel and walked out of the kitchen.

The adrenaline was pumping hard through Jae-sun's veins.

Heartbroken, enraged, he felt so helpless that he couldn't stop such a miscarriage of justice, nor do anything about it. He pulled Mari and Gun-ho to his chest, sobbing with grief. Ji-su was like his daughter.

She *was* his daughter.

Somehow, some way, he'd even the score.

Suddenly it hit him—tomorrow was Wednesday. They'd dump the bodies in the pit tomorrow morning, but wouldn't burn them until Saturday.

So tonight was the night. Gun-ho had to leave.

Jae-sun would smuggle Gun-ho onto that truck and get him out of this camp. From there, he'd be on his own.

As prisoners, they didn't have the luxury of grieving. They had to finish cleaning up the dining room and readying the kitchen for tomorrow morning's meal, or they might themselves be the recipient of the next bullet.

After they finished, Jae-sun asked the kids to meet him in the receiving office, the very office that they had been born in. He sat the kids down beside each other and faced them, sitting on a bucket.

He began to speak slowly. "Mari, Gun-ho, your mother—"

Jae-sun paused as he choked back his emotion.

"Your mother is gone. It is so wrong, what happened to her, and the time has come that we must do something. Gun-ho, these last few years I've tried to impart to you the knowledge you'd need to make your way to the South. Tonight, you must go. You may well die in the effort, and if you do, know that our lord Jesus Christ will receive your soul, just as he received your mother's. Then likely Mari and I will die here, too, so we'll see you in heaven. But if you survive—*if* you survive—then finish growing up, and somehow, some way, get in touch with Bill Johnson. He is in the United Sates Navy."

Jae-sun paused as he reached back to unclip his crucifix chain, then slipped it around Gun-ho's neck.

"If you find him, give him this. It will validate your story. Bill gave this to me when I was your age in Washington, D.C."

Gun-ho picked the crucifix off his chest and read the inscription on the back, then looked up at Jae-sun.

"You guys were close, huh?"

"Yes, close. Very, very close. So tonight, Gun-ho, we need to get you onto the truck. You must be strong enough to lie beside your mother and ride the truck to the pit north of the camp. They will likely lift the bed and let the bodies slide out, while both the guards remain in the cab. I do not know how far of a drop it is into the pit, but to avoid being hurt, you need to be aware of your surroundings, and once they begin to back the truck up to the edge of the pit, look to see if you can slip off in the center so they won't be able to see you in the side mirrors. You need to make sure you don't get injured so you can move on from the pit."

Jae-sun read Mari's face, eyes wide with fear; she'd just lost her mother, and tonight she would also lose her brother.

But it was their only hope.

"Now, Gun-ho, once the truck leaves, make your way out of the pit and wait for nightfall. You can walk from the pit east out to the beach, then turn north. Not too far up the beach, you'll come to a small town with a port. Find a small boat with oars. Then find as much fresh water as you can and take it with you. I have several pieces of dried fish for you. Hopefully, you'll get out into the Japanese current and make landfall on the southern tip of the Korean Peninsula or in southwest Japan before you run out of water. If you can rig up a sail, that would be good, but don't put up your sail until you can no longer see the shore."

Jae-sun could tell that Gun-ho was taking in all the details. They'd been over the plan before—many times before—but then it was only theory.

Now it was for real.

It was nearly 8:00 o'clock when they slipped out the door and down the steps beside the loading dock, making a beeline for the door of Block One. Jae-sun could see the back end of the truck parked at the end of Block One, where it was always parked.

The kids knew not to speak of the plan as they entered the block—the guards were known to recruit snitches.

Jae-sun rose at 4:00 a.m. and roused Mari and Gun-ho. He whispered into Gun-ho's ear. "Be sure to take water; you'll need lots of fresh water."

Gun-ho nodded, then hugged Mari. "I love you, sister. Stay strong. I *will* come back to get you! I *promise!*"

With that Jae-sun opened the hole behind loose planks he'd prepared weeks earlier and sent Gun-ho through. He watched him creep up onto the back of the truck to hide himself among the corpses.

Mari and Jae-sun walked out the front door of Block One at 5:00 a.m. The truck usually left at about 7:00, right after the morning meal. Jae-sun wanted breakfast to go smoothly. He prayed that Colonel Ji would stay out of the kitchen and not notice Gun-ho was missing.

Breakfast did go smoothly—it was the easiest meal, usually rice and fish.

Colonel Ji did not come into the kitchen. In fact, he didn't even make eye contact as Jae-sun served the meal in the dining room. As the last guard left, Jae-sun walked back to the loading dock door. He peered through the window of the door, which offered a direct line of sight to where the truck was parked.

The truck was gone.

Jae-sun glanced up and beyond Block One to the gate 300 yards to the south, and saw the rear of the truck exiting through the gate.

Gun-ho was on his way.

Chapter Twenty-eight

A taste of freedom

"What do you mean, you don't have a match? You were smoking a cigarette when we left the camp!"

"Yeah, Chol gave it to me."

"Well, don't look at me, I don't have any."

"Forget it. Let's go."

The clank of the empty Jeri-can thrown onto the bed of the truck rang in Gun-ho's ears.

Its engine started and the truck pulled away.

Gun-ho lay still, hidden by the charred remains he'd used to cover himself. Soon all Gun-ho could hear was the wind blowing. Jae-sun told him to do everything slowly—think, look, and listen.

Gun-ho gently uncovered himself from his hide and slowly crested the lower slope on the back side of the pit. He looked around in every direction and didn't see a soul, but he did see a big wide world, and he liked what he saw.

Jae-sun taught Gun-ho the gospels over the years and he had accepted Christ as his savior; there was no way he was going to leave his mother in this pit to be burned, she would have a proper burial. Gun-ho walked thirty meters from the back of the pit toward the ocean, which sounded wonderful; Jae-sun told him stories over the years about the ocean. Finding a flat spot behind a small sand dune out of sight of the pit, he took off his coat and set it aside, then crawled back down into the pit to find his mother's body among the dead. It was difficult, but he dragged her up the shallow slope at the back of the pit, then dragged her behind the small dune to the flat spot next to his coat. He then broke off a branch of a bushy plant nearby and went back and erased his tracks in the sand from the back of the pit with the branch. Satisfied that his tracks were covered he began to dig a grave in the sand for his mother. He gently laid his mother in her grave and tenderly buried her in the sand. When finished, whispering a short prayer while holding Jae-sun's crucifix between his fingers; Gun-ho put on his coat and walked toward the beach.

As Gun-ho got nearer to the ocean, the sound of the surf intensified. It was kind of exciting. He'd been experiencing lots of new things today—and he liked it. He stayed below the top of the sand mounds. Needing to be careful, he wasn't in the clear just yet, but this first taste of freedom tasted very delicious. Gun-ho noticed the little yellow flowers on the green bushes and the grass clumps growing on the sand mounds; and he loved the feel of the sand on his feet, and the freedom of the seagulls gliding on the wind over the beach.

Gun-ho paused for several minutes just inside the line of sand mounds where they give way to the beach. His first time seeing an ocean, he watched the surf roll onto the sand. He didn't know exactly how far he had to walk to the north to find the port, but he thought it best to make the hike at night—he'd have some starlight to navigate by after the sun ducked below the horizon.

Gun-ho retreated into the sand mounds and found a good hiding place to wait out the day.

As the last sliver of sun dipped below the land, Gun-ho cautiously crept out onto the beach, walking straight out to the edge of the water and turning left so the surf would erase his footsteps. He walked at a good clip for about an hour and a half.

Dim lights appeared way out in front—must be lights at the port, or the little town Jae-sun told him was there.

Gun-ho quickened his pace.

Closer to the lights, Gun-ho could make out a level line just above the waterline that jutted out into the ocean. This would be the jetty Jae-sun told him to look for. The docks and the boats would be on the other side of the jetty.

Gun-ho stopped about a hundred yards from the jetty and stood in the dark, just watching. If he walked across the top, he'd be visible— even at night. He wouldn't make that mistake. After assuring himself no one was on the jetty, he crept up to the bottom edge of the rocks that intersected the beach, following the bottom of the jetty up to the sand mounds. He peeked over the top edge, being careful not to expose himself. Gun-ho could make out two docks in the basin with several boats tied up along each side of each dock. The access to each dock was at the back of the boat basin to his left and down a ramp. He couldn't see the boats on the far dock, or the far side of the near dock all that well. He could, however, hear voices on the docks. Reasoning it was still before midnight, he decided that made sense. He would wait right where he was for a few more hours.

Gun-ho waited an hour beyond the din of the last conversation. Satisfied, he crept around to the back of the basin well back from the water, coming to a gravel road that paralleled the back of the basin. Little huts stood between the road and the water. One small yard light pierced the darkness between the docks, but its light would not reveal him on the far side of the road.

He looked down the center of the first dock for a boat. Seeing no prospects, he walked in line with the far dock and did the same. Now he could see a small rowboat out at the end of the first dock that had been obscured by a larger boat.

Gun-ho worked his way back in line with the first dock and silently crossed the gravel road. He stood at the top of the dock ramp and noticed that the tide was high—that was good. The outgoing tide would aid his departure. An old hose stretched from the first hut to the left of the top of the ramp. The hose ended at the end of the ramp at a fish-cleaning station with a trough that cleared the counter into the boat basin. He hoped the hose was a source of freshwater and not water pumped from the boat basin. A filet knife lay on the counter, and several pieces of course cloth pads hung over the rail.

Gun-ho quietly gathered six of the two-by-two cloth pads and took the filet knife. He made his way down to the end of the dock, relying on moonlight to avoid bumping into anything that might be heard.

He found the boat. It was perfect! It was a wooden craft about twelve feet long, with two oars and oar locks. It also had a wooden mast that hinged at the keel and rested in a yoke at the bow, when the sail was down. Gun-ho quietly set his things down set out to find a container for some water.

About halfway back up the dock, he spied two water containers sitting on the back of a small fishing boat. They must be water containers—the Korean script for water had been painted on the side of the first jug. They could be reached from the edge of the dock.

Gun-ho stood in the shadow of the boat on the jetty side and watched the boat with the water jugs for several minutes.

He cautiously stepped back into the moonlight and touched the first container. It pushed forward a bit with the slightest touch—empty. He touched the second jug—and it was heavy.

He smiled.

Gun-ho was small, but was strong for his size. The jug was about five gallons, so it would weigh about 45 pounds full. That was a lot, and it above his waist. He'd have to lift it ever so slightly and pull it back to get it to the dock surface.

His heart started to pound, and the adrenaline began to pump into his veins.

He placed both hands on the handle, lifted, and dragged the container ever so slightly.

It moved quietly on the smooth metal surface. Gun-ho gripped the handle again and made his move just as a dog on the boat barked and snapped itself back on its chain. Gun-ho was startled, but he didn't drop the jug. He set it onto the dock and retreated into the shadow.

The dog continued to bark.

Someone opened the door to the boat's cabin and yelled, "Shut-up!"

Gun-ho's heart was pounding, but the cabin door closed and the dog quit barking. Gun-ho stood stone-still for five minutes, then slipped back across the dock, retrieved the water jug.

He stood in the shadow and let his heart calm, then opened the jug and poured a bit of the fluid into his hand. He smelled it, then tasted the liquid—it was water. He followed the shadow line back toward the end of the dock until he got to the end of the big boat. He waited just a few minutes more, then stepped back into the moonlight and quickly covered the last fifty feet.

Gun-ho placed his supplies on the edge of the dock, then quietly stepped into the boat. It rocked slightly and made a gentle noise of water retreating from the movement. He set his water in the bottom, next to the mast. He set two pieces of the rough cloth near each oar-lock, and was about to untie when he heard a door open on another big boat. He slipped under the edge of the sail that was loose along the mast. A man at the bow of the big boat lit a cigarette, then stepped to the edge of the gunnel on the basin side and peed into the water.

Gun-ho waited.

The cherry of the man's cigarette flew out and landed in the water. Then the door opened and closed again.

Gun-ho reached over and untied the bow of his boat, then slid out from under the sail and untied the stern. He gently pushed the boat away from and toward the end of the dock.

The tide was starting to move, so after a few minutes, Gun-ho drifted thirty yards toward the jetty. Now in the shadow of the jetty, he lined each oar lock with two layers of cloth so the oars wouldn't rattle. Jae-sun had told him about oarsmen extracting George Washington and his army off Long Island in the dead of night, and how they lined the oarlocks with leather to quiet the rattle.

Well in the shadow and ten feet from the jetty, Gun-ho sat on the boat bench, grabbed an oar in each hand, and gently pulled.

After about ten minutes of rowing, he made the end of the jetty where gently rolling swells kissed the rocks.

Riding an outgoing tide, Gun-ho pulled one oar slightly harder and pointed his bow into the Sea of Japan.

Chapter Twenty-Nine

Why?

Leetia sat alone on the couch in her living room with the lights off. Andrew had been in bed a few hours. Art was still out fishing—he'd be back that coming Sunday. She watched the moonlight twinkle on the surface of Esther Bay. The tracks of her tears had dried.

She ran her finger around and around on the top of her wine glass. She really wished Art was home, but she'd decided not to radio him and tell him the news—out on the ocean, men had enough to think about just trying to survive. The news could wait until Sunday—but oh how she wished he were home to hold her.

Leetia woke at 7:30 Saturday morning. She sat up and looked out the sliding door. It was kind of foggy. When she stood up, she could see Andrew sitting on the beach down below the house a bit east of the shop piling. Leetia slipped on her fleece pants and a hoody, then walked down to the beach and sat beside Andrew.

She hooked her arm inside his and laid her head on his shoulder. "How did you sleep, honey?"

Andrew stared at the end of the waves lapping the beach.

"I slept fine—just a lot to think about."

"Yeah. Daddy will be home tomorrow. How should we break the news?"

"Mom, I think we should wait until we are alone up at the house. I'd like to hold off telling anyone else until after we go to Anchorage and have confirmation."

"That makes sense."

Andrew and Leetia watched the gentle wave action inside the bay creep toward their toes with the incoming tide.

Finally, Andrew broke the silence. "Mom?"

"Yes, Andrew?"

"I'd really like to make our trip to the Philippines next June. I sure hope the treatment they come up with doesn't keep us from going."

"Let's make that our goal."

Art ordered a new pollack fishing boat from a boat builder in the Philippines. It would be ready to pick up in June, ten months hence. They planned to travel to the Philippines in mid-May and stay with Leetia's sister and husband for a few weeks, then sail up to Alaska from the Philippines.

"Come on, I'll make you some breakfast."

Sunday morning at 10:15, Leetia picked up the binoculars and scanned the end of the bay, expecting Art's return.

Art's boat came into view.

She watched until the boat slipped into the entrance of the bay.

Leetia and Andrew put on their coats, walked down to the top of the ramp, and waited for Art to arrive.

*   *   *

Art saw Leetia and Andrew waiting at the top of the ramp. He eased the boat up next to the dock. Two of the guys hopped down and tied the boat off. Art told the guys to head up to the shop, take a shower, and rest up—they'd clean the boat up later in the day.

Art stepped off the boat and walked up the ramp to meet his family. As he approached, Leetia slipped under his left arm, and he pulled Andrew in for a hug with his right. They all stood there in silence for a few moments.

Leetia said, "Art, let's go up to the house."

Andrew turned as they reached the door. "Dad, we want to share the news from the doctor."

Art simply squeezed Andrew with a hug.

The Jacksons were seated at their dining-room table.

Andrew said, "Dad, the news from the doctor is potentially bad . . ."

Andrew avoided eye contact until the last word of his next sentence—leukemia.

As Art looked into his son's eyes, he tried to hide his anxiety, trying to be strong for Andrew. Art hugged Andrew as his son's eyes filled with tears. Art looked at Leetia with tears pooling in his own eyes. "I'm scared too, Andrew, but we're all in this together. We'll fight tooth and nail."

Andrew nodded while holding fast, his head on his dad's chest.

Leetia cleared her throat. "We need to go into Dutch Harbor tomorrow and catch the plane to Anchorage. They are going to run some more tests and hope to make a final diagnosis. The plane leaves at two, so we'll need to head in about ten or ten-thirty."

Art pulled his wife close looking to reassure her, but in so doing found solace in her love.

*   *   *

The Jacksons landed in Anchorage at 4:30 p.m. Monday afternoon. They checked into the Hotel Captain Cook. Andrew loved to walk the basement corridor and read the sequential artist panels showing the history of Captain Cook's voyages.

Once settled into their room, Art decided he was hungry.

"What do you guys want for dinner?"

"Lucky Wishbone!"

An iconic chicken and burger joint, The Lucky Wishbone sat at the east end of downtown—a must when one was visiting Anchorage. For one idyllic evening, the Jacksons got to live in their personal nostalgia, allowing themselves to ignore, if only for a while, the reason for their trip to town.

After a good night's sleep, the Jacksons arrived at the hospital fifteen minutes early.

The doctor called them back to a conference room and explained all the tests that they would be running, and of course they needed more blood.

The doctor assured them that they would get the samples right over to the lab, and that they would have a final diagnosis by that afternoon. They drew Andrew's blood, then poked and prodded, making observations and taking notes. After an hour, the doctors finished and asked the Jacksons to return at 4:30 p.m.

*   *   *

After a great sunny September day in Anchorage, the Jacksons arrived back at the hospital at 4:15. They checked in, and the receptionist invited them back to the same conference room.

As soon as the doctor came in, Andrew knew that the news was bad—actually, he knew before they ever left Esther Bay.

The doctor was neither dour nor chipper—like she was trying too hard to be normal. Leetia was seated at the end of the table with Andrew next to her at the corner, Art beside Andrew.

The doctor sat across from Andrew and cleared her throat. "The tests have come back positive for acute lymphatic leukemia." She didn't let the news linger. "We've had good success in treating this type of cancer, and the good news for you is we have found it early."

Andrew felt kind of sorry for the doctor. She had no way to know how the patients or their families would react. Following Andrew's lead, the Jacksons showed a measured, analytical reaction.

"What are the treatment choices for me?"

"The best protocol, at this time, is fourteen rounds of chemotherapy delivered twice a month. Each time, you will feel sick—sometimes very sick—for three days. The goal is for the chemo to kill the cancer cells and bring your white blood-cell count down to within normal. After that, we monitor your white count and hope and pray for the best."

"Emphasis on *the prayer*," Leetia added.

"Yes!"

"Will we need to move into Anchorage," Leetia wondered, "—during the seven months needed to receive all the treatments?"

"No, Leetia. We'll arrange for the chemo to be administered in Dutch Harbor. That way, Andrew can go right home afterward to be as comfortable as possible. Andrew, I want to say again: You *will* be sick, so be prepared and plan to take it easy."

Art said, "Doctor, we are—well, we *were*—planning to go to the Philippines in May to visit family and take delivery on a new boat. Should we change our plans?"

"Art, I don't see any reason to. We'll finish in March, and we'll take a blood test in April. If Andrew's white count is back within normal range, there is no reason not to resume life as normal. The next seven months, you'll just need to deal with how Andrew's body reacts to the chemo."

Leetia asked, "When will he get the first treatment?"

The doctor looked at her calendar. "Let's see, Leetia—this is the ninth of September. I'll arrange for you to take the first dose back to Dutch Harbor when you leave. Are you planning to head back tomorrow?"

"Yes, we should be at Dutch Harbor by noon."

"Okay, I'll make arrangements for them to administer the medicine in the clinic at two. How does that sound?"

The doctor followed the Jacksons into the waiting room, making small talk, and encouraging them toward the future.

The Jacksons drove the old Suburban into Dutch Harbor from the airport and parked in front of the clinic.

Art said, "Are you ready, buddy?"

"Yes, I am. Let's get it done, Dad."

The doctor administered the first dose. Art put on a brave face and took it well, staying with Andrew for the entire procedure.

They drove directly to the boat basin and headed back to Esther Bay.

Stepping onto the dock at Esther Bay, Andrew desperately reached for the stern to catch his balance. He held his stomach to calm the acid he could taste at the back of his throat. He retched, and lost his lunch into the bay.

It had started.

He walked up to the house, went to his room, and looked in the mirror.

You can handle this Andrew—you can do it!

Chapter Thirty

Looking Good

The next seven months went by quickly.

Aching, nausea, and just plain feeling bad six days a month became Andrew's routine. The doctor at the clinic in Dutch Harbor had explained that he was getting poison—just enough to kill the cancer, but not the patient. Andrew felt bad enough after each treatment—the doctor must be right.

Andrew's last treatment was administered on March 26th, 2009, and he was scheduled with the phlebotomist on April 7th.

They got the results of Andrew's white count on April 9th. The doctor looked up from the report. "Andrew, you are looking good!"

With the news, plans were full steam ahead to go to the Philippines on May 15th. Leetia surprised Andrew with the news that they would leave a week early and fly through Los Angeles to visit Disneyland, then to Hawai'i before heading to Manila.

"Oh, Mom, can Peter come with us?"

"Andrew, that's a great idea! I'll call today and check with his mama."

On Wednesday, May 6th, Andrew and Peter were standing in line at Disneyland to go on the *Pirates of the Caribbean* for the second time—they loved the ride.

The entire trip was a great time. In Hawai'i they got to visit Uncle Milt and Aunt Esther—lots of memories being made.

Five weeks since his last treatment, Andrew's eyebrows and hair were starting to grow back. He was thin, but not gaunt, just starting to gain some weight back. He didn't want to look sick when he arrived in Manila.

Peter's flight to Alaska left at 2:30 p.m.; and Andrew, Art, and Leetia's flight to Manila left at 4:30. After getting Peter situated, the Jacksons rode the bus over to the international terminal and checked in for their flight.

Andrew had never been to the Philippines, and he was excited to go. His mother's sister, Aunt Connie, married a Filipino man, Uncle Rene, and they lived in Manila. They had two kids—a boy and a girl, Jesse and David. Andrew's cousin Jesse was a year older than him, and his cousin David was a year younger. He'd only met them twice before.

Now that they were on the way to stay with this part of the family for two weeks, Andrew was thrilled.

They planned to leave Manila on the new boat and travel north to the south end of Japan, slip into the Sea of Japan through the Strait of Korea, then stop in Sapporo in northern Japan, then through the La Perouse Strait and on to Petropavlovsk in Russia, then east to Dutch Harbor. The entire trip should take 22 days.

On the flight to Manila, Andrew and his dad were making plans for the supplies they'd have to buy to provision the vessel for the trip back to Alaska.

The plane landed in Manila at 8:00 p.m. local time. Everyone was at the Manila airport to greet the Jacksons. After they cleared customs, they enjoyed a wonderful reunion. Leetia and Connie walked ahead of the group, Andrew and his cousins walked behind their mothers, and Art and Rene brought up the rear. After gathering the luggage, Rene brought up their van and loaded the whole group.

They headed straight to the Torres family home.

The next two days, they rested and got used to the time change.

Connie and Rene hosted a party in the Jacksons' honor that included Rene's extended family. They had a lot of fun. It was good to get to know the family that Connie married into in the Philippines.

On the third day, the Torreses took the Jacksons on a tour of the area and they visited a museum and some historical sites.

Everything was starting to feel normal.

*   *   *

On the fourth day in Manila, Rene, David, Art, and Andrew went to look at the new boat about an hour drive north. Andrew could hardly contain his excitement. The vessel proved better than expected. It would be the best pollack trawler working in the Bering Sea—170 feet long with a berth of 38 feet, 3,000 hp, and all the best electronics and hydraulic fish-handling technology. The boat builder would need two more days to finish the vessel and the paperwork; then Art could take it up to Manila Harbor and moor it at the transient dock so it would be close to the Torreses' home. The Jacksons planned to head north in ten days. Kenny would be arriving the day before departure to help crew the boat for the voyage back to Alaska.

The next day Art made arrangements at the Port of Manila to moor the new boat, *The Esther III*, at the transient dock for seven days. On the morning of the seventh day in Manila, Connie and Leetia drove Art, Rene, and all the kids back to the boatyard. Art, Rene, and the kids would sail the boat back down to the Port of Manila; Leetia and Connie would drive back and pick them up at the port in the afternoon. Before Connie and Leetia left the boatyard, Art arranged for a priest at the local Catholic Church to come.

The priest blessed the boat and offered a prayer, then officially christened her the *Esther III*. Art brought a bottle of champagne, so Leetia walked out onto a plank from the edge of the dock to break the bottle on the bow. She broke it on the first try, and everyone cheered.

Then Art, Rene, and the kids boarded the *Esther III*. Art walked onto the bridge, started the twin marine diesel engines, and with the twin screws and thrusters, he expertly eased the big boat away from the dock. He turned her on her axis, and headed for Manila Bay. It would be a three-hour trip to the Port of Manila. Rene, Jesse, and David were standing on the bow, enjoying the breeze, while Andrew stood on the bridge with his dad. They shared a smile as Art invited Andrew to move the throttles forward.

The trip across a portion of Manila Bay to the Port of Manila was smooth sailing. The new boat performed well—a few minor adjustments, but overall, a great first voyage. Andrew watched his dad gracefully pull the boat up next to the transient dock, and the dock boys tied it off. As the Torreses and the Jacksons disembarked, Art tipped the dock boys, and they all walked up to meet Connie and Leetia. Art hired a security company to keep an eye on the boat.

As soon as the security guy was briefed, everyone headed back to Connie and Rene's home.

*   *   *

On Wednesday morning, May 20th, Andrew woke to the wonderful aroma of frying bacon. He stretched on his futon bed in David's room and got up, ready to find the bacon. Andrew walked into the kitchen and sat down beside his dad.

"Good Morning, buddy. How'd you sleep?"

"Really good, Dad—really good. What are we doing today?"

"Well, Uncle Rene has some things he needs to do, so I thought we'd stay here and finish making our list of things we need to buy to provision the boat. We'll need sleeping bags and pillows, first aid, food, tools—lots and lots of stuff!"

The next day Art and Andrew went shopping. They bought two thirds of the dry goods and non-perishable items on their lists; it took the entire day. Art rented a box truck to put all the supplies in, and they went back to Uncle Rene and Aunt Connie's.

The next morning, they drove the box truck to the port and hired a crew to schlep the supplies down to the boat. Art and Andrew received them, then laid it all out, organized it, and put it all away.

Art hugged his son and kissed the top of his head. "I love you, son. We are going to have fun sailing this boat back home."

Andrew just looked up adoringly into his dad's eyes.

On the morning of May 22nd, Andrew woke, ready to go. They had another load to get and put away on the boat. Andrew cast aside his sheet and noticed bruises on his torso and on the inside of his arms from carrying the boxes. He didn't want his mother to worry; really, he wanted no part of her abundance of caution to get in the way of the voyage home. He decided to wear a long-sleeved shirt. He and his dad headed back to the marketplace to finish gathering the dry goods and hardware to provision the new boat.

The next two days, they hung out with the Torres and played.

On the afternoon of the 25th, Kenny arrived. Art and Andrew picked him up at the airport, took him to the boat, and relieved the security guys. He would live on the boat until they departed. Kenny was forty-two years old, but was still a giant of a man, and fit from a life of work. In whatever way one man can love another, Kenny loved Art Jackson. If Art asked him to watch the boat, nobody had better dare mess with that boat or they might end up with a broken neck.

On the morning of May 26th, Art and Andrew set out to buy all the perishable items. They stopped at the open-air market and bought fresh fruit and vegetables. Andrew loved the chaos of the open market—the food cooking on the sidewalk, the little kiosks the vendors had for their product, all the people and the bargaining back and forth. It seemed real—more real than the sterile supermarket with the neat packaging and prices marked on the shelves and barcoded on the package.

When they arrived at the port with the box truck, the men Art had hired lined up ready to receive a load. Andrew picked up a crate of oranges and handed it to one of the workmen. A piece of the wire holding the crate together scraped Andrew under his bicep. He flinched slightly, but successfully made the handoff. He rubbed the spot through his long-sleeve shirt and went back to grab another load. By 2:00 p.m., they had the perishable items put away in the refrigerators. The next day, May 27th, they'd try to be underway by 10:00 a.m.

That evening Connie and Leetia made a wonderful chicken-curry dish that everyone enjoyed. Most of all, they enjoyed the company of each other—except that at this feast the good-byes were already starting. The plan was to leave the house early to bid the Jacksons *bon voyage* at the Port of Manila.

Andrew bid everyone good night and went in to take a shower. He looked at the scrape in the mirror. It was tender and deeper on the upper half of a two-inch wound. The bruises on his torso and arms were still obvious. The cancer was back—he knew it. Another long-sleeve shirt tomorrow would be in order.

Andrew was up at 6:30 a.m., packing his clothes and checking his suitcase. The scrape under his arm felt warm to the touch and still tender. He put some Neosporin on the wound and covered it with a Band-Aid before putting on his long-sleeve Carhart t-shirt.

When they arrived at the port, everybody carried the luggage and boarded the boat. David and Andrew put his things in his berth and joined the others on the deck for final hugs. The Torreses returned to the dock and waved as the *Esther III* headed east toward the entrance of Manila Bay.

Blue skies welcomed their departure, and a seven-knot breeze from the south gently pushed them northward into the South China Sea. Art logged the first leg of the trip into the autopilot. They would travel north along the Philippines. Then as they left the South China Sea and entered the Philippine Sea, they would travel along the western coast of Taiwan, then head straight for the Strait of Korea and travel along the eastern coast of Japan, using the Japanese current that flows north in the Sea of Japan.

Andrew stood out on the bow of the *Esther III* as they exited Manila Bay. He was living his dream; he had so wanted to make this trip. As he leaned against the rail and enjoyed the moment, his mother walked up from behind and put her arm around him. She had to stand tall because Andrew was now as tall as his mother.

"Well, honey, we are on the way. This is what we've been dreaming about."

Andrew lay his head on his mother's shoulder.

"Thank you, Mom. This is beautiful!"

With the wind at their back, if the weather stayed good, they'd make the Strait of Korea in four days. Art and Kenny had worked out a plan to pilot the boat in six-hour shifts around the clock. At twelve knots, they were making good time. Andrew finished his dinner and helped his mom clean the galley, then decided to go to bed and read until he fell asleep.

Andrew woke the next morning and could hardly move his arm, and his throat was sore. He got up and looked at the scrape in the mirror. It was red and inflamed and puss was oozing out. He put some rubbing alcohol on a cloth and cleaned the wound, then put a new bandage on the scrape. He moved his arm around, and it felt better. He popped a throat lozenge into his mouth and walked up to the bridge. Kenny was piloting the boat—his dad's turn to sleep.

"Good Morning, Kenny."

"Good Morning"

Kenny pointed to the east. Andrew could see the coast of Taiwan. They would parallel Taiwan for a day, then head directly for the Strait of Korea.

Andrew went to the galley, made some coffee for Kenny, and took him a bagel, too.

"Thanks, Andrew."

"You're welcome. Kenny, would you do me a favor?"

With the bruising on his torso and by the way he felt, Andrew had known in his heart that his blood cancer was back, so he penned a letter to his folks.

Andrew handed a small sealed envelope to Kenny. "I'm not sure that my treatments worked, Kenny, so I believe I am still at risk of being very sick. If something happens to me, would you please give this to my mom and dad?"

Kenny looked at the envelope. "Do you mean if you can't do it yourself—like . . . if you die?"

"Yes, Kenny, that is exactly what I mean."

Kenny put the envelope in his pocket. "Okay, but you are going to be fine—right, Andrew?"

"Unfortunately, Kenny, none of us has such a guarantee."

As Andrew stepped out of the bridge and walked down the steps to the bow, he began to cough and the muscles in his neck ached.

At 9:00 a.m. Andrew looked back up to the bridge and noticed his dad was at the helm. He really was starting to feel worse, but he mustered a bright smile and waved to his dad. Andrew didn't want to alarm his mother, so he powered through how he was feeling and stepped from the bow deck into the galley, directly under the bridge. Leetia was in the galley, and Kenny had gone down to sleep.

"Good morning, Mom."

"Good morning, honey."

"Did you see Taiwan off the port side, Mom?"

"Yes, we are making good time. Andrew, honey, are you all right? You look a little pale."

"Yeah, I'm okay—just getting a bit of a cold."

For the next four hours, Andrew stayed in the galley, read his book, and hung out with his mother. He used several more lozenges to try to suppress his cough. His back and hips were also starting to ache, and the scrape under his arm was throbbing.

Leetia reached over and felt Andrew's forehead. "Andrew, you have a slight fever. Maybe we should give you some DayQuil to get ahead of it."

Andrew agreed, and his mother gave him a dose from the new bottle. The DayQuil helped Andrew feel a bit better, so he read until dinner. With either his dad or Kenny piloting the boat, they ate in shifts. Andrew ate a bit of food that he didn't have the appetite for, then took his paper plate to the trash burner. He hid from his mother the fact that his arm was killing him. Somehow he gathered the strength to help clean up the galley, then announced that he was going to bed early to keep ahead of his cold. He walked out the back of the galley, down to the stern deck, then stepped to the side where no one could hear him. He coughed up a big glob of crud and spit it into the sea. He *definitely* had more than a cold going on.

He walked down the stairs to his berth and curled up on his bunk.

At ten o'clock, Leetia opened the door to Andrew's berth.

"Andrew, honey, how are you doing?"

He turned his head toward his mom. "I'm okay."

Leetia felt his forehead and decided he needed another dose of something to block his low-grade fever.

She gave Andrew the medicine and some water, kissed his cheek, and bid him good night.

*   *   *

Sometimes ignorance is bliss.

Andrew's body was beginning to crash. His cancer being back, meant his immune system was seriously impaired.

The scrape under his left arm had introduced streptococcal bacteria into his body, and it was now raging unchecked in his blood and organs.

Andrew couldn't have known; he just knew his arm hurt. His mother didn't know because he had hidden the scrape from her. He didn't want anything to interrupt the trip.

In the end it wouldn't have mattered anyway—the leukemia would eventually win out.

*   *   *

At 6:30 the next morning, the third day on the water, Leetia opened Andrew's door to check on her boy. He was sleeping, but fitfully. She felt his forehead. He was burning up with fever. Leetia's heart pounded with the realization that something was seriously wrong.

She ran up the back stairs to the bridge. "Art, please come downstairs. Andrew is really sick."

Art used his binoculars to make sure the way ahead was clear, then followed Leetia down to the sleeping deck, letting the autopilot steer the boat.

Art and Leetia stood beside Andrew, and Leetia put her cool hand on his forehead. He opened his swollen, matted eyes.

"Hi, Mom." He tried to smile.

"Art, let's get his shirt off and try to cool him down."

Leetia lifted Andrew up at his waist, and Art pulled his t-shirt off over his head. When Leetia laid him back down, she gasped.

"Art, look at these bruises! The leukemia must be back!"

Andrew's left arm was inflamed. He lifted Andrew's arm, and they saw for the first time a nasty festering scrape underneath. "He's got more than the leukemia going on!"

"We gotta get him to a hospital."

"The closest place will be Nagasaki. It is a day and a half out, and we don't have the Coast Guard to call here. We'll have to deadhead for Nagasaki."

"Okay, get us there. I'll get him cooled down and hydrated."

Art nodded and charged up to the bridge to make a slight adjustment to their course.

Leetia gathered some plastic storage bags and put ice in them. She wrapped the bags in towels and packed them under Andrew's neck and beside his torso. She retrieved an eye dropper and began squirting little bits of water into Andrew's mouth.

As the hours passed, Leetia felt she was losing the battle. She just couldn't get Andrew cooled down. She frantically got more ice bags and put them between his legs and along the outside of his legs. She changed out the ice bags under his neck and along his torso.

He coughed violently, trying to clear his lungs, but he was having a hard time. His throat seemed to be closing shut. At noon, Leetia couldn't get Andrew to respond anymore. He was semi-conscious.

"Andrew, Andrew, stay *with* me. Don't go to sleep."

Andrew turned his head toward his mother, and forced a genuine smile, looking at her with slits for eyes. He raised his left hand at the elbow and tried to speak, but his hand flopped back down, and he uttered nothing.

Leetia kept talking to Andrew more frantically and began to rub an ice pack on his stomach.

"Andrew, baby, stay with me. Don't go to sleep. Stay with me."

Leetia raised his left eyelid; he was unconscious.

"Kenny," she called. "Go get Art! I really need him."

After a few long minutes, the door latch to the sleeping deck clicked, and Art filled the doorway.

He put his hands on Leetia's shoulders, and she turned to Art. "He is sick, Art. He is *really* sick."

*   *   *

Art put his fingers on Andrew's neck, but could not feel a pulse. His heart sank and tears began to fill his eyes.

He knew.

He leaned over at the waist and whispered into Leetia's ear. "He is gone, Leetia. Andrew is gone."

Leetia rested her head on Andrew's chest and began to wail.

Art got down on his knees behind his wife and held her as she cried. There was nothing else they could do—just grieve.

After several minutes, Art stood up and pulled his wife up, too. He gently took the bed sheet and covered Andrew's entire body. "Let's go upstairs."

Art sat Leetia on the couch in the salon and walked up to the bridge.

"Kenny, my boy is dead. Andrew has died."

Kenny turned and hugged Art, and Art sobbed again with grief. Art patted Kenny on the back, wiped his eyes, and looked around.

The sea was dead calm, like a lake.

Art pulled the throttles to full stop, then turned off the autopilot. "Let's go downstairs and talk to Leetia."

Kenny followed Art downstairs, and they all sat on the salon couch at a loss for what to do next. After several moments, Kenny reached into his pocket and said, "Andrew gave me this yesterday. He said if anything happened to him, I should give it to you."

As he handed the envelope to Leetia; she wiped her eyes with her tissue and broke the seal.

Dear Mom and Dad,

I know I am young and have not learned everything about this life. However, I've had much to think about these past seven months.

I love you both so much, but if you are reading this, I am gone.

Please know that I would much prefer to remain there with you, loving you, finishing growing up, marrying, having children, and enjoying all of us growing old together, but God has other plans.

Know that I am not afraid. I will be fine.

I know you are sad—very sad—but don't lose hope in life because your son, your only child, is gone. Find another in need of your love and bless them.

Mother, remember your promise to me.

We'll meet again in heaven.
Andrew

Leetia handed the letter to Art and buried her face in her lap.

Art gently rubbed her back as he read Andrew's letter. He finished, then after several moments, broke the silence.

"Leetia, what is the promise Andrew wants you to remember?"

Leetia sat up, blew her nose, and looked into her husband's eyes. "On the day we first got the diagnosis, he made me promise that, if he died, we'd bury him at sea. He wants to be buried at sea."

Art just nodded and handed the note to Kenny. "Leetia, I think we should honor his wish, and his wish is a good thing. The compressors for the big freezers are in Dutch Harbor, so we have no refrigeration until we get back. We either need to honor his wish now, or go into Nagasaki and fly his body home."

"I don't want to go to Nagasaki; I want to finish this trip for Andrew. We'll take samples from his body and put them in the little freezer so we can determine exactly what took him, and then we'll take pictures of his body and video the burial ceremony."

Art turned to Kenny. "Would you please put the long folding table on the bow deck and get some quarter-inch rope, a piece of canvas, and some lead? I'll go get Andrew."

Kenny nodded and walked out the stern side of the salon.

Leetia struggled through gathering samples of Andrew's fluids.

Art met Kenny on the bow deck. Kenny set up the table and spread the canvas over the tabletop like a tablecloth.

Art laid Andrew on the table.

Leetia took several pictures of him with her cellphone camera, then took off her crucifix and clasped the chain around Andrew's neck as Kenny and Art looked on.

Kenny placed ten pounds of lead at Andrew's feet.

Then Art and Kenny folded Andrew's body into the canvas and tied him in with the rope.

Art and Leetia stood on one side of the table and Kenny on the other.

Art uttered a prayer. "Father God, we commit the earthly remains of Andrew Gunnar Jackson to the deep and to your care, having faith in the resurrection and the light of the world, our Lord Jesus Christ. Amen."

Kenny picked up one side of the table and Art the other. They tipped the port end of the table down and let Andrew slide into the water, feet first over the side.

Several minutes passed as they stood there.

Finally Art said, "Kenny, I will take the helm until nine tonight. Go down and finish resting, if you can."

Leetia and Art walked up to the bridge. Art pushed the throttles forward, turned the boat back toward the north, and recalled the original course back to the autopilot. They were seven hours from entering the Strait of Korea.

Once the boat settled into its course, Leetia hugged Art. "I'm going to go down and take a shower."

"Okay, I'll be right here."

Leetia disappeared down the bridge stairs.

Art drove the boat through tears of loss and waves of grief.

Chapter Thirty-one

Gift of the Sea

Gun-ho reached the end of the jetty to the open ocean in the early morning of Thursday, May 21st, 2009. On a smooth ocean, on an outgoing tide, Gun-ho rowed hard to get as far from the shore as he could under the cover of darkness. Jae-sun told him to get as far south and east as he could and that the current in the Sea of Japan would take him where he needed to go.

In the dim morning light, Gun-ho felt a gentle breeze tease the hair on the back of his head, just as the sun peeked up to greet him from the water. He remembered from Jae-sun's stories that the sun rose in the east. He looked back toward the shore and saw only water. Gun-ho pulled the mast up and pinned it in the holder built into the bench. He trimmed the sail and felt the boat lurch ahead toward the rising sun, on the breeze coming from the west.

His sail full and his hand on the tiller, Gun-ho kept a steady pace east and a bit south. He reached his coat and slipped it on—it was cooler out on the water.

He retrieved the first piece of dried fish Jae-sun prepared for him. He ate half and drank his first cup of water—so far *so* good.

Gun-ho made notches with the filet knife on the rail of his boat to mark each day. On the morning of the sixth day, he was out of fish and nearly out of water. The weather had been good, so each morning he could sail toward the sun and a bit to the right. He felt he was heading in the right direction, but *still* no sign of land since he left the port behind.

On the afternoon of the seventh day, a squall blew up and Gun-ho experienced his first bout of bad weather. The force of the wind broke the mast as Gun-ho tried put it down.

The waves tossed him onto the broken mast pole and battered him around, but his boat stayed afloat.

In the fray, his water jug tipped over, and when the wind died down and the sun began to dip into the sea; Gun-ho had a broken mast, no freshwater, no food, and three inches of seawater in the bottom of his boat.

He bailed the seawater, then put on his coat, curled up under the loose sail, and fell asleep.

Gun-ho woke to the sound of a gull squawking above. He sat up and looked around. The sea was dead calm, and the sun was up. Gun-ho's lips hurt; they were cracked and flaking.

With no sail and no wind, he'd not be moving. There'd be no rowing that might expend the moisture in his body too quickly.

He got back under the sail out of the sun, and held Jae-sun's crucifix in his hand.

When the sun was low on the horizon, Gun-ho got up and sat on the bench—he was thirsty.

Just at sunrise on the morning of the ninth day, he could barely make out land to the east—*maybe*. As the sun rose, the glint off the water obscured what he thought was land.

He was so thirsty, he kept seeing and reaching for a glass of water sitting on the bench, but every time he reached, nothing was there.

His mind was playing tricks on him.

The sun was straight overhead—he was *hot!*

Gun-ho was dehydrated.

He lost consciousness.

*   *   *

Kenny hurried up to the bridge, taking steps two at a time. "Art, I'm sure sorry about Andrew. . ."

Art forced a half-smile and rubbed his tear-streaked face with his hands. "Yeah, Kenny. It's a bummer, he was such a *good* boy. . . . "

Art placed his hand on Kenny's shoulder. "Thanks for being here for me, buddy."

Kenny nodded and stoically assumed a watchful stance at the helm.

"Kenny, I'll be back at three."

Leetia lay sound asleep with an empty box of tissue beside her. The rise and fall of her steady breathing hypnotized Art—he felt so sad for her. He lay down on top of the covers and fell sound asleep. Mercifully, Art woke at 2:50 and turned his alarm off before it could wake Leetia.

Art exhaled deliberately, and all the events of the day before flooded back into his mind. He had a headache from all the tears he'd lost. Art swung his feet to the floor, still dressed in the clothes worn the day before. He looked over at Leetia still sleeping—he loved her, he had from the first time he saw her. He felt so sorry for her—and for himself. They'd survive, but it was going to be sad around the Jackson house for quite a while.

Art stepped onto the bridge at three.

"How we doing, Kenny?"

"Okay."

"You better go down and get some sleep."

Kenny nodded and walked through the door.

Art checked all the gauges and checked their course—everything was going just right. He just had to get through each shift. Art looked up at the picture of Leetia and Andrew he had brought from Alaska to put on the visor. Seeing the picture brought more tears to his eyes. He wiped them with the sleeve of his shirt and took two Advil.

Art reviewed the progress on their course. They had entered the Strait of Korea at midnight, leaving the Philippine Sea behind, and entering the Sea of Japan. He glanced at his watch—four in the morning, so they were four hours north of the Strait, heading for Sapporo.

At 8:45 Kenny opened the door of the bridge as Art looked out onto the ocean with his binoculars.

"Good Morning, Kenny. Did you get some sleep?"

"Yeah."

Art pulled the binoculars down and squinted out where he had been looking, then raised the glasses again. He handed them to Kenny. "Do you see that?"

Kenny raised the glasses. "What?"

"That—it looks like a small boat."

Kenny looked again.

"Yeah, it *is* a small boat."

"Kenny, go out onto the bow deck. I'll ease up to it and you look inside."

"Okay."

Kenny walked down the stairs and was heading for the bow when Leetia opened the sliding door from the galley. "Kenny, do you want some coffee?"

"Sure."

Leetia retreated to the galley.

Art began to slow the big boat way off from the little boat so that his forward motion would be faded by the time he eased up. Kenny stepped up to the bow rail just on the port side of the point, anticipating the best angle.

Kenny looked down into the little boat. He gripped the rail hard as he beheld a young boy—a young native-looking boy—with an *L* shaped scar under his eye, a crucifix around his neck, and bruises on his abdomen, lying in the bottom of the boat.

Art stepped through the door of the bridge. "Well, is there anything in the boat?"

Kenny paused and looked up at him, confused, then looked quickly back.

"Well?"

"It's Andrew—*Andrew* is in the boat!"

Good grief, Kenny. I hope Leetia didn't hear you say that.

A coffee mug shattered on the deck.

Too, late..

Leetia and Art reached the rail at the same time.

Leetia gasped and covered her mouth.

Art shook his head, thinking he was seeing things. "It's not Andrew—but, sure looks like him. Kenny, go to the back of the boat. I'll bring us about and back up to him so we can reach him from the stern."

Art charged back up the stairs to the bridge.

Kenny ran through the galley and down the back stairs to the stern deck with Leetia right behind.

Kenny hopped out onto the swim platform and reached for the little boat as it was coming up.

He grabbed it by the bow and tied it off to the cleat on the port side of the *Esther III*. Kenny stepped into the little sailboat and picked up the boy.

Art hurried down there just as Kenny handed him over the rail, then ran up the back steps and laid him on the couch in the salon.

*   *   *

Leetia felt his head and checked for a pulse. "He's alive, but he's cold."

She covered the boy with a fuzzy throw and tucked it around him.

Art handed her a moist cloth just as Kenny came through the salon door. Leetia squeezed some of the water out of the cloth onto his lips and tongue. His tissue soaked up the water. She handed Art the cloth and asked that he moisten it again. She squeezed more water into his mouth, and again his body quickly absorbed the moisture. Again, and again, Leetia gave the boy little bits of water and began to rehydrate him.

The heat for the salon discharged under the couch so the boy's core body temperature slowly began to rise.

Kenny paced back and forth across the salon. "Should I go back up and drive the boat?"

Art gently patted Kenny's back. "Good idea, Kenny, but first take everything out of that little boat, put it all on the stern deck, then let it go—cut it loose!"

"Okay."

As Kenny was exiting the salon, Leetia dabbed the moist cloth on the boy's cheeks. "What is going on here, Art? Why is this boy out in the middle of the Sea of Japan—all by himself?"

"My guess is, he is attempting an escape from North Korea. He probably was trying to get to South Korea, but the wind and current put him in our path."

Leetia looked back down at her patient. "That sounds plausible. What should we do?"

"Let's get him back on his feet. Then we'll find someone who speaks Korean and figure out if he has kinfolk somewhere."

Leetia was on her knees beside the couch, continuing to give tiny bits of water and dabbing his face with a moist cloth—he was sunburned. As Leetia gently patted his forehead, the gaunt boy stirred. "Mama? Mama?"

"Art! Art, did—*did you hear that?*"

"Yes—yes I did!"

Leetia sat on the couch and rested the boy's head on her lap. "We'll find your mama, sweet boy—we'll find your mama. Art, peel me an orange, please. He's going to need some calories."

Leetia continued gently stoking his forehead and temples with the moist cloth.

Art handed her the peeled orange on a paper towel.

She broke off the end of one of the orange sections and slipped the juicy bit into the boy's mouth.

His involuntary reflexes accepted the tiny bit of food, so Leetia put another little piece of the orange in his mouth.

Then another.

*   *   *

The food was like fuel in an engine. Gun-ho opened his eyes.

The first thing he saw was an angelic face.

Their eyes met.

She smiled. "There you are, sweet boy."

Gun-ho didn't want to take his eyes off her, but something moved and he turned his head.

A very big man was looking down at him.

Gun-ho tensed and tried to sit up.

"Help him up, Leetia. He wants to sit up."

Gun-ho strained again to sit up on the soft couch, and Leetia helped him get vertical.

He crossed his legs yoga-style under the throw and looked at Art, then back to Leetia.

Leetia offered him another section of orange.

He put it in his mouth. He couldn't believe something could taste that good.

Art poured a glass of water and gave it to Leetia.

The boy slowly took it from Leetia and drank the water.

Art said. "In Sapporo we'll need to find someone who speaks English *and* Korean so we can find out what is going on with our new friend."

"We're about three days away, right?"

"Ummm, maybe three and a half."

Gun-ho looked at Leetia, and then at Art, then softly addressed them. "I speak English and Korean."

Leetia and Art laughed together.

Leetia took his hand. "Well, that makes it easy!"

Gun-ho smiled as Leetia handed him another section of orange.

"What is your name?"

"Gun-ho—my name is Gun-ho."

"Okay then. My name is Leetia, and this is Art."

Gun-ho nodded. "Where am I?"

Art offered, "You're about thirty miles from the coast of Japan. Where did you come from?"

Gun-ho turned his gaze toward Art. "A prison camp in North Korea."

Leetia gave him another piece of orange. "Where did you learn to speak English?"

With her question, Gun-ho thought of Jae-sun, and then of his mother. Now that he was safe, or so it seemed, his emotions were closer to the surface.

His eyes filled with tears.

"A man in the prison camp, the man who protected me, educated me, and helped me escape—he taught me. His name is Jae-sun. He is still there. I hope to save him someday, he *and* my twin sister."

Leetia's eyes filled with tears.

She sensed the despair and hope all wrapped up together in his voice.

"Gun-ho, why were you in a prison camp? What offense could you possibly have committed?"

Still tearful, he answered, "I was—I was born there. My mother was kidnapped in Seoul when she was nineteen. The North Korean government prostituted her to a Russian military officer." Gun-ho told her the rest of his mother's story, concluding, "I was born a prisoner. Jae-sun delivered me and my twin sister."

Leetia listened to Gun-ho slack-jawed.

He drew a big breath and, as he exhaled, his chin was quavering with emotion. "The night before I escaped, one of the guards shot and killed my mother."

Gun-ho hung his head and tears fell into his lap.

Leetia scooted next to him and held him as he wept softly.

Art clasped his hands behind his neck and exhaled a big breath.

Leetia held Gun-ho. "You cry, sweet boy. We know what it's like to lose someone close—you cry. Let's get you something more to eat."

Gun-ho sat back up, and Leetia prepared some food and poured more water for Gun-ho.

After he was sated, Leetia said, "Let's go down and get you a shower and some clothes." She held out her hand.

Gun-ho took it and stood. He gathered his strength and balance. "Shower?"

"You know—a bath."

"I've never had a bath. Prisoners were not allowed."

"Well, now you are free, and you are welcome—more like *encouraged* to bathe."

Leetia led Gun-ho to the shower downstairs. She got him a towel and showed him how to adjust the temperature of the water.

Gun-ho felt the water coming from the shower head. "It is warm!"

"No cold showers here." She handed Gun-ho a bar of soap. "Now get those pitiful britches off and get into the shower."

*   *   *

Leetia's heart broke again as she gathered a fresh change of clothes from Andrew's bag. She knocked on the door and slid it open a few inches. Then handed the clothes in. "Gun-ho, put these on. They should be close to fitting you."

After a few minutes Gun-ho emerged from the shower room, carrying the socks Leetia had given him. "I've never had socks—or shoes."

Leetia was trying hard to imagine the hardship this child and everyone in the camp had to endure. She got a pair of Andrew's Nikes and told Gun-ho to sit on the step. He pulled on the socks, and Leetia showed him how to tie his shoes.

He stood up and looked down. "They feel good. Whose clothes are these?"

Leetia turned to avoid looking at Gun-ho as she answered. "Let's just say they are yours for now." She walked past him and mounted the stairs. "Let's go up and show Art."

When they walked into the salon, they found Art sleeping in the chair. He stirred awake with the sound of the opening door.

"Art, Gun-ho has had his first bath."

"You look refreshed."

"I am. Thank you."

Leetia made lunch for Kenny. "I'm going up to relieve Kenny, so he can eat some lunch."

"Okay. I'll be up in a bit."

Leetia walked out of the bow deck, glanced back at Gun-ho, then quickly closed the door.

*   *   *

A few minutes later, Kenny came through the room from the bow deck. He picked up the lunch and, as he turned to exit onto the stern deck, he came face to face with Gun-ho. "Hi, Andrew. You look like you're feeling better."

Gun-ho just smiled and looked at Art as Kenny walked out of the door. Gun-ho turned to Art. "Why did he call me Andrew?"

Art stood and walked to the table, then invited Gun-ho to sit. He studied Gun-ho's face. "How did you get that scar?"

Gun-ho told him what happened that day, concluding, "One of the guards raised his hand to hit my sister. She ran away. I tried to run the other way, but the other guard tripped me; then he kicked me. Jae-sun stitched up the cut."

Art listened intently and, when the boy was finished, he looked Gun-ho in the eye. "A long time ago, Kenny was injured in combat. He was in the American military. His injury affected his brain, so now his thinking is sometimes confused. The answer to your question is: Leetia and I have a son, well we *had* a son. He died. His name was Andrew. You and Andrew look like *you* could be twins. He also had a scar under his eye shaped like the scar you have."

"When did he die?"

"Yesterday. He had leukemia. We buried him at sea. Then we found you in that little boat on the sea this morning, so in Kenny's mind, Andrew simply came back."

"So, these clothes are Andrew's? That is why Leetia avoided my question about the clothes?"

"That's right."

Gun-ho looked at the floor, feeling Art's pain, unsure what to say.

Art cleared his throat, then said, "Um, I need to go up and drive the boat. Do you want to go out on the bow deck and see where you are?"

Gun-ho nodded.

Up on the deck Art pointed off the starboard side. "Japan is over there. We are heading north."

"Where are you going?"

"Home—back to Alaska."

*   *   *

Art walked up the stairs to the bridge and stood beside Leetia. She hugged Art. They looked out the bridge window and watched Gun-ho. He seemed to be trying to take it all in.

"I told him about Andrew."

"You *did?* How did *that* come up?"

"Kenny *called* him Andrew. Gun-ho asked me why, so I told him."

"Well, we're just going to take him home with us, then figure out what to do. Nobody is looking for him, and he is going to need someone to help him face his future. When we get to Sapporo and the consulate comes to check our visas, the paperwork will be correct. We'll just call him Andrew."

"That sounds good to me."

"I'll go see if he's hungry."

Chapter Thirty-two

What a World

Art and Leetia were anxious to get home and sort everything out. Art figured out fast that Gun-ho was bright and street smart, concluding Gun-ho had to be savvy and tough to have survived. Art explained to him the security requirements of different countries, and that he'd have to feign being Andrew to fool the customs agents. Gun-ho understood perfectly and nailed the role.

When they arrived in Sapporo Harbor, the customs people came down to interview them. Art assured them that they were only there to fuel the boat and they'd be on their way to Petropavlovsk and then to Dutch Harbor. The customs people looked at their passports and didn't even hesitate when checking Andrew's—Gun-ho really did resemble him.

Sailing from the East in the Bering Sea, they were glad to see the rocky point that announced the entrance to Esther Bay. It was June 17th, 2009, exactly 22 days since they departed Manila Bay, but so much had changed in that short amount of time. Leetia and Art were both ready to be home.

Art eased the new boat up to the dock at 4:15 in the afternoon.

Gary and Bert came out to tie the boat off and to check out the new vessel. They rolled the stairs up to the *Esther III* so everyone could disembark.

Leetia came down the stairs first, and Gun-ho followed her.

Art stayed on the vessel, knowing the guys would want to check her out.

*   *   *

As Leetia stepped onto the dock, she warmly greeted Gary and Bert and told them she needed to get up to the house.

As Gun-ho stepped onto the dock, Art was looking on from above.

Gary patted Gun-ho on the back. "Hi, Andrew. You look great. Your hair has grown back, and you're gaining weight."

Leetia looked up at Art sadly.

As Gun-ho and Leetia walked up the ramp, Gun-ho turned toward Leetia. "May I see a picture of Andrew—would that be all right?"

Leetia put her arm around Gun-ho. "Of course, you can. You and he really do look alike, but the scar on your face ends any doubt in anybody's mind that knew Andrew. The scars are nearly identical."

As Leetia and Gun-ho walked into the house, Leetia made the snap decision to put Gun-ho in the guest room; she still had some feelings to work through, and she wanted to preserve Andrew's room and his things. Leetia gave Gun-ho a tour of the house and told him to make himself at home.

An hour later Art walked in and reported that everyone loved the boat. Their goal was to have it ready in August to work in the *C pollack season.*

*   *   *

After dinner, Gun-ho stepped onto the deck and took in the view of Esther Bay and the Bering Sea beyond, so many questions racing through his mind. Paramount was how he'd get back to North Korea to save Jae-sun and Mari.

What could he do?

How would he prepare?

The North Korean government was *horrible*—denying so many people basic human rights.

Gun-ho felt blessed. Had the Jacksons not found him, he would be dead—a possibility Jae-sun prepared him for.

As all these thoughts paraded through his mind, he held Jae-sun's crucifix tightly.

*   *   *

Art and Leetia discussed what should happen with Gun-ho. They hadn't decided on anything, mostly because they were still gripped by grief, but life goes on and eventually decisions must be made.

In this moment of privacy, Leetia reached over and held Art's hand.

"Art, I put Gun-ho in the guest room because I didn't want to diminish Andrew's memory. But I've been thinking, I think we could help Gun-ho by raising him as our son—not replacing Andrew, but honoring Andrew's memory by helping Gun-ho save his sister."

"I think you're right, and it's what Andrew would want—and I like the kid. Despite his terrible circumstances, he doesn't have an ounce of malice, and he is very bright."

Art and Leetia were sitting at the dining-room table when the sliding door opened, and Gun-ho walked in.

Gun-ho sat down to Art's left. "How old do you have to be, to be considered an adult in this country, to be able to make decisions that would be recognized by the government?"

Art answered, "Well, generally speaking, you are an adult when you turn eighteen, but to be able to legally consume or purchase alcohol you must be twenty-one. You are probably about twelve—do you know your birthday?"

Gun-ho thought for a moment. "I do not know the exact day because the guards ruined the calendar Jae-sun kept in his berth, but I do know I was born in the spring of 1997, late in the evening, on a day when there was a partial solar eclipse. Jae-sun told me this."

"Well, we can look that up on the internet."

"The internet?"

"On the computer, there are search engines you can access on the computer that will retrieve just about anything you want to know. Why do you want to know when the government considers you an adult?"

"Well, since I did not perish on the ocean, my goal as long as I am alive will be to return to North Korea and try to save my sister and Jae-sun. I do not know just yet how I will do that, but I believe I won't have much of a chance until I am considered an adult."

"It will help to be a warrior, too."

Leetia chimed in. "Gun-ho, in the meantime you'll need a place to call home and people you can rely on. Art and I want you to know that we'd love for you to stay here and rely on us." She smiled with tears in her eyes. "And, as you know, we are missing our son."

Gun-ho looked down at his hands folded on the table, then looked up at Art and Leetia. "The night I left the prison camp, I had to lie next to my mother's body and pretend to be another corpse. Jae-sun is like a grandfather, but I've never had a father, so I would be grateful to stay here and learn how this wonderful world works. I will honor the memory of Andrew, and I will be blessed to have a mother *and* a father."

Gun-ho reached across the table to hold Leetia's hand and placed his other hand in Art's tender grip.

*   *   *

One month later the guys had the *Esther III* ready to go catch pollack. The morning Art departed with the crew, Leetia and Gun-ho took the Boston Whaler into Dutch Harbor and caught a plane to Bethel. Leetia correctly reasoned that Gun-ho had not received any vaccinations. She still had connections at the hospital; she could get Gun-ho the shots he needed without a record. She also asked them to check his blood type—*O negative*, just like Andrew.

Gun-ho was indeed a wonderful and unique person, but legally he had assumed Andrew's identity. That was the best route—otherwise he'd technically be an illegal alien. He and Andrew looked so much alike it was remarkable. Gun-ho was about to go into puberty, and adolescence always blossoms a person into a new look.

Art would be out fishing for a month on the first working trip of the *Esther III*, so Leetia decided she would take Gun-ho on a trip and show him a little of his new country.

They left Bethel and travelled to Seattle. Leetia took Gun-ho to the Space Needle and other sites of the big city. They flew to Washington, D.C., and toured the White House. They visited the Smithsonian, and they visited the South Korean embassy. When the tour guide, a Korean national, and Gun-ho were speaking Korean, Leetia thought, *Wow, he really is fluent in English and Korean.*

When they stepped back outside, Leetia said, "Wow, Gun-ho, nice job with the tour guide. Did he say anything interesting?"

"He talked about the history of the building, but the important thing is, Jae-sun lived here—*he was here!* Somehow, someway, I must go back to save them!"

"You will, honey. You will."

It was almost September when Leetia and Gun-ho arrived back at Esther Bay. Leetia had Gun-ho tested for grade level when they passed through Anchorage. She was surprised at the results, because for his age Gun-ho would be starting seventh grade, but he tested at an 11th grade level. He was very smart, and his mentor, Jae-sun, had given him very good fundamentals.

Leetia took Gun-ho to the library in Anchorage, and they signed up to borrow materials from Anchorage through Dutch Harbor. Gun-ho had a voracious appetite for reading and learning, and Leetia kept him challenged with home-school lessons above his grade level.

By December, Leetia felt Gun-ho had caught up to the culture. He had computer skills. He loved music. He read anything and everything. He excelled at the school lessons Leetia set up for him, and he knew how society worked.

By December 15th, it was time to go visit Uncle Milt and Aunt Esther in Hawai'i. Gun-ho had grown three inches. Leetia didn't know if the sudden improvement in his diet sparked puberty or if it was just time, but he was growing.

Leetia and Art had not told anyone of Andrew's passing. Only Art, Gun-ho, Kenny, and she knew; and Kenny simply assumed Andrew had come back in the little boat—Art didn't even try to convince him otherwise.

At this point Leetia didn't know if she would even tell anyone— what good would it do? This way her folks still had a grandson, Milt and Esther still had a grand nephew, and Andrew's cousins still had a cousin. She didn't see any upside in letting them all in on the truth.

When they arrived in Hawai'i, Milt and Esther greeted everyone and they assumed, like everyone else, that Gun-ho was Andrew. They made over him and showered him with praise at how much he had grown and how healthy he looked.

Gun-ho stepped over to Leetia, hugged her, and smiled a knowing smile.

Her eyes welled with tears, and she smiled with pride—Gun-ho was almost a head taller than she.

Late in the afternoon Leetia and Esther were enjoying a glass of wine on the veranda, Milt was napping, and Gun-ho and Art were play-ing in the swimming pool. They were wrestling in the water and having a good time.

For whatever reason, God needed their son, but he also gave them another.

Chapter Thirty-three

Hope

Colonel Ji came into the kitchen. "Where is the boy?"

"When I woke yesterday, he was gone. He was inconsolable the night his mother was killed. I am sure he was captured by the guards and met the same fate as Ji-su."

Jae-sun hung his head to sell the story.

"Colonel Ji, may we have more help in the kitchen? This is more than Mari and I can do and maintain the service you deserve."

Colonel Ji walked back toward the dining room. At the door, he turned. "I will send you someone."

Jae-sun thought to himself, *Good. I'll be able to continue Mari's education.*

Despite his faith, at times, Jae-sun was tired and depressed about being a prisoner. Mari didn't know it, but she kept Jae-sun going. The hope elders have for the young people in their lives does give one a purpose. Since Mari was born in the prison camp, she didn't have any other experience to compare, but Jae-sun's hope of one day giving her a life beyond the camp kept him going.

A month after Gun-ho's departure, Mari and Jae-sun were cleaning the kitchen after the evening meal. "Jae-sun, do you think Gun-ho is alive?"

Jae-sun walked over to Mari and put his hands on her shoulders.

"I do, I really do. I pray for him each day. He made it past the pit— otherwise, we would have overheard the guards talk about him. He must have made it out of the port—otherwise, they would have brought him back. If he had been killed at the port, we likely would have heard about that in the dining room, too. So he made it out to sea."

"When will he come back?"

"Mari, I cannot know for sure, but I know if there is any way possible, he *will* come back after he becomes a man."

"When is that?"

Jae-sun smiled. "Well, that is different for different people. Some boys never become men—real men—but if Gun-ho gets into the right circumstances, he'll try to come back when he is eighteen. That is six more years. In the meantime, we'll do our job well, and we'll make sure you are educated for the time you'll be free." Jae-sun hugged Mari and tried to reassure her.

Mari returned the gesture.

The next afternoon, Colonel Ji walked into the kitchen. A young woman with two black eyes followed behind. Jae-sun estimated her to be about 20 years old.

"Geon Jae-sun, this is your new helper." Colonel Ji turned and walked out of the kitchen.

Jae-sun turned to the young woman. "Hello, child. What is your name?"

The young woman was very shy, but with eyes downcast, she finally said, "Ae-jung."

"Ae-jung—that's a pretty name. My name is Jae-sun, and this is Mari."

Ae-jung looked over at Mari and smiled.

Mari walked over and held Ae-jung's hand. "How did you get those bruises around your eyes?"

Ae-jung looked down at the floor. "One of the guards did this to me."

Jae-sun could tell she was terrified, so he walked over and gently lifted her chin.

"Well, they won't do this to you again."

As they were preparing the morning meal, Jae-sun, Mari, and Ae-jung heard voices coming from the dining room, which was not unusual. It was seven, and the guards were gathering for their morning meal. At the sound of a particular voice, Ae-jung froze and was clearly terrified.

"What is wrong, Ae-jung?"

"That sounds like the guard that beat me."

Jae-sun looked through the kitchen window and noticed a new guard that he'd not seen before. "Ae-jung, crouch down behind the prep table and look toward the door. When I open it, look through the legs of the prep table into the dining room and tell me if you see the guard."

Ae-jung nodded and crouched down, out of view.

Jae-sun waited until he was sure Ae-jung had a line of sight, then lifted a stack of plates and backed into the door, opening it to provide a clear view. He let the door close behind him and set the plates on the table.

He walked back into the kitchen. "Is that him?"

Ae-jung nodded, turning white with fear.

All the guards were mean, but some were particularly vindictive—psychopathic. Jae-sun decided he'd keep an eye on this one. He would keep Ae-jung back in the kitchen. He and Mari would do the work in the dining room.

As, Jae-sun and Mari finished setting the table. Jae-sun surreptitiously observed the new guard. When the guard noticed Mari, he stopped talking and watched her intently, like a predator watching prey.

Jae-sun knew he had a problem.

He couldn't lose Mari like he had Ji-su. He needed to be careful.

Overseeing the kitchen was left solely to Colonel Ji, and fortunately he never let guards enter the area. Security of the food was important to Colonel Ji, and he trusted no one, so the kitchen provided some degree of sanctuary.

Over the next several days, Jae-sun observed the new guard. He heard him called *Chol*.

When Jae-sun needed help in the dining room, he always had Mari work the side of the table opposite of where Chol was seated. However, every time Mari was in the dining room, Chol watched her in a way that was creepy, even for a guard. Jae-sun decided he needed to do something.

This *cobra* had to go.

The following day, Colonel Ji came in and told Jae-sun that he would be gone for the next two days for his semi-annual trip to Pyongyang. Because the guards feared Colonel Ji, Jae-sun always dreaded his departures—his presence kept things stable.

Jae-sun thanked him for the news, and Colonel Ji left.

After the noon meal the next day, the kitchen waste for the hogs needed to be taken. Jae-sun didn't want Mari or Ae-Jung to be outside, so he decided to take the waste himself.

As Jae-sun was emptying the waste into the hog pen, he noticed some mushrooms growing in the shade within reach of the hogs. The fact that they were undisturbed indicated to Jae-sun that they were a poisonous variety. Jae-sun looked them over, then used a stick to pluck them out of the ground and pop them into his wooden pail.

Maybe he could use these to sideline Chol.

*   *   *

Chol knew Colonel Ji was gone.

His obsession with Mari was driving his thoughts. He told his partner that he needed to go back to their barracks and that he'd be back, but his true intention was to go to the kitchen.

He walked quietly into the dining room and stole up to the kitchen door.

Looking through the window, he saw Mari cutting vegetables—
But wait!

There at the prep table sat Ae-jung, his first obsession. She used to work in the factory. He had cornered her in a mechanical room, intending to rape her. After beating her, he was about to live out his fascination when two other guards walked into the room. The interruption gave Ae-jung an opportunity to flee.

Colonel Ji assigned her to a different prison block, or so he thought.

Another chance to strike!

*   *   *

Mari was startled by a man crashing into the kitchen.

He grabbed Ae-jung by the hair, pinning her against the end of the prep table.

Mari was trapped by the side wall of the kitchen. She had to get by him to escape.

Ae-jung screamed, "Run, Mari! Run!"

Mari remembered the lessons Jae-sun taught her: observe, evaluate, then act.

Everything was going through her mind instantly.

She jumped onto the counter to get around Chol, then grabbed a kettle and started to run, swinging it wildly.

Crash! An entire shelf of cooking utensils got knocked to the floor.

Ae-jung was screaming.

Chol held Ae-jung's hair with one hand and with the other doubled his fist and landed an adrenaline-charged punch into Mari's stomach.

The punch knocked the wind out of Mari and slammed her on the floor.

As Mari tried to catch her breath, Chol turned his full attention back to Ae-jung.

He slapped her hard and told her to stop screaming.

She screamed louder.

He ripped off her clothes and smashed her onto the end of the prep table.

Mari gasped for air.

Holding her down by the neck, Chol stood between Ae-jung's legs.

* * *

Jae-sun came into the receiving area through the back door just in time to hear the crash of the utensils. He rushed to the back door as Chol was attacking Ae-jung.

Jae-sun rushed up from behind and swung his wooden pail as hard as he could down onto Chol's neck and back.

The blow knocked Chol to the floor, landing him on the floor next to Mari.

* * *

Mari regained her wind. She found the paring knife she'd been using to cut vegetables.

Chol rose to his hands and knees, trying to get his wind back, the top of his head pointed toward Mari.

With a reflexive adrenaline-fueled strike of her own, Mari slipped her thumb over the end of the paring knife handle and buried the blade into Chol's neck at the base of his skull.

Chol's body instantly went limp, and he fell dead.

With the knife standing up in Chol's neck, Mari sat back, watching blood ooze onto the floor.

Mari looked up at Jae-sun, then back at Chol.

Jae-sun took off his smock and handed it to Ae-jung.

"Mari, are you all right?"

"Yes, but *he* isn't! Jae-sun, what are we going to do?"

"Okay, I am sure he made some excuse to be away from his patrol because he knew Colonel Ji is gone, so we have some time. Ae-jung, are you all right."

"I am fine."

Jae-sun looked at her face, which was red from being slapped.

"Mari, remove the knife, then you and Ae-jung take off his uniform and boots. Mari, we must clean the blood off the floor and rinse the towel you use very, very well. Ae-jung, fix your clothes, then put the kitchen back in order They will be looking for him eventually. We *must* have everything looking normal."

*   *   *

Jae-sun took Chol's uniform and boots and hid them in the bottom of the freezer. Within a few minutes they had the kitchen cleaned up and the utensils restored to order. Jae-sun told Mari and Ae-jung that it was important to act normally.

They finished preparing the evening meal and served it without incident.

Jae-sun wished they could simply put Chol's body onto the truck with the other casualties, but that would never work. They'd be seen trying to get the body to the truck, and that would be the end.

He had to dispose of the body some other way.

Jae-sun finally faced up to the fact that he'd have to dismember the body, freeze the parts, and take a little bit at a time to the hog pen—let the hogs do the work. He smiled to himself when the thought *one piece at a time* entered his mind because it made him think of the old Johnny Cash song "One Piece at a Time".

He might not have thought of that song or Johnny Cash since he heard it in 1976.

The mind is a funny thing.

Chapter Thirty-four

The Plan

The lawn out back of Milt and Esther's place offered a lush and inviting place. Gun-ho sat cross-legged on the grass, looking out over the ocean, thinking about Jae-sun and Mari.

Art walked out onto the veranda and down onto the lawn. "Thinking about Korea?"

Gun-ho looked up at Art. "Yeah, Mari and Jae-sun."

Art sat down near Gun-ho. "You're really bright, Gun-ho, and you learn quickly, but before you go into a place like a prison camp, where everyone in authority will kill you on site, you not only have to be smart to survive, but you also have to be skilled in the art of warfare. You'll have to develop the skills and strength to kill the enemy—all of them. Do you understand?"

"Yes, I do. You were a soldier, right?"

"I was. That's how I met Kenny. I was with him on the mission when he got injured. We were Navy SEALS, an elite force within the US Navy."

"If I wanted to become a SEAL, what could I do to prepare?"

"Well, that's the right question. You'll need to acquire the skills of a SEAL to approach the coast and come ashore without being intercepted. The training requires six months. You can join the service when you are eighteen. After you get your first assignment, you could take some leave and accomplish your personal mission to North Korea."

"I think I'll be thirteen on my next birthday, so I could join in five years! Right?"

"That's right. In the meantime, continue learning, reading, and improving your mind. You are really starting grow. We'll make sure you stay in good shape the next three years, and in the last year before you turn 17, we'll really make sure you are in tip-top shape. If you're already in good shape when you start the training, you'll have a lot more fun."

As Gun-ho watched the sun sink into the ocean, he turned to Art. "Deal!"

Gun-ho and Art walked up to the house. Gun-ho played a game of cribbage with Uncle Milt.

*   *   *

After breakfast, Leetia make a list of items they needed for dinner. "I need to go into Kahului—would anybody else like to go?"

Gun-ho perked up. "I would."

Art and Milt declined. Esther asked if she could send a list, too.

"It's you and me, honey. Let's go!"

As Leetia turned the car into the parking lot of the grocery store, Gun-ho pointed at a U.S. Navy Recruiting Station in the same shopping center. "Mom, I need to go into that store for a minute—okay? I'll find you next door in a few."

"Sure, but don't join up just yet."

Gun-ho walked into the recruiter's office and smiled at the receptionist. "Good morning."

"How can we help you, young man?"

"I'd like some information about the Navy SEAL program."

The receptionist picked out the brochures from the filing cabinet. "Here you go—I hope we'll see you in a few years to enlist."

Gun-ho looked at her and smiled. "You can count on it. Thank you."

Gun-ho walked over to the grocery store to find Leetia.

She rounded the dairy case and called to him, "You didn't join up, did you?"

"No, but I got some information."

Leetia hugged Gun-ho. "You'll make a *good* SEAL."

*   *   *

The Jacksons returned to Esther Bay in late January.

Art decided it was not too early to train Gun-ho with firearms. On the way through Anchorage, Art bought 2,000 rounds of 7.62 X 51mm cartridges and 2,000 9mm handgun rounds. When they arrived at Esther Bay, he set up a multi-distance shooting range down the beach toward the east. He and Gun-ho built a covered shooting station with a target downrange at 25 yards for handguns; 100 yards for rifles; as well as 300-, 500-, and 700-yard targets for rifle.

Art wanted Gun-ho to be prepared for a very, very dangerous place. Gun-ho would go when he felt he was old enough anyway, so Art decided to train him—to give him the skills he needs, so he'd have a chance of returning to them.

They finished the shooting station on a Saturday afternoon. Art saw Leetia watching them from the house. He knew she approved— she'd asked him to make sure Gun-ho was prepared.

Art followed Gun-ho as he pushed the wheel cart up the beech toward the shop to put the tools away.

Leetia stepped out onto the deck and called down to them. "Dinner time."

Art acknowledged her with a wave of his arm.

Minutes later, Art and Gun-ho walked in the back door. The wonderful smell of grilled red salmon greeted them. Leetia served the salmon with asparagus and brown rice.

Art served Leetia and passed the salmon platter to Gun-ho. "Gun-ho, have you read the U.S. Constitution?"

"Yes, I have. It was one of the first things I got from the library. Jae-sun told us several times in his stories that the U.S. Constitution is perhaps the single best political document ever written."

"Well, I hope to meet Jae-sun someday, because he's right. One of the things that truly sets us apart from other countries is our right to keep and bear arms—the Second Amendment. Don't ever let anybody tell you that individuals keeping and bearing arms is outdated or that it was somehow included in the Constitution so eighteenth-century folks could go hunting. The Second Amendment is specifically included to stave off tyranny—the tyranny of a government gone amuck. A corrupt government will think twice before oppressing the people for fear of an armed rebellion. History shows plenty of examples of governments disarming the people, then oppressing them. The result is sure—thousands, sometimes millions of people perish before things are set right. North Korea is a great example."

"So, if the population is armed and a rogue politician tries to take our liberty, the people can defend themselves?"

"You got it. Tomorrow I'll train you on gun safety and how to shoot. Once you have that down, you can practice and practice. I'll make sure you have as many rounds as you want—practice makes perfect."

Leetia looked at Art. "Mom and Dad called. They want to come to Esther Bay on March 6th, so they can be here for Andrew's birthday." She looked at Gun-ho, and they shared a moment of understanding.

"That sounds fun. Dad, did you ever look up on the internet the date a partial solar eclipse happened in 1997? From here on, my birthday will be Andrew's birthday, but I'd still like to know the date when Mari and I were born."

"No, but let's look it up next time we go into Dutch Harbor."

Gun-ho helped Leetia clear the table and wash the dishes.

The next morning Art coached Gun-ho through his first shooting experience with a rifle and a handgun.

Art stressed the importance of ear and eye protection. He showed Gun-ho how to set up a spotting scope so he could see his success on the targets. After their first lesson, Art taught Gun-ho a checklist of safety steps, and how to clean and lubricate his weapons. Art was impressed with Gun-ho's need for organization and neatness.

He shot 100 rounds every third day, and by June he was good—very good.

Art was proud of Gun-ho's marksmanship. *He's a better shot than me—and that's okay!"*

On March 6th, Andrew and Lillian—Leetia's folks—were scheduled to arrive in Dutch Harbor.

Art said, "Let's go in early, guys. We'll drive by the library and figure out Gun-ho's birthday."

"Oh, good idea!" He smiled in appreciation.

They arrived at the boat basin two hours before Andrew and Lillian's plane was scheduled to land. They drove the old Suburban over to the library. Except for the librarian, they had the place to themselves. They walked over to the PC at the end of the first book stack and Leetia sat down.

Art and Gun-ho were standing to her right, looking at a map of Alaska mounted on the endcap of the second book stack. They were studying where Manokotak is on the map.

Leetia gasped!

"What's wrong, honey?"

Her eyes met Art's with confusion and awe. She stood up, pushed the chair back with the back of her knees, and walked toward the windows.

Art and Gun-ho looked at each other, then walked over to the computer screen. The only partial eclipse visible from North Korean in 1997 occurred on the morning of March 9th.

"Looks like Andrew, Mari, and I were born on the same day!"

Art gently gripped Gun-ho's shoulders. "Well, how about that!"

Leetia hugged Gun-ho, weeping softly. Art embraced them both. "Let's go get your folks."

*   *   *

Gun-ho appreciated Leetia quizzing him on all things relating to her folks—he had it down. Andrew had called them Gram and Poppy, because that is what his cousins in Manokotak call them. Leetia drew a layout of her folks' home and the village of Manokotak.

Clear on the names of his cousins and his aunts and uncles, Gun-ho was ready.

"Does Poppy play cribbage?"

"Doesn't everybody? Yes, yes, he does. He is very good."

As the Jacksons watched from inside, Andrew and Lillian descended the stairs from the airplane. Gun-ho was genuinely excited about the idea of grandparents. He watched them intently as they crossed the tarmac toward the door to the terminal. As they entered, Gun-ho trotted over to take Lillian's shoulder bag.

"Hi, Gram. Hi, Poppy."

Lillian reached for her hug. "Andrew, look how much you've grown! You are taller than me and Poppy!"

"And Mom!"

"There's Leetia's boy." Poppy patted Gun-ho on the back.

Leetia's eyes filled with tears as she watched. She hugged her folks, and Art warmly greeted his mother- and father-in-law.

Gun-ho turned to his grandfather. "How's everyone up in Manokotak?"

"Everybody is doing fine. Peter has been out on the trapline with me many times this winter. We've got about 200 marten and probably 30 beaver so far. It will be a good year."

At home, Gun-ho took the wheel cart down to the dock and wheeled the luggage up to the house.

Lillian watched Gun-ho pull the heavy load up the steep ramp. "Leetia, look how strong that boy is—wow! He takes after you, Art! He's just thirteen years old, and look how strong he is."

Gun-ho carried his grandmother's suitcase to their room. "We're having halibut for dinner tonight—that's your *favorite*, right?"

"Especially the way your mama makes it."

Two hours before dinner, Gun-ho goaded his grandfather. "Poppy, do you want to play cribbage?"

Gun-ho was very good with numbers. He could figure his chances with each hand dealt. If the cards were running his way, he could compete with anyone.

Neck and neck in the first game, Gun-ho needed seventeen to go out, and it was Poppy's crib. Gun-ho received two jacks, a diamond and a spade, a king, a five, a seven, and a three. He threw the seven and the three into Poppy's crib and cut the cards for Poppy to turn.

He turned a queen of spades.

Gun-ho smiled to himself. Even if he didn't peg a single point, he was out by one with the right jack. During the play, he didn't peg a single point, but he counted first. Poppy was four points out as Gun-ho laid his cars on the table and counted seventeen; he was out by one.

"You little beggar!" Poppy laughed with delight.

For Gun-ho's birthday, Leetia prepared a moose roast that her folks brought with them from Manokotak. Bert, Gary, and the entire crew were in port, so all were invited to the birthday dinner. After dinner, Leetia brought out a birthday cake and they all sang.

Gun-ho made a wish—because Leetia told him that's what folks do—and he blew out the candles.

For his birthday, Lillian and Andrew Kashevarof brought their grandson a rifle; a .338 Lapua Magnum with Deviant Action, a composite stock, a Swarovski Z6i 3-18X50 P BTL scope, and five hundred rounds. Amazed, Gun-ho looked at the rifle in the open gun case. He opened the action to render the gun safe and picked it up—it was so light. He admired it, then handed it to Art to inspect and turned to hug his grandparents.

"Thank you so much."

"So, Leetia, do you think he can come up to Manokotak and go moose hunting this fall?"

She looked to Art. "Well, Dad, I think he better, so we can have some moose in the freezer."

Art handed the rifle to Bert, then discreetly leaned over to Andrew.

"That is a six-thousand-dollar rifle the way it's set up!"

"Last fall, one of Johnny Johnson's high-dollar clients brought his New York attorney, who had never been hunting. He wanted to have the best of everything. He brought that gun up, and Johnny got him onto a monster moose up the Nushagak with that rifle! He was so happy with his trip, he gave all his gear to Johnny, said he had a great time but wouldn't be needing it anymore, and left. Johnny gave me the rifle, so I thought we'd just give it to Andrew."

"Well, that is quite a rifle—thank you."

"You're welcome and thank-you for letting him come up to go hunting this fall. I'll take him and Peter up the Nushagak. They'll have fun."

*   *   *

Leetia's folks left Esther Bay on Friday, March 12th, to go home. The next morning, Leetia got up to make coffee, looked out the kitchen window, and saw Gun-ho sitting on the beach in the same spot she'd seen Andrew a year and a half earlier. The déjà vu overwhelmed her.

She put on her coat, walked down, and sat beside Gun-ho on the sand. "What's up, honey? Are you okay?"

"Better than okay! I cannot believe how blessed I am. I'm really starting to understand many of the things Jae-sun would weave into his stories. He told Mari and me the nuclear family was the foundation of a successful society. We had no way of knowing firsthand what that meant, but I—I've been given a chance to experience having a family. I've never had a birthday party before, I've never had grandparents that bring gifts . . . and I never had a bed before you found me. Mom, I really believe God had a hand in my good fortune—there is no other explanation."

"Gun-ho, I am sure of it. Just remember the source of your blessings and stay true to your goal, because I want to meet Mari."

Leetia hugged Gun-ho. "Come on up to the house. I'll make you some breakfast."

*   *   *

The next five months went by quickly. Gun-ho faithfully shot his rifles every third day. By mid-August he consistently put a group inside a 4" circle at five-hundred yards. He also consistently put a group inside a five-inch circle at seven-hundred yards.

He really liked the gun. It was light and very, very accurate. He planned to take it up to Manokotak with him to hunt with Poppy.

Gun-ho found a military backpack in the shop. He wanted to build muscle, so he loaded it with thirty pounds of rock; and every time he shot his rifles, he would pack it down the beach to put up and retrieve his targets. By the end of the summer, he could tell the difference in his strength.

Gun-ho and Leetia left to go to Manokotak on August 27th. First, they had to fly to Anchorage and then back to Dillingham. Andrew's friend, Johnny Johnson, picked Gun-ho and Leetia up at Dillingham with his Cessna 185 to hop the 25 miles over to Manokotak.

Lillian and Andrew rode their Honda four-wheelers over to the village airport to meet Leetia and Gun-ho. Johnny Johnson lined up with the gravel runway on a beautiful late-summer afternoon to land at Manokotak. Gun-ho sat in the right seat next to Johnny. He enjoyed everything—the scenery, the small airplane, the wildlife from the air, everything!

Johnny expertly landed the plane on the gravel runway and pulled off to the side near where Lillian and Andrew waited. Andrew loaded all the gear and luggage into a meat trailer hitched to his four-wheeler.

Gun-ho rode to the house with Poppy, and Leetia rode with her mother.

Leetia had drawn him a sketch of the house, but Gun-ho waited so he could follow Leetia inside and take her cues until he was familiar with everything.

When they walked through the door, the house smelled so good and felt very cozy—it made an instant memory in Gun-ho's heart.

Gun-ho explored the small three-bedroom home in the village, built on wood piling. From the living room adjacent to the front door, he headed straight back to the kitchen and dining area. An oil-burning stove made kind of a boundary between the living room and dining room. The bathroom was the first door down the hall before three small bedrooms beyond. *This is the home Mom grew up in— a home full of love and good memories.*

Leetia's older brother and his wife lived in Bethel. Leetia's sister and her husband lived in Manila, but Leetia's two younger brothers, Harold and Frederick, and their wives lived in the village.

Harold and Fredrick married sisters, Nelda and Nadine. Peter's mom and dad were Harold and Nelda; and Gun-ho had one other cousin, Fredrick and Nadine's daughter, Lilly, nine years old. Lillian had invited everyone over for dinner.

Just as Gun-ho was beating Poppy at their first game of cribbage, Peter arrived and burst into the house to greet his aunt Leetia and his cousin Andrew. "Hi, everyone!"

Leetia told Gun-ho that Peter and Andrew had been close, but Peter had not seen Andrew since they went to Disneyland together fifteen months earlier. Andrew had lost his hair and eyebrows. He was thin and just starting to rebound from the chemotherapy.

Gun-ho calculated he needed greet Peter warmly and engage him right away. He hopped up and hugged Peter. "Hi, Peter. How are you doing?"

"I'm fine, Andrew, but how are you? You're looking a lot better since Disney. Wow, you are *tall!*"

They sat around the table eating beans and biscuits, sharing, laughing, and enjoying each other's company. Gun-ho misted with emotion. He looked across the table at his mother and shared the moment in an instant . . .

This is what makes life—*family.*

Chapter Thirty-five

The Hunt

On the morning of August 31st, Johnny Johnson arrived at the Manokotak airport right on time.

Johnny would be flying them up the Nushagak to a remote air strip next to the river where Poppy had a boat positioned. They would travel downstream on the river for about forty miles; then Johnny would pick them up at another bush airstrip.

Lillian organized all their food for the trip. They planned to camp along the river for three or four nights. Johnny would fly them and all their gear back to Manokotak. If they did harvest a moose—or two—it might take three or four trips from the lower rendezvous point to get everything back home.

Poppy sat in the right seat next to Johnny. Peter and Gun-ho rode right behind Johnny and Poppy. They stowed the gear behind Peter and Gun-ho, plus in the cargo pod under the airplane.

Gun-ho's heart pounded as Johnny slowly pushed the throttle forward, ever increasing the *rpm* of the engine. The plane rolled forward as the powerful Lycoming engine spun the propeller faster and faster. The wings found their lift with plenty of runway to spare, and Gun-ho once again enjoyed the view from above. The flight took just thirty or forty minutes. As Johnny flew high over the section of river they were going to travel, they counted six legal bull moose. Gun-ho and Peter high-fived as Johnny descended to the bush runway where they'd camp the first night.

The plane came to a stop near the north end of the runway. Johnny shut down the engine, and everyone exited. Peter and Gun-ho set all the gear well away from the airplane. When all was accounted for, Johnny shook each of their hands. "Good luck, guys."

He hopped back in his airplane, turned onto the gravel runway, and forced the throttle forward. Gun-ho watched in awe as the 185 quickly found lift inside of a hundred yards. The plane disappeared in the distance.

Poppy said, "Okay, boys, lets carry this stuff to the river and set up camp."

Gun-ho followed Poppy to the bank of the Nushagak, only fifty yards from the end of the runway. Their boat waited, moored to a willow on the bank. Gun-ho admired the craft, a 24-foot flat-bottom open-river boat with a fifty-horse Yamaha outboard motor. Gun-ho imagined them all heading downriver come morning.

Poppy built a fire and warmed the dinner that Gram had prepared in advance for her hunting party—hard biscuits and moose stew from last year's harvest. It was good—very good.

Gun-ho sat indian-style on a flat rock. He made eye contact with Peter and Poppy. Poppy winked, showing his satisfaction. Gun-ho felt happy, truly happy.

He understood pain and suffering—the absence of hope, but for the sheer will of Jae-sun's inspiration.

But this. This was joy—pure joy. Family, belonging, the love of a grandfather, everybody around a campfire, a hunting trip.

Gun-ho and Peter washed the dinner dishes in the Nushagak, then set up their tents. Gun-ho crawled into his sleeping bag at ten o'clock, just after the sun dipped below the horizon. He listened to the faint sound of the Nushagak seeking Bristol Bay. It was a slow river here, so one had to listen hard. Gun-ho prayed as he did every night for Mari and Jae-sun.

He slipped into peaceful slumber.

*   *   *

Gun-ho awoke to the sound of a magpie squawking about something. He stretched his legs out straight and consulted his watch in the stash sewn into the tent above his head: 6:15. Gun-ho crawled out of the tent in his skivvies and stepped into his tennis shoes, then walked several feet away and watered a bush. The sky hosted a low overcast with fog along the river. Just a few degrees warmer, and the fog would dissipate. Gun-ho quickly dressed and repacked his tent and sleeping bag. Poppy walked up with an armload of firewood.

"Good morning, Andrew. You ready to kill a moose?"

Gun-ho had to get used to people calling him Andrew. "You bet, Poppy. Let's go get 'em!"

"I'll make some coffee and get us something to eat. That will give time for the river fog to clear. You can carry all the gear we don't need for breakfast down to the riverbank, if you want." He walked to Peter's tent. "Hey, Peter! Time to get up."

Peter groaned his reluctance to leave the comfort of his sleeping bag. Soon enough, he appeared at the opening.

"Good morning, everyone!" Peter was always in a good mood.

A breakfast of hard biscuits and dried salmon would stick with them. By 8:15, they had everything loaded in the boat, and the fog was beginning to lift.

Peter untied the boat and hopped onto the bow. He scampered back to the stern with Gun-ho and Poppy, lightening the bow on the sand bar. Poppy slid the Yamaha into reverse and backed the boat out into the river. He moved the transmission lever forward, and they were off. Thrilled, Gun-ho scanned each bank, back and forth.

Poppy didn't put the boat on step, as there were still some fog patches. They just idled along. They travelled all day the first day and made about twelve miles.

They didn't see a single moose—just birds. At nearly five o'clock they came upon a high gravel bar and decided to stop for the night.

Peter and Gun-ho unloaded the gear, gathered some firewood, and set up the tents. Poppy heated some food. After a second-but-enjoyable feast of moose stew and hard biscuits, Poppy told Gun-ho and Peter the story of the first moose he killed.

He was picking blueberries on the slope above the village with his grandmother when he was twelve years old. "When I was eleven, my mother was pregnant with her fourth child. It was September, and the baby would come in late October. My mother got really sick one day, so she had to go into Bethel to see a doctor. The plane crashed, taking my mom and dad and the pilot. After that, my two little sisters and I went to live with my grandparents."

Poppy sipped his coffee and continued.

"Almost a year later, we were picking blueberries, and my grand-father was boiling his traps, getting ready for the trapping season. My grandfather was a kind man. He always found ways to help me feel important and needed. I guess he didn't want me feeling sorry for myself. Anyway, as grandma and I walked by where he was working, he picked up his rifle and said, 'Here, son, take my gun.' He put that rifle in my hand, and I knew he really trusted me. It was an old open site, lever action, 30-30 carbine. As grandma and I walked up the hill, I felt so proud, carrying his gun, protecting grandma. We had our baskets full of berries and were getting organized to walk back down to the village, and I looked up to see a nice bull moose walking toward us in the brush. My grandmother grabbed my arm and whispered into my ear. 'Andrew, I want you to shoot that moose—we need the meat!' We stayed low in the brush next to a big rock. My heart pounded in my throat. I knelt on my knees next to the rock and took a rest.

"The moose came within thirty yards of us. Grandma squatted behind me. She poked my side just below the armpit and said, 'Hit him right here.' I pushed the safety off, exhaled, took aim, and squeezed the trigger. He turned to his left and ran down the hill, back toward the village. I jumped up on the rock to see the direction he took. I said to Grandma, 'I missed him.' She said, 'No, you didn't. I heard the bullet hit and saw him bunch up; we'll find him by and by.' She was very calm and matter-of-fact."

Poppy sipped his coffee.

"We walked down the slope back toward the village and dropped down that last little bench to the runway level, and sure enough, there we found him, lying dead fifty yards from the runway. We walked back to the house, got my grandfather, and butchered that moose right there. My grandfather started the old runway dozer and hooked an old skid trailer onto the back. All we had to do was lift the meat onto the trailer and pull it right into the village, easy-peasy, lemon-squeezy."

Gun-ho loved the story. He wanted to ask more about the plane crash, but decided to wait for another time. "Poppy, that was a great story. Maybe we'll get our moose tomorrow."

Gun-ho crawled into his sleeping bag. The tent door was folded back a bit.

He admired his grandfather sitting by the edge of the fire, on the bank of the Nushagak River.

*   *   *

Gun-ho opened his eyes. The dim light of pre-dawn told him morning was nigh. He lay snug in his sleeping bag and stretched. The current of the river lapping the side of the boat reminded Gun-ho he had to pee, so he unzipped the door of his tent and crawled out into the brisk morning and found a bush.

Feeling much relieved, Gun-ho crawled back into his warm sleeping bag and drifted back to sleep. An hour later, Gun-ho heard the crackle of Poppy's fire. He peeked out and saw Poppy getting ready to heat up some breakfast. Gun-ho got up, dressed, quickly rolled up his gear, and slipped it into his waterproof bag.

Peter also got up and rolled up his gear.

Low on the horizon but rising, the sun sent rays through the tree-tops, brightening the area all around—it was beautiful.

After breakfast Gun-ho gathered the dishes to wash. The gravel bar they camped on was on the inside of a bend in the river. Beyond the bend, the river straightened for 500 yards, then curved into another bend, which had a sandbar on the inside. Where the trio camped, the trees on the bank shaded them from the morning sun. Downstream, the river alternated between glistening and fading into shaded areas as the sun's golden morning light found its way through the trees along the east bank of the river.

Standing on the gravel bar, Gun-ho's eyes were drawn to motion in the water down at the next bend. He squinted, leaned forward, and witnessed an amazingly huge bull moose emerging from the river, then standing on the sandbar in the morning sun. He shook the water off his body, which created a visible mist like an aura around the impressive creature.

Gun-ho calmly set the dishes down and walked over to his gear stacked near the bow of the boat. He grabbed his tent-roll and his rifle.

As he turned to walk back, he whispered, "Look, Poppy! Our first moose!"

Poppy turned and looked. He lifted his field glasses and let a low whistle out as he exhaled, communicating how impressed he was with the animal.

Gun-ho set his tent bag down, lay prone on the gravel bar, and took a rest over the tent bag. Gun-ho could feel Poppy's incredulity.

"Andrew, that is five-hundred yards—easy five-hundred yards."

He pulled the field glasses down. "If you wound him and he runs a half mile from the river, we'll have to pack him back—it won't be easy."

"Well, I'll just hit him at the base of his head—then he'll die where he stands."

Poppy put his glasses up, smiled, and glanced at Peter. Tongue in cheek, he said, "Well, wait until he steps onto the bank, so we don't have to butcher him in the sand."

Gun-ho caught the gentle sarcasm and smiled.

"Okay."

The bull moose stood where he shook off the river water for two full minutes. It seemed to Gun-ho that the moose was enjoying the warmth of the morning sun. Gun-ho had optimal conditions. He was still in the shade—no glare in his optics.

He was very comfortable, and his rest was the perfect height and steady. Gun-ho watched as the bull took two steps toward the green bank, stripped the leaves off a low bush, and munched. With effortless ease, the moose mounted the three-foot elevation between the sandbar and the green bank, then stood broadside to Gun-ho. He took two steps and stopped, then turned his gaze away, revealing the amazing width of his antlers and exposing the base of his skull to the muzzle of Gun-ho's rifle.

Poppy exhaled another low whistle as he watched the big bull through his field glasses.

Gun-ho's crosshairs found his preferred target.

The moose's head was up high, looking at something to its left.

Gun-ho slowly exhaled and gently squeezed the trigger.

He didn't even hear the rifle—his concentration was so deep. The bullet found its mark and severed the ungulate's spinal cord right at the base of his skull. The moose literally dropped where he stood, dead before he hit the ground.

"Jesus, Mary, and Joseph—Andrew, you got him! Nice shot!"

Peter was so excited he jumped up and pumped his fist in the air several times. "What a shot, Andrew!"

*   *   *

They quickly gathered up the gear and pushed off the gravel bar. Poppy headed the boat downstream, then nosed up on the moose's sandbar. Peter tied the boat off to a log imbedded in the sand.

They stepped on the green bank and admired the moose. Poppy pulled the antlers up straight, pulled out his tape—a 68 ½-inch spread!

Poppy set up the tripod and joined the boys in a picture. Then Gun-ho and Peter each sat in a palm with their feet touching in the middle— it was an impressive photo.

"Okay, boys, now the work starts. Andrew, bring me the green bag from the boat, please."

Gun-ho fetched the bag and gave it to Poppy. They all worked to lay the moose over on its left side. Then Peter and Gun-ho watched in awe as Poppy slit the moose's hide from under its chin, along its belly to its anus.

He slit the hide up the inside of a leg Gun-ho held up until he intersected with his initial incision. Poppy asked Peter to hold up the moose's back right leg the same way.

He skinned the entire right side of the moose and spread the hide out on the ground behind the moose. He explained to the boys that the front legs are attached to the moose's body with glide joints—held only with muscle and tendons, no bone. He asked Gun-ho to lift the hide-less front leg up again, then cut the muscle and connective tissue. As he cut, Gun-ho could lift the leg higher and higher until it was vertical. Poppy asked Gun-ho to step behind the moose and pull as he cut the remaining tissue, completely detaching the front quarter from the body.

Poppy retrieved a game bag from his pack, rolled it down like a long sock, and set it on the flesh side of the hide with the open end up. He separated the tendon above the right knee from the leg tissue, making a handhold. He had Gun-ho hold the front quarter vertical while he pulled the bag up and over the entire front quarter.

He easily split the front knee joint open with his knife and popped the bottom part of the leg off at the knee. He tied the game bag at the severed knee, then asked the boys to put the front quarter on the bow of the boat.

Poppy's handywork left their meat clean—not a hair, not a speck of sand or piece of moss—just clean. Gram would be impressed.

Poppy asked Peter to hold up the right back leg, then began cutting the muscle and ligaments next to the moose's body cavity. He explained to the boys that the hind leg was attached bone-to-bone with a ball joint. "Much like our own hips."

Peter raised the hind leg higher and higher until it was nearly vertical. A pool of blood gathered in a depression in the moose's body cavity right where the hind-leg bone connected to the moose's pelvis. Poppy pressed his knife down on the edge of the blood pool and let it drain onto the ground.

"The ball joint is right here."

He cut slowly and carefully so as not to puncture the body cavity. He found a bright joint cap made of cartilage, and touched it with his blade. It popped open with a distinct noise revealing a bright white ball joint in a socket.

He asked Peter to step directly behind the moose and continue to hold up the leg. He used the fully exposed ball on the head of the femur as a handle, and lifted as he neatly cut the top of the hind quarter off the moose's body. When it released, he cut another handhold behind the tendon at the knee, and set the hind quarter onto the flesh side of the hide and put that quarter into a game bag, equally as clean as the first.

Poppy set his knife on his green bag, then directed the boys each to lift the moose's left legs and roll the moose over onto the hide that was stretched out on the ground.

Poppy lifted the antlers and turned the moose's head as the boys lifted. Using the long legs as levers, the moose's body easily rolled. With the left legs now up, Poppy skinned the left side of the moose and removed the quarters just as he had on the right.

Poppy used his knife to slice a path for a rope under the moose's spine on the front side of his hump. Poppy asked Peter to get his come-a-long from the boat. He pulled the cable off the pulley and attached it to the other end of the log embedded in the sand. He hooked the come-a-long onto the rope loop and used the it to pull the moose's carcass up onto its belly.

He expertly carved the two back straps off the length of the spine, one off each side. With the back straps safely in game bags Poppy retrieved a very, very sharp saw from his bag and cut each of the ribs on each side of the spine from just in front of the hump to the rump. He then cut the spine across just behind the rope loop. He tied a rope around the spine just behind the horizontal cut of the spine.

He asked Peter and Gun-ho to pull back and up on the spine. He cut the connective tissue on the underside of the spine as the boys lifted with the rope. When the entire spine was perpendicular, the tenderloins were exposed. Poppy carved them out, one on each side on the underside of the spine, then cut the spine away from the carcass at the rump.

He removed the rib cages, removed the head, then had the boys pull the neck forward while he cut the tissue just behind the brisket, all the way across, releasing the neck and brisket from the gut pile that remained.

Poppy showed Gun-ho how to record the date of the kill on his moose tag. He purposely put it back in his wallet for safekeeping. By noon, they were all cleaned up and idling down the river with their moose in the boat.

They made the rendezvous point by noon the next day.

Johnny Johnson had the party, their gear, and their meat home by 4:00 o'clock.

Chapter Thirty-six

Contentment

Jae-sun awoke.

He was buoyed by an overwhelming feeling of peace and confidence in the future. He lit his candle and marked his calendar, part of his daily routine—March 10th, 2015.

Jae-sun assumed something good must have happened somewhere. He got up and meditated for his devotion. He roused Mari and Ae-jung, and they all prepared the meals for the day. Jae-sun's attitude was infectious.

By eight-thirty, the morning meal was over, and they were preparing ahead for the noon and evening meal. Jae-sun's waste bucket was near the dock door, so he walked through the back door of the kitchen to retrieve it. No sooner had Jae-sun walked out of the kitchen, than Colonel Ji walked in from the dining room.

Ae-jung sensed that he was looking for Jae-sun. "Good morning, Colonel Ji. Jae-sun is in the back."

The colonel nodded his reply and walked back to the loading dock.

Jae-sun picked up his wooden bucket and was heading back toward the kitchen when Colonel Ji walked through the door.

Jae-sun greeted him cheerfully. "Good morning, Colonel."

The colonel looked straight into Jae-sun's eyes. "How do you do it? How do you maintain such a positive attitude?"

"Colonel Ji, I have learned the secret of contentment."

Colonel Ji scoffed. "Contentment, how can you be content? You've been in this prison camp for eighteen years! I took over this camp two months before you arrived, so you've been here as long as I have. I fight having a bad attitude every day."

Jae-sun invited Colonel Ji to sit down.

"Colonel Ji, that's the trouble with living under a brutal dictator— only those in the top tier have any opportunity for happiness, and that is uncertain, even for them, based on the whims of the dictator. The difference between you and me is, I have seen and experienced true freedom, liberty, self-determination. I can be content because I have hope of returning to freedom someday. You, however, have no hope—not in the position you hold, crushed under the thumb of a dictator, trapped by your false sense of security within this brutal system. Because you don't know the truth of life beyond the borders of this horrible country, by your measure, your circumstances are better than most, surely better than the prisoners here. It wouldn't even occur to you to leave and see what life could be like where freedom exists. Even if you wanted to, you wouldn't be allowed, and you would most definitely be punished for even considering such a thing. That should tell you something."

Colonel Ji looked at the floor, knowing somewhere deep down that Jae-sun was right.

"Colonel Ji, the genesis of the United States happened under the boot of tyranny. Great Briton foolishly and arrogantly took the people in their colony in North America for granted. When they had enough, a rebellion started, which was summed up in the Declaration of Independence that the leaders presented to the king. That document declares that all men are created equal and that they are endowed by their creator with certain unalienable rights and that among those rights are Life, Liberty, and the pursuit of Happiness. That is what I believe. I've lived in such a system; that is what gives me hope. The Americans helped South Korea create a free and vibrant country. Someday

I'll leave here and resume my life. In the meantime, my duty is to Mari and to Ae-jung."

Colonel Ji stood up, took a deep breath, and smiled. "Well, take me with you when you go."

He turned on his heel and walked out.

Jae-sun walked back into the kitchen and set the waste bucket on the floor beside Mari.

"Is everything all right? What did the colonel want?"

"Everything is fine, Mari. The colonel is curious about freedom, about what life would be like in a free society. Someday maybe we'll show him."

"Well, to do that, we must survive. It seems like the supply to the camp is being decreased, and the food isn't as good. I think there is something wrong out in the country—shortages or something. I remember a story you told Gun-ho and me about Joseph, when he worked for the Pharaoh in Egypt. He saved food when they had more, to sustain the kingdom when there was less. I think we should dry food and hide it, so if there really is a shortage and it gets worse, we will be able to sustain ourselves."

"Mari, that is an excellent idea! We'll have to be very cleaver in how we conceal the dried food. If we are found out, we'll be executed."

Chapter Thirty-seven

Eighteen at Last

Dinner would be ready in about ten minutes, so she walked out and rang the bell on the eaves of the house adjacent to the door from the kitchen.

Gun-ho and Art were in the shop, preparing gear for the March halibut opening. Art heard the bell, even though the shop door was closed—he was hungry.

"Let's go eat, Dad, I'm starving."

"Me, too!"

They took off their coveralls and washed up in the shop sink, then walked out into the brisk early March evening.

Gun-ho ran his fingers over the tablecloth his mother put on the table—*good dishes, too.*

Gun-ho towered over his mother and delivered a genuine hug. "Geez, Mom, it's just us. You didn't have to use the good stuff."

"Sweetie, you only turn eighteen once, but you won't be back here until late tomorrow night, so we need to have a special dinner tonight."

They gathered around the table to enjoy the seafood alfredo Leetia prepared with shrimp and scallops that Gun-ho caught in the bay.

Art and Gun-ho deferred to Leetia to serve herself first.

"What time are you guys leaving tomorrow morning?"

Art passed the broccoli to Leetia. "The plane leaves at seven-thirty, so we need to leave here at five-thirty. We arrive in Anchorage at ten, so we should be at the recruiting center by eleven."

"Where did you sign to join the Navy, Dad?"

"In St. Paul, Minnesota. I got there on a Thursday morning, and I had to fly out to California the following Monday. One of the guys in the class got hurt in a car wreck, and I got to fill his spot, so once I signed up, I had to ship right out. My mom didn't like it very much, but she understood."

Leetia wiped away a tear.

"Mom, I'm not leaving in three days. I'll be back late tomorrow night. I don't have to be in California until May 15th."

"I know, but you're going to be out *fishing* with Dad most of the time." She smiled to affirm her innocent tease. When time came to fish, her boys had to go, and Gun-ho had become a very valuable part of the crew. Replacing him would be hard. "Gun-ho, you're all grown up and about to set out to achieve your goal . . . you've never wavered—I'm so proud of you."

"Mom, without you and Dad, I'da never made it. Hopefully, I can get back into North Korea sometime next year. I know they're okay!—I just know it."

"I know it, too."

*   *   *

At 5:30 the next morning, Art and Gun-ho left Esther Bay on the way to Dutch Harbor. Gun-ho was piloting the boat.

As he pointed the bow to the east, Art slapped him on the back. "By the way, happy birthday!" Art smiled and pulled his cap down to sleep.

They arrived at the Unalaska Airport with time to spare and boarded the plane for Anchorage. The recruiter's office knew they were coming. Gun-ho appreciated his dad talking to his contacts in the Navy over the last year.

He'd already passed his physical—all he had to do was sign his name.

They rented a car at the Anchorage airport and drove to the recruiter's office, arriving at 11:00.

He invited Gun-ho and Art to sit down in the conference room. At 11:10, the recruiter opened a folder and took out the proper documents.

"Sign here and here, please." He handed his pen to Gun-ho.

Gun-ho picked up the pen, and his heart filled with satisfaction. He could imagine himself coming ashore in North Korea and walking back through the sand dunes from the surf to get to the prison camp.

As he put pen to paper, he looked over at Art. "It is four-fifteen tomorrow morning in Korea right now. Jae-sun is just about to rise and start his day. I wish I could tell him about this particular bit of progress."

He signed: *Andrew G. Jackson.*

"You can tell him about it firsthand, soon enough."

The recruiter stood and offered his hand to Gun-ho. "Congratulations, Mr. Jackson. Welcome to Uncle Sam's Navy."

As Gun-ho shook his hand, he wondered if the woman in the recruiter's office in Kahului still worked there; he wagered she wouldn't recognize him now.

Art and Gun-ho left the recruiter's office and drove to the gun store and bought some ammo, then stopped by the quilt store and filled Leetia's list. They bought more gear for the halibut opening, and by the time they had everything gathered up and ready to ship, they just had enough time to return the rental car, then catch the plane back to Unalaska. They turned their boat into Esther Bay just at dark. They used the lights on the shop to guide them to the dock.

Gun-ho walked into the house at 10:30 with his mother's wish list from the quilt store. Leetia was dozing on the couch. He sat and put the bag of sewing supplies and fabric next to her, then let her sleep. He'd tell her about the day in Anchorage tomorrow.

For now, Seaman Jackson was going to get some sleep.

*   *   *

The halibut opening came and went. Art and his crew were blessed with a great catch. Gun-ho had been home a week when May 12th rolled around on the calendar. He was on the 8:00 flight out of Unalaska to Anchorage and then on to California. He had to check into the SEAL training facility no later than May 15th. He would arrive two days early.

The alarm on Gun-ho's watch went off at 5:00, but he had abandoned the notion of sleep an hour earlier.

Leetia got up and made coffee. She needed one more hug before Gun-ho departed.

He tried to cheer his mother. "Mom, I'll be home for Christmas!" He hugged her one last time. He put his hands on Leetia's shoulders and looked her in the eye. "Thank you, Mom. I love you."

He followed his dad out the door.

Art and Gun-ho had plenty of light at 5:30 in the morning. There wasn't a breath of wind, and the water was flat. They made it to Dutch Harbor in forty-five minutes.

Just before boarding, Art took Gun-ho's hand. "Take care of your team, son, and they'll take care of you. You're ready—you'll do fine."

Gun-ho embraced his dad. "Thanks, Dad. I'll see you in December."

*   *   *

Gun-ho checked in with the chief and received his barracks assignment. He picked a bottom berth. They informed him mess would be served at 18:00, leaving time for a run.

Gun-ho enjoyed running—it made him feel good. Per Art's advice and mentorship, Gun-ho arrived in excellent tiptop shape. At home, he'd run down the beach a mile, then along the creek that emptied into Esther Bay, then up a trail he'd cut over the years to the foothills of the island, up the ridge above the house, then back down through the alder brush to the house. For the last year, he'd been running the four-mile course with a fifty-pound pack.

Running on this path now, adjacent to the Pacific in the warm California sun, he felt really good—three women sunbathing on the grass just checked him out.

The next day, several more guys arrived. One of the last walked through the door late in the afternoon. He seemed to be wondering where to land.

Gun-ho excused himself, stepped out, and extended his hand. "Hi, my name is Andrew Jackson; I go by Gun-ho. There's a berth for you right here."

The man smiled a bright smile and grasped Gun-ho's hand. "Thanks, friend. I'm Hershel Epps."

"Nice to meet you, Hershel."

On the 15th, 242 men were present at muster. Training was grueling, but Gun-ho was prepared, and so was Hershel.

Gun-ho admired the fact that Hershel was in excellent physical shape and a natural athlete. The only thing Hershel didn't like was the cold-water training. Gun-ho teased him about that.

Gun-ho thought the water was much warmer than the Bering Sea, the water he'd been pre-training in.

Of the 242 men starting the class, only 75 would graduate.

Hershel and Gun-ho would be among the very best.

*   *   *

Leetia and Art flew to California for the graduation ceremony. Graduates were allowed to leave the post to meet with family the evening before. The Jacksons decided to go out and enjoy a steak.

At dinner, Art told Gun-ho that Uncle Milt had passed away the day before they arrived in California.

Despite the news, dinner tasted great, and Gun-ho got to hear the rest of the family news. The plan was to fly to Hawai'i and hold a Celebration of Life event for Uncle Milt. They would stay with Aunt Esther through the holidays; then Gun-ho would need to check into his team assignment on January 12, 2016.

In the meantime, Gun-ho couldn't wait to fill in his folks on the last six months.

Chapter Thirty-eight

Team 3

Gun-ho received his team assignment right before graduation; he'd be on SEAL Team 3, based in Pearl Harbor, Hawai'i.

As Gun-ho and his folks boarded a plane bound for Maui, he was thinking about reporting to his team, looking forward to the continued training and missions. But first they'd gather for a Celebration of Life where Gun-ho would have an opportunity to eulogize his great uncle. Gun-ho and Milt had grown close over the last six years. He loved the man.

Everyone who knew him did.

*   *   *

Gun-ho arrived early to Pearl Harbor on January 12th. He checked in with the chief and got his housing assignment. Herschel was also assigned to SEAL Team 3.

Gun-ho's phone dinged; Herschel was at the gate. Gun-ho decided to wait for Herschel at the housing office; that would be his first stop.

When Herschel walked through the door, he saw Gun-ho and flashed a big smile. "Hey, Jackson, how you doing?"

"Just right, brother!" They shook hands and body slammed.

The commander walked through the front-office lobby where Gun-ho and Herschel stood talking. Both Gun-ho and Herschel snapped to attention and saluted the officer.

"At ease, men." He offered his hand to Herschel, then to Gun-ho. "I'm Commander Flynn. Welcome to Team 3."

Gun-ho and Herschel introduced themselves, and after a short visit, the Commander excused himself.

Training and preparation at the base in Pearl Harbor proved very interesting for Gun-ho. He learned much about tactics and weapon systems developed and used by the SEALS.

On July 12, 2016, Gun-ho's platoon received orders to deploy to Afghanistan to support regular Army operations. In the same platoon, Gun-ho and Herschel arrived at the post together.

Gun-ho walked off the plane into a hot and dusty Afghani day, shouting over his shoulder to Herschel, "This is paradise, brother!"

"Well, it ain't cold."

"Not yet anyway."

They settled into their quarters, then explored the remote base. The Army had built a security perimeter with sand mounds and fencing, so their patrols began either by truck or helicopter.

As summer gave way to fall and fall to winter, the days grew much cooler and shorter, and the nights were cold—but still dusty.

On January 20, 2017, Gun-ho, Herschel, and two other SEALs—Alvarez and Schultz—flew out via a UH-60 Black Hawk helicopter to provide support for a rescue-and-recovery operation in the mountains to the east. A seven-man Army detail patrolling ridgetops was ambushed by a group of Taliban fighters. With one soldier killed and one injured, the entire patrol was pinned down by the enemy.

As the helicopter lifted off, Gun-ho felt for the chain holding Jae-sun's crucifix, then checked his gear and weapons.

Gun-ho's senses were on high alert.

He looked over at Herschel and nodded; this trip could be their most dangerous operation since being deployed. He had studied maps of the area, but it would be good to see it from above.

As the Black Hawk pilot began to descend and position the bird, the helicopter crew could see the fix their Army brothers were in: pinned down on a narrow ridge. The ridge continued to their north, albeit at a much steeper angle. To the south, the ridge descended, but continued for several miles. The patrol was pinned down on a relatively flat piece of the ridge about thirty meters long. They had cover from the south behind several large rocks and the descending topography. The crew in the helicopter were all connected via intercom in their helmets.

The pilot shouted warnings of enemy fighters 200 yards to the south; the enemy were intent on wiping out the pinned-down Army patrol.

The intercom buzzed with news of sixteen Taliban, but Gun-ho couldn't see them from his position on the starboard side.

Thirty meters above the ground, the pilot shouted, "Incoming!"

He banked hard to the left, which swung Gun-ho around toward the cockpit.

A rocket barely missed them, low by two meters, exploding into the west face of the mountain.

The two-man enemy crew worked to reload the rocket launcher and have another go.

Gun-ho dove prone onto the helicopter floor, hooked his toes onto the starboard-door threshold, found the shooter in his sights—

And killed him with the first shot.

Gun-ho missed the loader, who was frantically trying to shoulder the weapon and become the shooter.

Gun-ho took aim again—

And killed the second man.

The pilot shouted through the intercom. "Good shooting, whoever did that!"

Gun-ho shouted to Alvarez and Schultz. "Cover that launcher! Don't let any of those bastards pick up that weapon!"

The pilot landed so Gun-ho and Herschel could exit the starboard door and help their Army buddies load.

Alvarez and Schultz kept up blistering cover through the port door of the bird.

Four of the Army guys loaded the body of their fallen comrade. Gun-ho and one of the Army guys helped their wounded brother load while Herschel provided additional cover from the nose of the Black Hawk.

Everyone could hear the co-pilot's directive through the intercom. "We're loaded—let's go, go, go!"

Herschel ran back to the starboard door of the Black Hawk just as the pilot was spinning the rotors.

Gun-ho positioned himself at the front starboard doorpost.

Herschel lunged through and caught his balance on the door threshold.

Just as he turned to position himself at the aft doorpost, an enemy bullet slammed his chest. His flak jacket stopped it, but it knocked the wind out of him and stumbled him backwards.

Gun-ho reached for him.

A second round hit him in the left side.

Just above the point of his pelvis, it ripped through flesh and hit the rail of his pack. It knocked him backward out the helicopter door just as the rotors were catching lift.

Gun-ho watched helplessly as Herschel fell backwards six feet to the ground.

Gun-ho spun his pack off, threw it to the ground, and jumped—now a drop of ten feet. His rifle still in hand, Gun-ho took position behind the eastern-most rock on the ridge point and trained his sights on another enemy fighter attempting to fire the rocket launcher.

*　　*　　*

As the helicopter flew along the west face of the mountain range, one of the Army guys was shouting without the aid of the intercom. "Man down! Man down!"

The co-pilot spun around. "Who's hit?! Who's hit?!"

The Army platoon leader reached up and grabbed a headset. "The SEAL—the brother!"

"Epps? Epps is hit?"

"Epps—yeah Epps! He fell backwards!"

Alvarez and Schultz turned.

Alvarez shouted, "Where's Jackson?"

"When Epps got hit, Jackson threw his pack out and jumped!"

"What the hell do you mean, *he jumped?*"

"I'm telling you, Epps got hit! He fell, and Jackson jumped down to help him!"

The pilot yelled through the intercom. "Son of a bitch—*damn it!*"

Now safely away from the fracas, the Black Hawk was protected by the obtuse curve in the mountain range.

The Army leader shouted, "Jackson just saved our lives! Soon as he hit the ground, he took out another Taliban trying to launch a rocket. The guy's head exploded in a cloud of pink, and the rocket exploded into the ground!"

"Well, I hope his luck holds up. It's too late to go back now—

"We don't have enough fuel."

*   *   *

Gun-ho wasn't sure how many enemy were left, or if they knew that two from the helicopter crew were still on the ridge. Discerning he had a few seconds, he tended to Herschel, who was just coming to. Checking him out, he ripped off Hershel's flak jacket and shirt, finding where the first round hit. Herschel had a huge nasty bruise and probably broken ribs. Gun-ho exposed the wound where the second round hit. It was bleeding, but Gun-ho could tell it was a flesh wound. The bullet had not entered

Herschel's body cavity. Relieved, he began applying pressure to slow the bleeding.

Fully conscious now, Herschel worked his way up on his elbows. "What happened, Jackson?"

"You got shot, that's what! Twice. Your jacket stopped the first round, but the second one caught you in the side. You'll be okay in a couple of days—nice dive out of the chopper, too. I'll give you a nine-point-six for that!" He checked Herschel for a concussion. "We'll have to keep an eye on you—you hit the ground pretty hard."

"Chopper got away okay?"

"Yeah, yeah they got out okay. They'll be back in the morning to get us."

"How'd you get left behind, man?"

"You pulled me out when you fell, you asshole!"

"You bailed out, didn't you, Jackson? Thanks, man!"

Gun-ho winked at Herschel as he finished dressing the wound. "I gotta go check on our friends down the hill before dark. I think there were sixteen of them when we arrived. I think we got ten of 'em, so we could still have six guys down there."

Gun-ho retrieved his field glasses and worked his way out to the edge of the east rock again, then looked down the hill, but couldn't see anyone in his field of vision. He eased his way up on the rock to get a higher view. Five enemy stood together, seemingly discussing their situation.

They were gesturing wildly and seemed confused about what to do. They apparently didn't know anyone was still up the hill—they were fully exposed.

Gun-ho moved his position to the west between two of the big rocks where a smaller rock was pinched between them. The small rock provided a great rest back in the shadow of the large rocks. Gun-ho watched them, hoping they would decide to head back down to the camp the Army patrols had verified in the next valley, south and east about eight miles from their location.

About forty minutes until dark, it looked like a decision had finally been made.

They retrieved their weapons and started up the ridge to look for bodies or gear left behind that they could exploit.

Gun-ho patiently watched through his scope as the five Taliban worked their way up the ridge, no doubt toward his and Hershel's location. The guy in the lead reminded him of Major Lee, the guard in the prison camp who kicked him so many years ago—he had the same turned-down mouth.

Too bad for these Taliban—if Gun-ho held any empathy, it evaporated.

He waited until they were about seventy yards out.

When they all lined up, he painted his crosshairs on a shirt stain over the lead man's heart.

He squeezed his trigger—

Boom!

The lead man crumpled. The second man grasped his throat, blood squirting through his fingers, then fell across the lead man. The third man spun back and dropped to his knees.

Three men down—one round!

The other two turned and ran.

Gun-ho caught one in the back of his head with a second round, but the other enemy fighter made it to cover.

Gun-ho watched.

After two full minutes, the fighter emerged five hundred yards out, running down the ridgetop trail.

Gun-ho squeezed the trigger.

His third round missed high.

The fighter turned left and followed the trail along the east face of the far mountain. The trail departed from the ridgetop at that point because the next peak south had impassable rock formations.

Now at 800 yards out, Gun-ho gave him one last scare. The bullet hit the foot path just ahead, making him recoil and fall to the ground.

He popped back up and began running faster.

At his rate of travel, he'd be back at his camp in about two hours. That meant that by daybreak, he'd be back with help—maybe *lots* of help.

Gun-ho dismounted his hide and got some water for Herschel.

Chapter Thirty-nine

A New Direction

President Trump arrived early, even though he'd gone to bed so late. The inauguration balls he committed to attend kept him up, but now sitting at his desk in the Oval Office, he savored the moment. He had a full day ahead, signing executive orders, which would begin the process of changing the policy direction of the country, deviating sharply from the Obama years.

After a few moments alone, President Trump's peace was disturbed by a sweet voice asking if he wanted a cup of coffee. The president accepted the offer. Mr. Miller and Mr. Flynn tapped on the door, and the president waved his men into the room.

After reviewing the roster of items for him to sign, the president looked up. "Mike, do we have human intelligence in North Korea?"

The already embattled national security advisor crossed his arms. "I don't think so, Mr. President. Our guys stick out like a sore thumb over there."

"You mean we don't have any Korean guys on our side—you know, good red-blooded American Koreans that we can get in there?"

"I don't think so, Mr. President."

President Trump looked at both men. "You know, Barrack told me last week that North Korea is going to be our toughest problem. I don't know if he's right about that, but I'd still like to solve that mess!" He paused for ten full seconds.

Neither man responded, nor did he expect a reply.

"Mike, what about the elite services—you know, Rangers, SEALs, RECON guys—guys like that. Let's find out if any of those guys have a candidate we can insert into the North."

"Well, I doubt somebody like that is out there, but even if there is, those guys don't do solo missions. They are team oriented, but I'll put out a call."

"Thanks, Mike. Not service-wide, though—just to the elite commanders. Let's keep this inquiry pretty quiet."

"I'll take care of it, Mr. President."

*   *   *

Head of the command structure for the Navy SEALs, Admiral Johnson read an email to the elite services of the Army, Navy, Marines, and Air Force:

Gentlemen:

Needed, a human asset, fluent in the Korean language, with Korean features, for consideration of a special assignment.

Best:

Mike Flynn
National Security Advisor

The admiral couldn't imagine what was afoot, but he forwarded the email to each of his team commanders.

*   *   *

Commander Jake Flynn—no relation to the national security advisor—opened the email from Admiral Johnson and read it at 1:00 p.m.

Hawai'i time on January 21, 2017. *Well, Mr. Flynn, if I were twenty years younger and a little more Korean-looking, I'd be your man.*

Flynn did speak fluent Korean as his first language. His grand-mother, Soo-ah Erickson, had taught him to speak Korean before he learned English. She watched him every day when he was a baby while his mother worked in the family business. Commander Flynn was 25% Korean, but his Scandinavian and English genes blended him well with his Caucasian peers.

Commander Flynn read the next email from Afghanistan. Seems two of his boys were missing in action. He needed to get to the bottom of this.

He didn't like losing his men.

*   *   *

As darkness fell and the temperature dropped, Gun-ho hoped Alvarez and Schultz would be back tomorrow. He couldn't take a chance that the Taliban would re-group and make it back up to the saddle by morn-ing. There could be a hundred of them up here.

Gun-ho decided to reposition Herschel to the top of the peak behind them. That way the helicopter could pick them up from the north side of the peak and have complete cover from any enemy in the saddle to the south.

Herschel was cold, but his wound looked good.

"Come on, ole buddy, we gotta get you up there. It's a better place for the helicopter if our local friends come back." He helped Herschel up to his feet and supported him from his left side.

It took about thirty minutes to make it to the top.

"I gotta piss, man!"

"Good, that means everything is working. We gotta keep you hydrated."

Gun-ho set him up out of the wind under a rock overhang on the north side of the peak. He laid out a space blanket for groundcover and covered Herschel with the ponchos and the other space blanket.

"You comfy, Herschel?" Gun-ho smiled, pleased with his jab.

"Four-star, man—send by room service, would ya?"

"Listen, Herschel, I gotta go down there and build a surprise for our friends. You get some sleep."

Gun-ho ran down the steep slope on his heels. But for the lack of alder brush, it reminded him of running the ridges above Esther Bay. He didn't think he'd run into any grizzly bears up here, but maybe a few grizzly guys.

Gun-ho made it back to the packs. He collected two pounds of plastic explosive from each pack. Plus, they each had a four-frequency ultra-sonic trigger switch with two caps per frequency. He could set up sixteen charges.

He walked around the two guys he'd killed.

The third guy still clung to life. Gun-ho ended the man's misery with his blade.

He made it down to the rocket launcher, finding twelve unused rockets.

Gun-ho could see three-hundred yards to where the trail left the ridgetop. It followed the east face of the mountain and disappeared around the curve in the moonlight. If the enemy made it into the saddle, they could spread out and eventually overtake him and Herschel on their perch. But to get to the saddle, they'd all have to come up that trial along the mountain face, and they'd all be lined up in a nice little row.

There, he would strike.

Gun-ho lifted the crate of rockets onto his shoulder and made his way down the trail to where it rolled off onto the face of the mountain. The ultra-sonic triggers had a range of 1,500 yards. He walked down the trail to a point easily seen from 800 yards back. He made a depression in the scree of the cut bank at about knee height. In the depression he buried one of the rockets with some plastic explosive and a trigger cap, then placed seven more charges going up the trail, one every twenty yards. His charges covered 160 yards of the cut bank. Gun-ho climbed up the mountain above the cut bank and placed eight more charges parallel to the first row. Every other one also had a rocket for extra kick.

He was ready.

At 3:00 a.m., he walked back up through the saddle to his original hide 800 yards from the furthest charge. With the curve of the mountain coming toward his location, the closest charges, farthest up the trail, were about 700 yards away.

*　　*　　*

Commander Flynn requested a call be routed through to Major Dillon at the Army outpost where his SEALs were assigned. When the connection was made, Flynn picked up his phone. "Major Dillon, what's going on over there?"

"Good morning, sir." He briefed the commander on what led up to the current situation. "The time of day," he continued, "and fuel level prevented the helicopter from returning. The pilot made the right call. We likely would have lost thirteen all together. We are going back first thing in the morning with two helicopters to retrieve Jackson and Epps. We've also requested a drone to help cover us if we encounter more enemy."

Commander Flynn listened carefully. "That sounds good, Major. Thank you. I really appreciate your effort."

"You're welcome, sir—we want to get your boys back. Oh, by the way, you should know that Jackson is a great shot. He took out a two-man rocket launcher crew at 200 yards from a moving helicopter with three shots. He jumped out and popped another guy trying to man the launcher to get one more shot off at the helicopter. Without Jackson out there today, it might have been a different story."

Commander Flynn laughed.

"Thanks for letting me know—he is a good kid. I'll see if we can get some satellite time to give you guys advance knowledge of what you're flying into."

"Thanks, Commander. That'd be great."

Commander Flynn made an urgent request to SENTCOM for eye time over the area.

$$* \quad * \quad *$$

Now 4:00 a.m., Gun-ho could still see his special piece of the trail even with the moon almost gone.

At 6:00, the sky beyond the next mountain range to the east began to brighten. The sun wasn't up by any means, but the dim of early morning light appeared.

At 6:50, Gun-ho detected motion on the trail.

Through his field glasses, he observed a string of enemy making their way. The lead guy was about sixty yards from the first charge. They were moving slowly but steadily. Gun-ho could count them. One, two, three—82 men in a line about fifty yards long.

The sun still wasn't above the horizon, but the sky quickly brightened.

When the lead guy reached the middle of Gun-ho's trap, he climbed up and stood on top of one of the large rocks.

Gun-ho perched himself on the ridge at the top of the saddle on the horizon, exposing himself like a beacon, framed in an aura of morning light, a light breeze moving from east to west.

Gun-ho could hear their chatter on the wind.

The lead man advanced 2/3 into the zone, then suddenly halted, stopping the line behind him.

They had seen him.

The view amused Gun-ho as news of his appearance travelled down the line. The lead guy looked at him through his own field glasses.

Gun-ho lowered his field glasses, smiled and waved to the leader, then reached into his pockets and retrieved the frequency switches. He ran his thumbs down the array of switches on each holder, each about the size of a Snickers bar.

The charges beside the cut bank and those on the mountain above the enemy procession all exploded within milliseconds. The entire line disappeared, engulfed in a shrapnel-riddled cloud of dust.

Seconds later, forty feet of the mountain above the trail collapsed, sliding down and burying everything and everyone below.

Gun-ho hopped down off his rock, grabbed the packs, and headed up the hill to Herschel.

*   *   *

Four miles out, two Black Hawks were flying side by each. Commander Dillon had ordered them into the air by 6:30 so they could retrieve Epps and Jackson before the sun rose above the horizon.

One of the pilots radioed the other. "You see that, someone is standing on the top of that ridge, right on the horizon."

"Yeah, I see—that's weird. Hey, look through your scope. See that string of guys on the next mountain? There must be a hundred of 'em!"

"Yeah, yeah, I see 'em. Wonder what's up."

Just as the words left his mouth, the entire mountain exploded in a cloud of dust.

"That's what's going on! Your buddy on the horizon just brought that mountain down on their heads! Wow!"

*   *   *

"Major Dillon, this is Airman Collins at Nellis." The major leaned back in his chair.

"Yes, airman, go ahead."

"Major, I have the coordinates in sight from the drone. In thirty seconds, I'll be in firing position. I see one guy standing up on the horizon and approximately eighty men working their way up toward him. Stand by—Oh my god! Major Dillon, the entire enemy force has just been engulfed in a massive explosion! Oh my god!"

"Did the Black Hawks hit them?"

"No, sir. The Black Hawks are out of range. I'd say your guy on the ground just gave them a little IED medicine on their own trail!"

*   *   *

"Commander Flynn, I have SENTCOM on the line."

Sitting at his desk at 6:45 p.m., Flynn was expecting the call from SENTCOM, as it was 6:45 the following morning in Afghanistan. Commander Flynn picked up his phone.

"Jake, this is Bill—Admiral Johnson. We have the satellite image up. I'm going to put you on speaker so you can hear the observer."

"Thanks, Bill."

The observer described the scene and said, "The man on the ridge is pinging a biometric that indicates he is Seaman First Class Andrew Jackson. Another biometric is pinging 200 meters to the north, indicating Seaman First Class Herschel Epps, but he is not in view. There are two Black Hawks from Forward Base Charlie approaching from the west. A drone from Kandahar is approaching from the northeast—"

"What? What happened?"

A major explosion! It appears the entire area has just erupted, source unknown. The drone has not fired. The helicopters are out of range. Seaman Jackson has just moved his position. It appears that he is moving up toward Seaman Epps. The enemy threat has been eliminated."

Admiral Johnson picked up the phone. "Jake, it looks like your guys are in the clear, thank God. You know, Jake, I've met Seaman Jackson's dad. He was a SEAL, too. Those Jacksons are warriors—

"*Real* warriors."

Chapter Forty

Desperate Times

Mari was determined to keep Jae-sun and Ae-jung alive, but they were very ill. Jae-sun suspected cholera. Supplies to the prison camp had virtually dried up; less and less food was being delivered to the prison, and no fuel had come in the last two months. Many of the prisoners had died over the winter, and half of the guards had been re-assigned elsewhere. Not having fuel to boil water or to cook had allowed cholera to sweep through the population. Mari surreptitiously removed wood from the side of the buildings and used it to boil water to keep Jae-sun and Ae-jung hydrated. She also made an antibiotic brew with garlic.

Major Lee Dae-du was in charge of the camp now, so any autonomy they enjoyed under Colonel Ji was gone. A mean and vindictive tyrant, Major Lee framed Colonel Ji, implicating him falsely of stealing food, making him a prisoner in the very camp he'd overseen for twenty years. The last time Mari saw him, he didn't look so good. Jae-sun had a soft spot for him, so Mari worried about him, too.

Somewhere Mari kept finding the strength to persevere, but daily she prayed that Gun-ho would arrive soon. She knew deep down that he *lived*, and in that belief, she found hope to continue.

For two years Mari had been drying fish and making it into fish meal. She kept all the small containers she could find, packing them with meal and a bit of rice. She would hide them in the rafters above the kitchen receiving area. It was a good thing she had, because lately the protein and calories added to Jae-sun's, Ae-jung's, and her diet had helped to sustain them. Mari figured what she had set aside would last about two more months; after that they'd have trouble surviving.

Mari had Jae-sun and Ae-jung fixed up in the receiving office behind the kitchen. She'd prepared a fish, cabbage, and rice broth and was feeding Jae-sun. She was encouraged, as it seemed he felt much better.

"Mari, did you mark my calendar today?"

"Yes sir, it is February 12th."

"Gun-ho will be here soon; I can feel it."

"I hope so, Jae-sun. It's hard to imagine how we can survive much longer. More people died last night. I saw the guards throw the bodies onto the truck."

"Thank-you, Mari. I've had enough. Please take care of Ae-jung."

"Okay. How are *you* feeling?"

"Much better. I think I'd like to get up and walk."

"That's good. You *must* be feeling better."

Jae-sun walked into the kitchen and back.

Mari was feeding Ae-jung.

Jae-sun put his hand on Ae-jung's shoulder. "How are you feeling?"

Mari smiled as her eyes met Ae-jung's.

"I'm feeling much better, Jae-sun, thanks to Mari."

Jae-sun patted her shoulder.

"Mari, I need to go check on Colonel Ji."

Reluctant to share their precious resources, she fought her own feelings of selfishness. "I know you do. Let me send something for him with you—

"Maybe it will keep him going a bit longer."

*   *   *

Jae-sun tucked the bit of food and some clean water under his shirt and slipped out into the darkness.

With infrequent electric power, no fuel, and fewer guards, it was safer now to move about the camp.

Jae-sun quietly slipped in through the barracks door. He felt his way down to Colonel Ji's berth. Even with few prisoners now, he still had to be wary of spies and snitches.

Jae-sun gently shook Colonel Ji Soon awake. "Soon, come outside."

Soon followed Jae-sun out the door. They slipped along the wall to the corner and stepped around, out of the moonlight.

"Soon, how are you doing?"

"Jae-sun, what are you doing over here. You're taking a big risk!"

"I'll be fine. How are you doing?"

"Frankly, I'm having a hard time."

"The best revenge is to get you out of here alive; I brought you some fish and some clean water."

Soon was very hungry and on the brink of dehydration. "Thank-you, Jae-sun."

"Soon, do you remember the boy, Mari's brother?"

"I sure do. He disappeared the night Major Lee shot his mother."

"Yeah, that's right, but he didn't exactly disappear on his own. From the time he and Mari were babies, I educated them and painted them a mental picture of freedom and the world beyond. I prepared him from a young age to leave this place so he could bring help. He's been gone eight years, so he should be all grown up now. I *know* that he survived and he *will* be here soon. When he comes to get Mari and me, I want *you* to come with us."

Soon hung his head.

"Jae-sun, I have a hard time being as optimistic as you, but if you make a plan, I'd be pleased to go with you, friend. I'd rather die any-where but here."

"Okay then. You stay alive. I'll bring you more food tomorrow night."

Jae-sun looked around, then quietly slapped Soon on the back and slipped into the night. He made it back and petitioned his God for deliverance.

Chapter Forty-one

I Think I have Your Man

Gun-ho made it back to Herschel with the packs just as one of the Black Hawks hovered so they could board. The other Black Hawk remained aloft to watch for trouble.

Gun-ho helped Herschel onto the helicopter. "Hey, try not to fall out this time." Herschel just smiled.

* * *

Gun-ho's deployment ended two weeks later. Herschel went to Germany to get healed up. Gun-ho and the rest of the platoon arrived back at Pearl Harbor late on the 15th of February. The next morning, he received word that Commander Flynn wanted to see him at 1000. He walked into the commander's building right on time.

"Good Morning, Jenny. I'm here to see Commander Flynn."

"Welcome home, Seaman Jackson. The commander is expecting you."

As Gun-ho entered his office, the commander stood behind his desk, smiling broadly. "Welcome home, son. Welcome home!" He motioned for Gun-ho to sit. "I just wanted to tell you what a fine job you did out there, son, and to hear all the details!"

Just then Jenny's voice came over the intercom. "Commander Flynn, I am so sorry to disturb you, but a courier requires your signature."

"Okay, I'll be right up." As he walked toward the door, the telephone on his desk rang again. "Grab that call, Jackson. I'll be right back."

Gun-ho picked up the receiver. "Commander Flynn's office."

A sweet voice speaking Korean wished the commander, "Happy Birthday, Jake!"

Without even thinking, Gun-ho answered in Korean. "Hello, ma'am. This isn't Commander Flynn. I am Seaman Jackson, one of his men. Commander Flynn will be right back."

"Oh, this is Soo-ah, the commander's grandmother. Seaman Jackson, what do *you* do?"

Gun-ho replied in Korean. "Well ma'am, I do what Commander Flynn tells me to do."

Soo-ah laughed. "Are you Korean? You speak the language so well—where did you grow up, Seaman Jackson?"

"I grew up in Alaska, ma'am, out near Dutch Harbor."

Just then Commander Flynn stepped back into his office. He looked dumbstruck.

"Oh, ma'am, here he is."

He handed the phone to the commander. "Sir, it's your grandmother. Happy birthday, sir!"

Commander Flynn told his grandmother that he would call her back shortly. "Seaman Jackson, I didn't know you spoke Korean."

"Uh, um—my dad has an old Korean guy on his fishing crew. He taught me to speak Korean from the time I can remember.

"You speak so well. Anyway, tell me about the mission."

*   *   *

Commander Flynn thought about the email he received from Admiral Johnson last month. This Jackson kid might be what they wanted. He actually speaks Korean, and he looks Korean—at least Asian.

After Gun-ho left, Flynn responded to the admiral's original email so there would be no confusion. *Admiral Johnson, I think I have your man.*

*   *   *

Admiral Johnson read the email from Commander Flynn. It vexed him because Mike Flynn had resigned a few days earlier. He contemplated what to do. Since no one had been appointed to replace Mike Flynn just yet, Admiral Johnson called him to get his take. The only person Admiral Johnson knew at the White House—or more accurately who *used to be* at the White House—was Mike Flynn.

Admiral Johnson dialed the number.

General Flynn answered on the first ring. "Flynn."

"Mike, this is Bill."

"Hi, Bill. What can I do for you?"

"Mike, I don't know what's going on, or why you had to leave, but I need your take on an email I just received."

"Yeah, it's a rotten deal. We'll talk about it sometime over lunch. What do you have?"

"You still need that Korean-speaking asset for a special assignment?"

"Yeah, that's something the president wanted me to send out. Whatta ya got?"

"Well, one of my commanders just told me he has your man. What shall I do with this information?"

General Flynn paused briefly. "I don't trust Preibus to follow through." He paused again. "Bill, send a message to Hope Hicks. Tell her you have information the president wants regarding North Korea. You can rest assured that she'll relay the message. If he wants what you have, either Hicks or the president will contact you."

"Okay, Mike. Consider it done. I'll look forward to that lunch date."

"Sounds good, Bill. I'll be in touch."

Admiral Johnson emailed Hope Hicks: *President Trump asked for information regarding an issue having to do with North Korea through former National Security Advisor Flynn. I have his answer. Please advise.*

*   *   *

Admiral Johnson came to full attention. Receiving a call from his commander-in-chief?—that just didn't happen every day!

"Yes! Yes, Ms. Phelps," he told the president's secretary. "Absolutely!"

"Very good, please hold for the president."

The next words Admiral Johnson heard made his heart skip.

"Admiral Johnson, President Trump here. I haven't had the pleasure, but thank you for reaching out."

"Yes, sir, Mister President, the pleasure is all mine."

"I'd like to meet you and hear what you've got. Come over to the White House tomorrow morning—say, 10:00 o'clock?"

"Yes, sir, Mr. President."

After the admiral hung up, he dialed Commander Jake Flynn.

He wanted to be prepared.

*   *   *

"Jake, tell me what I need to know."

Commander Jake Flynn told Admiral Bill Johnson about Seaman Jackson's abilities.

"Well, how does a boy from Alaska even become fluent in Korean?"

"He told me his dad has an old Korean guy on his fishing crew, and that he learned the language as he grew up."

"Well, that's all well and good, Jake, but the president wants someone who also *looks* the part."

"Thing is, Bill, he *does*. He's Alaska Native. He'd definitely fit right in. What does the president have in mind?"

"I'll let you know tomorrow morning."

The next morning Admiral Johnson arrived at the White House at 0930. He was checked in and taken to the anteroom. At precisely 10:00 o'clock, he was taken into the Oval Office and introduced to President Trump.

"Mister President, it is a pleasure to meet you, sir."

"Admiral—Bill—it is great to meet you! What a great job you're doing; I've heard good things. Tell me, Bill, what do you have for me?"

He briefed the president about Jackson.

"This is the thing, Bill—I want to put an end to the shenanigans this fat little tyrant in North Korea is pulling. I need information, so I'd like to get someone in there before I really start holding his feet to the fire."

Admiral Johnson tried to mask his concern—without much success. "Mr. President this kid has a lot of moxie. I saw him take out 80 Taliban single-handed by using his brain, but good grief, Mister President, that could be a suicide mission."

"I agree, Bill, but if he is successful, it could be a huge deal for the entire region—hell, for *the world.*"

The president paused for a moment.

"Let's do this. Bring this kid to Washington, but don't tell him why. Have him put through a battery of tests to confirm that his is fluent—speaking, reading, and writing. Also, give him a psychological test to make sure he can take the stress. Then I want to meet him and personally lay out the mission."

Admiral Johnson was apprehensive, but agreed.

When he returned to the Pentagon, he called Commander Flynn and explained the mission. "Jake, the president wants to put Kim Jung-un in checkmate. I agreed to bring our man to Washington and check him out. What do you think?"

Commander Flynn paused a moment.

"Well, Bill, he's a sharp kid. With the right support, I think he could pull it off."

"Okay, send him out, but don't tell him what's up. The president wants to make sure he is up to the task. I'll have a liaison handle him on this end, and if he checks out, we'll go over to see the president."

"I'll have him there tomorrow night."

*   *   *

Gun-ho received word to report to Commander Flynn again. He thought to himself, *Second time this week—hope I didn't screw something up.*

Commander Flynn was every bit as affable as he'd been before.

"Seaman Jackson, you need to be in Washington tomorrow night. Grab your gear and be at the airfield at 1800 hours. I'm sending you in *my* plane directly to Washington."

Gun-ho stood up, and smartly saluted. "Yes, sir."

*   *   *

The plane touched down on the airfield at the Navy base in Annapolis, Maryland, at 1730 on February 19th.

A liaison officer greeted him. "Welcome to the east coast, Seaman Jackson. I'm Captain Rodgers."

Seeing her rank, Gun-ho replied with a crisp salute. "Thank you, ma'am."

"I've come to take you to your quarters and to inform you of the schedule. I will be escorting you to each of your test appointments over the next week." She motioned toward the black Suburban waiting on the tarmac.

Captain Rodgers's driver opened the car door for her as Gun-ho made his way around to the other back door.

In the car, Gun-ho turned toward the Captain. "Ma'am, may I ask what my assignment is?"

"At this point, all I can say, Seaman Jackson, is that you are being considered for a special mission. You'll be given a series of tests at

Langley, the CIA headquarters, to determine if you are qualified. I will deliver the results to the correct personnel. Then we wait."

"That sounds good, ma'am. I'll be ready at 0600 hours Tuesday morning."

*   *   *

CIA Agent Marks received her assignment to begin surreptitiously running their first test on Gun-ho to see if he could be distracted from duty. She would try to get him to agree to dinner off the base, then get him into a hotel room and, with his guard down, charmed by her feminine wiles, drug him and leave him safely sleeping through his 0600 appointment.

Her secondary goal was to get him to boast about the places he'd been and the things he'd done. She would subtlety try to get him to commit to spending some time in the afternoon visiting the local points of interest off the base. She'd reel him in one event at a time.

When the officers watching him figured out he'd be heading to the gym, she donned provocative workout clothes. Dark and slender, with waist-length silky black hair, she possessed black eyes that held the attention of any man she toyed with. Powder-blue spandex emphasized her perfect bottom and long, shapely legs. She wore a white-and-blue-striped sports bra that created eye-catching cleavage and showcased her trim waist.

As she exited the dressing room, she admired herself in the mirror one last time and thought, *Poor bastard. He doesn't stand a chance.*

*   *   *

Gun-ho was working out by himself, doing chest and arms.

A gorgeous woman with long dark hair pulled back into a pony-tail walked into the gym and immediately commanded the attention of every man—and of a few women.

She walked over to Gun-ho and sweetly inquired, "May I lift with you?"

Gun-ho struggled to give her face full attention—a difficult task given the quality of her sports bra. "Yes, ma'am, I'm working my arms."

She playfully admonished Gun-ho, "Yes, *ma'am?* I'm not your fifth-grade teacher."

"That's for sure, ma'am." He flashed her an approving smile.

She held out her hand. "Hi, I'm Sharon."

Gun-ho gently shook her hand with his own massive paw. "I'm Seaman Jackson. Nice to meet you, Sharon."

"It is certainly nice to meet you, Seaman Jackson. Do you have a first name?"

She looked doe-eyed into his gaze. She held him in her spell.

"It's Andrew, ma'am—Andrew Jackson."

Gun-ho thoroughly enjoyed his workout, enhanced by all the flirtatious banter and sexual tension.

"Hey, it's 11:30, Andrew. Do you have time for lunch?"

"That sounds good, ma'am—I mean Sharon."

They agreed to meet at the café on the base in 45 minutes.

Gun-ho ran to his quarters to shower and change, then arrived at the café first. While intrigued, he was in no danger of being distracted from his duty. Jae-sun had repeatedly explained to him, in detail, the biological disadvantage men have with respect to women. His folks in Alaska had reinforced this truth, each in their own way. Gun-ho had an unwavering underlying single purpose: get back to North Korea and rescue Mari and Jae-sun. The life experiences Gun-ho had endured had reinforced his resolve, girding him from being turned by a pretty face and a sweet voice.

Gun-ho seated himself in the back corner of the room with a view to the door.

When Sharon walked in—*wow!* She wore a pale green chiffon blouse with a plunging neckline, black slacks, and open-toed heels. Even her toenails were perfect. Beautiful green barrettes held her hair back on each side, framing her angelic face.

As she approached, she smelled *soooo* good.

Gun-ho stood.

She walked up and leaned in for a hug. "Hi, Andrew."

They ordered lunch and had an enjoyable conversation. Gun-ho artfully dodged questions about his military exploits.

He sensed a tender trap, but carefully avoided taking the bait.

After they finished lunch, Gun-ho felt a need to spend some time writing letters to family. Despite being flattered by the seemingly genuine attention from this handsome woman, he had no intention of leaving the base with anyone other than Captain Rodgers. He wanted to leave, but he didn't want to be rude, so he devised an exit strategy.

"Sharon, this rendezvous has been wonderful."

He stood, leaned down, kissed her on the cheek, and whispered in her ear:

"But I'm gay, and I've got to go."

*   *   *

Even though her earpiece was hidden from view by her hair, Gun-ho's whispered words were picked up loud and clear by Agent "Sharon" Marks's team out in their van. The observers, both men—and both gay—laughed when they heard Gun-ho's declaration. They high-fived each other, knowing that they'd never stop teasing her over this epic fail.

Agent Marks was speechless. The fifty-dollar bill he'd slipped onto the table confirmed he was leaving, and she couldn't do a thing about it. She *knew* he wasn't gay. She had many gay friends and considered her *gay-dar* top notch. No, he had just shut her down the best possible way.

She watched him walk away and found herself wishing he *hadn't* been a mark. *What a man!*

As he walked to the door, she waited for him to look back.

He didn't.

Chapter Forty-two

I'll Do It

The CIA facility impressed Gun-ho, or at least the parts of it he'd been exposed to. He hoped that the results they received gave them the confidence that he could handle whatever the mission required. The last tests they conducted were language tests. Gun-ho wondered if all of this happened because of the conversation Commander Flynn overheard him having with his grandmother. In any event, his classical education at the feet of Geon Jae-sun shined through. The test indicated complete fluency of the Korean language.

Having finished with four days of testing, Gun-ho and Captain Rodgers walked down a hallway, heading for the car to drive back to Maryland. As they made the corner, they encountered a group a people talking in the foyer. One person in the group—none other than Sharon Marks! Gun-ho had the advantage of seeing her first. He had enough of a side view to know for sure. She was sent to Maryland last Monday to try to throw him off! He would have some fun with this.

Gun-ho and Captain Rodgers walked around the group; Sharon's back was toward them. When he passed her right side, he paused.

"Oh, hi, Sharon. Thanks again for lunch the other day. I had a great time."

Then he walked on, leaving her stunned, no doubt.

She excused herself and trotted up behind them. As she passed his left side, Gun-ho paused. Sharon clasped his right hand in hers and squeezed, leaving him holding her card, which he quickly pocketed. "Andrew, I had a good time, too. Please call me when you can."

She briskly turned and walked away—two points for Sharon, maybe three.

Gun-ho was still smiling when he stepped into the car for the two-hour ride back to Annapolis.

*   *   *

Admiral Johnson read the test results in the attached report. It wasn't confusing; Seaman Jackson had clearly proven to be a remarkable individual. The report indicated he was very loyal and possessed an enhanced sense of duty—dependable, absolutely dependable. He can process appropriately the deaths of the enemy by his hand; he is not a psychopath. He has empathy, he is kind, he deals with stress extraordinarily well, and he has a very high pain tolerance. On top of all that, he is completely fluent in Korean. Admiral Johnson concluded the president needed to know that the man "checks out." He emailed Hope Hicks and asked that she let the president know. Hope Hicks assured the admiral that the message would be delivered late Friday afternoon, February 24th.

True to her word, the president's call came late in the afternoon. "Hello, Admiral. I got your message. So, the bottom line is, the kid is up to the task. Is that correct?"

"Yes, sir, Mister President. He is a remarkable individual."

"Well, let's talk to him. You probably heard that General McMasters is the new National Security Advisor; I'll want him in the meeting. What will your schedule allow, Bill?"

"Any time, Mister President, I'm available anytime."

"Well, let's do it Sunday afternoon at 2:00 o'clock. That way we won't likely be under any time pressure like we might on Monday."

"You got it, Mister President. I'll come exactly at 2:00 and have his liaison officer bring him in at 2:15."

Admiral Johnson called Captain Rodgers's cellphone. She picked up on the second ring; she could see the Admiral calling.

"We just returned to Annapolis about twenty minutes ago," she told him. "I dropped Seaman Jackson, and I'm on the way home."

"He *is* a remarkable individual."

"Well, that doesn't surprise me, sir. Just in the time I've spent with him, I can confirm he is something special."

"Well, here's the thing, Jeri—you need to have him at the White House at 1:45 on Sunday afternoon. I'll have your clearance worked out and waiting at the gate."

"Yes, sir. I'll have him there."

*   *   *

Gun-ho's mind ran wild. The language testing let him hope that this mission may have something to do with Korea. He'd read all the headlines—a lot of news about the region lately. The slightest possibility brought Jae-sun and Mari to his mind. Gun-ho decided to go for a run.

After returning to his quarters, Gun-ho stood in the shower, leaning against the back wall with the top of his head resting on his arms folded on the wall. The water massaged the back of his neck as he watched the water drip off the end of Jae-sun's crucifix. He prayed for their well-being, and that whatever the military was about to ask of him could be leveraged to take care of *his* business, too. Gun-ho fell asleep, trusting that the hairs on his head were counted.

Gun-ho was ready and waiting when Captain Rodgers's car pulled up at 11:40.

"Good Morning, Seaman Jackson. How'd you sleep?"

"I slept great! Where are we going, ma'am?"

"The president wants to personally lay out a special assignment for you. I am not aware of details, and that's done on purpose—you know, *need to know.*

"Wow, ma'am—have you ever been to the White House?"

"No, this will be the first time."

"Will you be in the meeting?"

"No, you'll be in the meeting with the President, General McMasters, and Admiral Johnson."

Gun-ho stiffened at the news. "Is that Admiral *Bill* Johnson?"

"Yes, have you met him?"

"No, ma'am. My dad has, though."

Gun-ho was in awe as they drove through the gate onto the grounds. He hoped he'd be able to tell his folks about being at the White House and meeting the president.

They exited the vehicle under the porte-cochere and were invited into the White House. The young man that greeted them was very friendly. He offered them drinks and showed them to a very comfortable waiting area.

Captain Rodgers couldn't help tapping her finger on her water glass. "They will come here to get you very shortly, and I will be here when you are finished." She was being very professional, but Gun-ho could tell that she'd like to have met the President.

"Okay, ma'am. I'm depending on that."

The President's secretary, Jennifer Phelps, walked into the room. She introduced herself to Captain Rodgers and then to Gun-ho. "Seaman Jackson, please follow me." She turned and said, "I'll bring him back in about an hour, Captain Rodgers. Please make yourself at home."

Gun-ho caught Captain Rodgers's eye and acknowledged her accurate prediction.

At exactly 2:15 Ms. Phelps led Gun-ho into the Oval Office. God does, indeed, work in mysterious ways. In eight short years he'd come from a prison camp in North Korea to the White House and an audience with the president.

"Mr. President, this is Seaman Andrew Jackson. Seaman Jackson, it is my honor to introduce you to President Trump."

Gun-ho's heart pounded as he shook the president's hand. "Nice to meet you, sir."

"Thank you, Jennifer. Andrew, may I call you Andrew? Geez, I hope they checked you out; you could kill me with your bare hands." President Trump smiled at his own joke. "Andrew, I want you to meet these gentlemen. This is General McMasters, and Admiral Johnson."

Gun-ho shook their hands and greeted them warmly; he was trying to stay calm as he shook the Admiral's hand. Jae-sun's last words to him were to find this man, this man right here!

Admiral Johnson told the president and general of Gun-ho's recent exploits in Afghanistan. Then the admiral turned to Gun-ho. "I've met your dad, son. He's a great guy—top notch."

"Thank you, sir. I agree."

President Trump invited the men to sit in a circle around a coffee table.

The president sat to Gun-ho's left. The admiral sat to his right, with the general straight across.

"Andrew," began the president, "the reason I asked you here today is I need to get someone, maybe someone like you, to go into North Korea to gather some intelligence, and if the opportunity arises, to ruffle a few feathers."

Gun-ho could not believe what he'd just heard! He nodded and tried hard to seem interested, but not overly excited.

"Now, I appreciate this is going to be a very dangerous mission. If they catch you, they'll kill you. That's why I wanted to have you in and lay everything out and make sure you understand that this is completely your choice. I won't blame you if you tell me I am crazy. I just asked the guys here to see if we had anyone qualified, and you popped up. But, Andrew, I want to stress, you—"

Gun-ho cut the president off, looking him dead in the eye. "I'll do it. I *want* to do it."

The President looked at Gun-ho, then at the others, then turned up his palms. "He *wants* to do it."

"Sir, I have *no* conditions, but I do have two requests."

"Name 'em."

Gun-ho stood up, took one step toward Admiral Johnson, reached behind his neck, and unclasped the chain holding Jae-sun's crucifix. He held it out to Admiral Johnson. Johnson looked blankly at Gun-ho and opened his hand, then took out his glasses for a closer look at the crucifix.

He turned white and gasped. "Where did you get this!"

The President said, "Bill, are you all right? Let me get you some water."

"Jae-sun gave it to me and told me to find you, sir, and now I've found you, thanks to the president."

President Trump gave the water to Admiral Johnson. "Seaman Jackson, what's going on here?"

Admiral Johnson answered before Gun-ho could. "Mister President, I gave this crucifix to my dearest friend, Geon Jae-sun, when we were twelve years old. We grew up together here in Washington. His dad worked for the first ambassador to the United States from South Korea. When the war broke out, they had to extend, so Jae-sun and I grew up together. He was my dearest friend until 1997, when he went missing. We think the North Koreans kidnapped him." He took a long breath, then turned to Gun-ho. "Seaman Jackson, please explain!"

"Mister President, General, Admiral, I grew up near Dutch Harbor, Alaska, but I didn't get there until I was twelve. Admiral, you are right; the North Koreans put him in a prison camp—the prison camp I was born in. My birth mother was kidnapped the same year. She was just eighteen years old. In North Korea they prostituted her to visiting Russian military advisors. When she became pregnant, they sent her to the prison camp where Jae-sun is."

"You mean he's still there!"

"I'd bet my life on it. He made sure I spoke both Korean and English fluently as he groomed me to be smuggled out of the camp someday. He wanted me to find my way to the United States and to find you, sir."

The powerful trio sat in rap attention.

Gun-ho told the story of finding his new family in Dutch Harbor, where he grew up. "I am theirs, and they are mine. They guided me toward a life that would give me the skills to eventually go back to North Korea and rescue Jae-sun and Mari."

President Trump nodded. "Andrew, do you think they are still alive?"

Admiral Johnson interjected. "You bet they are, sir. Jae-sun—he's a fighter, and smart."

"So, Mister President," Gun-ho continued, "I *want* to go to North Korea and do the mission. The Navy has given me the skills to succeed, but once I've accomplished the mission, may I go back to that camp and rescue Mari and Jae-sun?"

The President smiled. "Deal!" He extended his hand. "From the look on Bill's face, he's going to have the entire U.S. Navy sitting twelve miles off the coast, waiting for you!"

"You're damn right!"

After more discussion, President Trump wound things up. "Andrew, we're gonna let the CIA prep you for this mission. When they say you're ready, you'll go."

As they stood to leave, General McMaster turned to the President. "Sir, we'll have to name the mission. What do you think?"

"Let's call it *Counterpunch!* They threw the first punch by kidnapping; we'll punch 'em back harder—or you will, Andrew! Hey, what was your second request?"

"Oh, sir, I was wondering if you'd come out and meet my liaison officer."

"Sure, I will."

Chapter Forty-three

Planning and Preparation

On the ride back to Maryland, Captain Rogers kept strangely quiet. Finally, she turned to Gun-ho. "Seaman Jackson, I want to thank you for your thoughtfulness. I don't think I've ever met someone as perceptive and kind as you are; I really appreciate you."

She paused for a moment as if trying to get control of her emotions. "I don't know what they are planning for you, and I shouldn't know, but if you ever need anything—anything at all—I want you to call me. I will help however I'm able."

"Thank you, ma'am. I already have your number memorized." He smiled.

"Admiral Johnson wants to have lunch with you tomorrow. I'm to take you to the Pentagon. After that, you'll be assisted by others."

"What time will we be leaving?"

"0930 to be on schedule."

The car pulled up to Gun-ho's quarters and he hopped out. "Thanks again, Captain. I'll be ready to go at 0930. Good night."

Gun-ho walked into his room and began to process his good fortune. He cautioned himself not to be too excited. He needed to be deliberate, thorough, and smart. This was truly the opportunity of his life, the catalyst that would allow him to fulfill his life's purpose. He'd need to bring all the education, training, and mentorship he'd received from Jae-sun, his folks, and Uncle Sam's Navy to be successful. He had the right attitude—just a bit of luck, and soon he'd be enjoying the company of Jae-sun and Mari *in freedom*.

Gun-ho was ready and waiting at 0930. Captain Rodgers had clearance to direct her driver to enter the secure parking garage attached to the Pentagon. Two junior officers were waiting in the garage. Gun-ho stepped out of the car, grabbed his bag, then leaned through the open car window.

"Thank you, ma'am. I appreciate all your help."

"You are welcome. Godspeed." She motioned her driver on.

The junior officers led Gun-ho up to Admiral Johnson's office. One of the officers nodded at the admiral's receptionist, and they walked directly into the office.

Looking out his window when Gun-ho entered, the Admiral turned and smiled. Gun-ho saluted. The Admiral invited him to sit.

Johnson opened his hand and let Jae-sun's crucifix dangle from his fingers. "Seaman Jackson, I would like to give this back to you, so when you make it to that prison camp you can return it to Jae-sun. You tell him that I *will* be waiting offshore for your arrival."

Gun-ho slowly reached over and accepted the crucifix, then put it back around his neck.

"Son, I know you haven't been with him for eight years, but tell me how Jae-sun was doing before he smuggled you out. Was he holding up?"

"Admiral, he was doing well. They work him too hard, but in that job, he has access to the calories he needs to stay healthy. Also, he is very disciplined, so he used order and organization to lighten his load and make time for educating Mari and me. He taught us everything. In the last eight years I've benefited so many times from the lessons learned at his feet."

Admiral Johnson listened intently and smiled knowingly. He clearly admired and held affection for Jae-sun.

"The last words he said to me were, 'If you survive, finish growing up, then go find Bill Johnson. He'll know what to do.' Then he sent me through the hole in the wall adjacent to the corpse truck."

"Well, it looks like the president set things up for us pretty well. This afternoon you're going to head down to Langley and work with the CIA. They will brief you on their goals and give you the tools to accomplish them. Once you arrive in the North, we'll be monitoring progress through your biometric signature. We'll give you the means to communicate with us at the time of your choosing, so we can coordinate your recovery."

"That sounds good Admiral, and I want you to know that I believe with all my heart that he is alive and well. We're going to get him outta there!"

"I appreciate your attitude, son, and I share your faith. Now let's get you down to Langley to work with the spooks for a bit, and then we'll get you into North Korea."

After arriving at Langley, Gun-ho's handlers took him to a large room approximately eight by fifty feet. The room featured a huge screen in the middle of one of the long walls. It appeared to be a virtual map of the entire northern hemisphere. Desks and worktables filled the area, with analysts working at each. One group intently watched him as the handlers walked him to a large office in the back with windows on three sides and a complete view of the room and the screen.

The gentlemen who led Gun-ho to the office were dismissed, and Gun-ho was invited inside by a grandfatherly type.

He extended his hand. "Hello, Seaman Jackson. I am Agent Hans Kramer. I am the director of this unit, which has the responsibility of keeping an eye on China and North Korea."

"Very nice to meet you, sir."

"I appreciate the respect, son, but call me Hans. You're in the military, but you are being lent to us to accomplish a specific goal, and we are going to do our damnedest to help you be successful—but you have no superior officers here, so call me Hans.

"Okay, Hans, please call me Andrew."

They shook hands again.

Agent Kramer invited Gun-ho to sit. They were sitting on the same side of a worktable so they could look together at a large computer screen.

Agent Kramer brought up a satellite image of North Korea. "Andrew, you have been given *Top Secret* clearance. Your badge will be delivered here shortly."

Gun-ho recognized the jetty adjacent to the port he left from eight years earlier. After he arrived in Alaska, Gun-ho had continuously studied everything about North Korea he could get his hands on to prepare for the day when he could go back, including geography. This image on Hans's computer was the best he'd ever seen.

Hans moved his cursor about twenty miles north of the port. He enlarged the area to reveal a very large and long building adjacent to what looked like several launch pads. "Andrew, this is an image of a missile prep and launch facility. We can see all around it from the satellite, but we'd like to see inside. That's where you come in."

Gun-ho nodded. "You want me to get inside of that facility?"

"No, I want you to position yourself up here on this ridge and fly these cute camera drones we have—they look like little birds. I want you to position them in just the right places. All the images will feed via an infrared pulse system to a transmitter built into a drone about the size of a sparrow. You'll need to anchor the transmitter drone near a vent in the roof so it can deploy an antenna. All the images will be sent to the transmitter drone every two minutes, where they will be compressed and sent up to the satellite every twenty-four hours. If you are successful, we'll know what's going on inside that building before Kim Jung-un does!"

Both men chuckled at the prospect.

"The other thing we'd like you to do is to cause a little damage at this facility." He moved his cursor inland about 100 miles.

"This is going to be a great deal more difficult. It is not right on the coast like the *launch* facility. This is a *test* facility. We'll think about how to import damage over there for a few days. Hopefully we'll have you out of here in a week. The Navy will position you and all your gear favorably so you can approach the coast. Now, once we get you in, we must get you out. I've been briefed on your secondary mission, so if you are successful in recovering your people, this ship right here leaves the port every Thursday morning at 08:30. It is a garbage scow. If you can make it back to there, you may be able to hitch a ride, so to speak, and redirect the scow's path to international waters before the Norks know what is going on."

"That seems like a good option. Do we have a schedule?"

"Yes, we do."

He handed Gun-ho the schedule.

"It is getting late now, so the guys supporting you will take you to the motor pool and get you a vehicle, and then take you over to one of the agency condos nearby. That will be your home while you are here this week. Be back here at 0800 in the morning and we'll get started in earnest."

Someone tapped on the door. Agent Kramer opened it and received an envelope, which he handed to Gun-ho. "Here is your badge. Your clearance is higher than all the people out here on my team, but it hast to be. You're being sent into the jaws of the tiger; you'll need every advantage to avoid being chewed up."

He smiled a wry smile to finish off his point.

As Gun-ho moved toward the door, he asked, "On my way in here, one group of people on the left as I came toward your office were really looking me over. What is their interest?"

"That group is the North Korean intelligence group. This mission is *Top Secret* and they weren't read in, so their noses are a bit out of joint. They'll be okay. I'll see you here tomorrow morning, then."

Gun-ho simply nodded and walked out, but he was wary of jealousy—an emotion that can cause trouble.

Gun-ho's support team met him as he emerged from the office. They took him to the motor pool where he checked out a Chevy Suburban—a *black* Chevy Suburban. The vehicle made him think of home and the old Suburban his folks kept at Dutch Harbor. The support team suggested that one of them drive a separate car into the community near Langley and lead Gun-ho to the address. The other support team member rode with Gun-ho.

After driving for about ten minutes, they arrived at two rows of townhouses. Each row had ten units with each garage set back from the next to break up the front elevation of the building, the second row directly across from the first with a wide boulevard between. Lights on the side of each garage door illuminated each drive-pad.

Gun-ho's passenger suggested he use the garage-door opener and drive the vehicle into the garage, which he did. The lead vehicle parked on the drive-pad, and the driver walked into the garage through the open door. Gun-ho's support team led him into the condo and showed him around. Assured that he knew his way back to Langley, they bid him good night and left through the front door.

Gun-ho held his stomach. During the tour he noticed there were no groceries. He decided to walk over to the market and get a few things before turning in.

Gun-ho rose at 0530 and drove back over to Langley, carrying his uniform and wearing his workout clothes. He headed directly to the gym. Gun-ho just finished his first set when he noticed someone approaching. He looked up to see the familiar face of Agent Sharon Marks; her back to the others in the gym.

"Smile and gesture, like we are having a friendly conversation."

Gun-ho did as she asked.

"Andrew, you need to watch your back. There are those here who have been politicized. They were not happy with the results of the election, and frankly they are capable of inappropriate things. I don't know what leadership has planned for you, but rumors are that you were handpicked by the president and that you could be here spying on the spies, so just watch your back."

As she turned, she smiled big and waved to sell the tone of the interaction with Gun-ho.

Gun-ho decided to notch up his awareness. He finished his workout, showered, and reported to Hans Kramer's office at 0800 as instructed.

The first day of Gun-ho's training focused on the technical aspects of the drones. He learned how to care for and troubleshoot both types of drones. They also took him to a practice facility where building mockups of various types were constructed. Gun-ho practiced flying both drones; he was very good. The technology was superior. Both drones used the same controller, which had a small screen so the operator could see what the drone was seeing as it flew. The operator could fly the drone to the desired location, command it to grip a perch, and then position the camera to the desire view. Once in place, each camera drone could then be switched remotely to *operational* mode and begin sending photographs to the transmitter drone. By the end of the day, Gun-ho considered himself an expert drone driver.

By eight o'clock Gun-ho was ready to head home. He'd been thinking all day about the inland test facility, so he decided to stop by Hans's office on the way out.

Hans was still in his office, the big analyst arena empty. Gun-ho tapped on the door and heard Hans's voice inviting him in.

"Hi, Hans. I have a question about the test facility."

"Shoot."

"Have you observed any vehicle movement between the launch facility and the test facility."

"Yes, yes we have. Once a week, pretty reliably, there is a supply truck that leaves the launch facility and heads inland to the test facility. He unloads and then heads back to the launch facility. Then once a month or so a big flatbed truck brings rocket components from the test facility to the launch facility. What do you have in mind?"

"Well, I was down in the lab today learning about the drones. Those guys down there are something. They can build anything you want. I was thinking if they could build me a bomb that I could plant on the truck, with an ignition switch that is triggered via a GPS signal, we could do real damage to the test facility without going inland—very discreet."

Hans thought for a moment, then a moment more. "The trucks are usually staged outside of the launch facility in the early morning hours before departure. If you could get onto the grounds of the launch facility undetected—no easy feat—then I think your idea would work. Talk to the lab guys tomorrow and see what they think."

"Will do, Hans. Good night."

As Gun-ho pulled onto the road adjacent to the gate of the Langley campus, he noticed headlights instantly illuminate the road three hundred yards beyond the gate. It seemed odd to Gun-ho, because the road was straight for almost a mile either side of the gate. That meant that either someone was pulled off for some innocent reason, or that his vehicle was being followed.

He decided to go with the latter.

Gun-ho kept his eye on the lights behind him. They held back quite a ways, but after as many turns as he'd taken, the lights stayed right with him.

Coming up on his right, a warehouse building sat on a cross street very close to the road.

He wheeled right and quickly turned behind the far side of the building and doused his lights, watching as his tail went by.

He pulled back onto the roadway, and as he negotiated a curve, his tail approached a red light. His tail was in the left lane and another car was in the right. Gun-ho pulled up behind the other car and noted the license plate of his tail. When the light turned green, Gun-ho turned right and went directly home—unrattled, but aware.

The next morning Gun-ho repeated the routine of the previous day. He was in the gym by 0600. After his workout, he showered and headed down to the lab to continue his personal seminars on his weapon systems.

Gun-ho's instructor was Agent Ben Forbes, a very bright guy. He and his team could dream up any number of cleaver weapons.

Before getting started with Ben's agenda, Gun-ho posed his question: "Hey, Ben, can you make me a bomb that will ignite upon reaching a particular GPS location?

Ben smiled. "Sure, how big do you want it?"

"Oh, I suppose about eight or ten pounds. I have to carry it and attach it to the frame of a truck, so it needs some pretty good magnets—ones that will hold for a hundred-plus-miles trip."

"Can do. Let me get the boys working on that before we start."

He briefed Gun-ho on the packaging and transportation details of the drones. Gun-ho would be deployed from a surfaced submarine in an inflatable boat. However, as he approached the coast he would deflate and submerge the boat in fifteen meters of water, then using sort of an underwater jet ski travel submerged up a river adjacent to the launch facility. His gear and weapons had to be packed to remain dry.

By the end of the day, his third day at Langley and his second full day in the lab, Gun-ho felt he was ready. "Okay, chief, what's next?"

"Well, Seaman Jackson, we have some new skookum personal body armor for you to check out. It is very thin, bulletproof, and designed to be worn under your wetsuit. It is getting late—here, take this piece home and check it out; we'll wind up in the morning and finish setting things up with the Navy to get you inserted."

Gun-ho took his drone manual and the body armor and headed out. He stopped and discussed with Hans the possibilities of his plan for the test facility. At 1900 Gun-ho headed out of Hans's office.

As he walked by the part of the arena where the North Korea team worked, he noticed one man surreptitiously watching.

He exited the arena and headed for the elevator.

*   *   *

Doug Collins, Agent Doug Collins, was a capable guy, a very capable guy, but he'd become corrupted by partisanship. Allowing himself to be compromised by the political appointees at the agency, now he was hopelessly but willingly caught up in misplaced efforts to resist the president. He'd bet heavy on the other team before the election and participated in some very dark efforts to see her elected; and after she lost, he was wedded to the resistance.

This latest slight, some upstart from the Navy, handpicked by the President to do who knows what inside the agency, just couldn't be tolerated. Something had to be done.

As Gun-ho walked by with aplomb, Agent Collins's anger raged. He had a plan in place to eliminate this threat. His people were in place. He'd done something similar before the election when some idealistic kid inside the campaign had the temerity to smuggle Democrat secrets out and give them to the world. A little street crime, another unsolved murder in Washington, D.C., and the threat was eliminated. Round two was surely in order.

Before Gun-ho had reached the elevator, Agent Doug Collins placed a call, setting the plan in motion.

*   *   *

Gun-ho's commute to the condo was uneventful. As far as he could tell, he wasn't followed. Gun-ho turned onto the drive lane of the condo project from the roadway. The lane ran about 200 feet, treed on each side. It emptied onto the wide boulevard between the two rows of townhouses. Gun-ho's condo was on the left side of the boulevard, the seventh unit down.

As he entered the boulevard, he noticed a vehicle with the dome light on well back in the visitor parking area. He couldn't see the plate, but the vehicle looked like the same one that had tailed him the night before. Gun-ho noted the event and reached down to confirm that the master switch on his dome light was off. That's how he liked it, so the light would not come on when his vehicle door opened.

Gun-ho turned left onto his drive-pad and punched the garage door opener. The forty-watt lamp on the garage-door operator dimly lit the interior.

He pulled forward until a hanging tennis ball kissed the windshield. Gun-ho reached up and pushed the opener again to close the door. It started down, but jerked right back up like something was in its path. He decided to get out and check the door path, then close the overhead door from the switch by the entry.

He grabbed his coat and draped it over his left arm, then grabbed the piece of body armor and his drone manual and held them with his right hand against his body. He opened his Suburban door with his left hand and stepped out. He shifted the manual to his left side, intending to use his right hand to close the car door.

As he turned, he came face to face with a slight, well-dressed man standing at the back of his vehicle.

The man raised his right arm to reveal a suppressed pistol.

The assailant squeezed off two quick rounds, hitting Gun-ho on the left side of his chest.

The force of the bullets knocked Gun-ho backward into the hinge part of the open car door. Gun-ho hit the back of his head on the door window frame, which caused him to bite his tongue.

The light timed out and the garage went completely dark.

Gun-ho went down, dropping his manual, coat, and the body armor. Catching his breath, he tried to feel the wound, but couldn't find one. The manual and Ben's armor had stopped the bullets.

Now he was just pissed.

He put his left hand on the running board, his right hand on the car-door handle, and stood up.

On the left side of the garage, he found a ten-foot stick of conduit leaning against the wall. He grabbed the conduit, peeked out the door from the shadows, and saw his assailant walking casually away.

He was in the middle of the boulevard making a path back toward the visitor parking area.

Gun-ho's anger doubled at the thought that his assailant didn't even think he had to run; he was just walking. Gun-ho dashed out of the garage with the conduit in his right hand, holding it like a javelin. He found his stride and launched the twenty-pound conduit with an adrenalin-fueled throw. The makeshift weapon hit the man on the left side of his back.

It hit him full force, knocking him to the ground. His face smacked the storm grate in the middle of the boulevard.

Gun-ho closed the gap in an instant, kicking him hard on his right side, crunching ribs.

Gun-ho secured his hands with his belt and searched him for weapons, finding the pistol in a chest holster and a military knife on his belt. Gun-ho secured the weapons and dragged the man by the collar back into his garage. He pulled him to the front of the garage, turned on the overhead lights, and closed the door.

Gun-ho considered every angle. What should he do next? He needed to find out if another person was in this guy's vehicle.

The would-be assassin began to moan.

Gun-ho secured his hands better with Ty-wraps and duct tape.

The assassin winced with pain as Gun-ho moved him around. He also secured his legs at the ankles and at the knees. He sat the man up and leaned him against the steps going into the house, then stepped in front of the man.

"What's your name?"

The man looked up at Gun-ho with his left eye; his right was swollen shut from the fall.

"Mickey Mouse."

Gun-ho was not in the mood for sarcasm. He walked into the house and retrieved the fire poker. He knelt in front of the man to cut his ankles and knees free. He duct-taped the fire poker handle to one of his ankles and duct-taped the shaft to the other so his feet were held twenty-four inches apart. Gun-ho stood the man up and tied a rope to his hands, which were clasped behind his back, then threw the rope over a bike hook embedded in the ceiling.

Gun-ho raised the man's arms up behind him until he cried out.

Gun-ho pulled out the man's wallet and phone, then set them on the hood of his Suburban. He reached into the backseat and pulled out his gym bag, setting it on the floor. He stood in front of the man, unbuckled his trousers, and let them fall to the poker. Then he pulled down his underwear, stood up, and flipped open the man's knife, holding it under his nose.

The man's left eye opened wide. "Come on, man, don't do this!"

Gun-ho picked up the man's wallet. "Once again, what is your name?—and your answer better match the ID in this wallet."

The man looked at his wallet. "Gene. My name is Gene Hamilton. Don't cut me, man! Please!"

The ID said Gene Hamilton was Agent Gene Hamilton. Confused, Gun-ho looked back into Gene's left eye. "You're supposed to be on my side. Who sent you here, Gene?"

Gene's face twisted with pain, and not from his wounds. He didn't want to answer the question.

Gun-ho flipped the knife back open, waved it again under Gene's nose, then reached down and used the back of the blade to pick up the end of his penis. Gene recoiled at the touch of cold steel.

"Gene, I don't have a lot of time, so we're gonna have to move this along."

Gene Hamilton started to groan, anguished by his choices.

Gun-ho slid the back of the blade down the inside of his left thigh. He blurted, "Collins. Doug Collins is running us."

"*Us?* You got someone *else* in your car?"

Gene was crestfallen. The look on his face confirmed the answer.

"Who's out there, Gene? I need a name."

"Jimmy. His name is Jimmy Kelly. Don't hurt him, man. He's just a kid."

"Yeah, what's that make him? Twenty-three? Twenty-four?"

"He's twenty-four."

"Well, I'm twenty, you prick, and you tried to kill me! Your friend's level of pain will be directly proportional to how well he cooperates! What's the security code on this phone?"

"Twenty-four thirty."

Gun-ho gagged Gene, then grabbed his sweaty tee-shirt out of the gym bag and pulled it over Gene's head. Gun-ho retrieved the garage-door opener from his car, walked over, and turned out the lights in the garage.

Through the dark he said to Gene, "Don't run off. I'll be right back."

Gun-ho punched in the security code on Gene's phone and read a recent text to Jimmy. He locked the phone again and put it in his pocket. Grabbing his night-vision binoculars, he walked out the back door.

He walked through the back gate and onto the bike trail behind his building. The trail crossed at the end and ran along the back side of the other building across the boulevard. He crept to the far end of that building until from the shadow he could see the assassin's vehicle. With his binoculars, he observed Jimmy sitting in the driver's seat. He had his left hand on the steering wheel, thumping it with his thumb. Gun-ho unlocked Gene's phone and sent a text.

"Finished. Almost there."

Jimmy reached for his phone.

Gun-ho crept along the bike path beyond the condo building so he was positioned at a 45-degree angle behind the driver's door.

In the shadows, he received a text back on Gene's phone: *About time!*

Gun-ho sent an emoji, so Jimmy's eyes would be on the phone.

He rushed the SUV from Jimmy's blind spot. Fifteen feet out, he used Gene's pistol to blow the drivers' window out.

Exploding glass stunned Jimmy.

Gun-ho grabbed the back door post with his right hand, doubled his left fist, and swung a hook into Jimmy's face. He pulled him out onto the ground and subdued him.

Jimmy was still semi-conscience from the initial punch, much less the second and third. Gun-ho tied his hands, knees, and feet, and secured his weapons. He shut the car door and picked Jimmy up, throwing the big man over his shoulder and walked directly back to his garage door.

Gun-ho opened the door with his opener, walked in, shut the door, and turned on the lights. He set Jimmy on the garage floor across from Gene. He decided to call Captain Rodgers. He stepped into his vehicle so he could keep an eye on his prisoners and they couldn't hear the call.

It was 2030 when Captain Rodgers's phone rang. "Seaman Jackson, how are things going down there?"

"Captain Rodgers, I've had an exciting evening and I need your help."

"What's going on, Seaman?"

"There is a rogue group inside the CIA. Agent Kramer, the guy who oversees my mission, told me their noses were a bit out of joint because I was given a higher clearance. They were not read into my mission. However, their noses are more than a bit out of joint—they tried to kill me tonight."

"What! You're telling me that someone from the CIA tried to do you harm?"

"Damn right. One of them shot me—twice!"

"Are you okay?—I mean, are you wounded? Where are you hiding?"

"I'm not hiding, and I'm fine.

"What about the shooter? Where did he, uh, *they* go?"

"I got 'em in my garage, both of them!"

"Are they okay? Did you kill them?"

"They're a little banged up, but they'll be okay. One of 'em told me they are being directed by an Agent Doug Collins, so what do you think I should do, Captain?"

"Stay right there. I am going to call the admiral, and he'll send NCIS to take them into custody and sweep up this Collins creep. I will call you after I talk to the admiral."

"Yes, ma'am. I'll stand by."

*   *   *

NCIS finished processing the scene at 0215 and left. Agents Jimmy Kelly, Gene Hamilton, and Doug Collins were in the brig, and an investigation was underway to determine how far the rot had spread.

Gun-ho looked in the mirror at his bruise as he headed to the shower. In that moment, he whispered a prayer

"Father God, thank you for this deliverance. I'll take it as a sign that you are blessing my mission. In Jesus' name, amen."

Three days later Gun-ho landed at Sasebo Navy Base in southern Japan to load his gear onto a submarine.

Chapter Forty-four

Implementation

At 10:00 a.m. on Sunday, March 5, 2017, Gun-ho stood on the sail of a Seawolf class submarine with her commander, making their way out of the harbor at Sasebo. They would be in position fifteen miles off the coast of North Korea in ten hours. Gun-ho descended into the boat and made his way to his quarters as they turned northwest out of the harbor entrance. The captain of Gun-ho's mission support team suggested that he rest for the next eight hours. The plan called for Gun-ho to be launched from the submarine under the cover of dark at 2300. That would give him seven hours to make it into position before dawn on March 6th.

Gun-ho lay down on his bunk and thought about everything that had happened over the last month. He went over the mission in his mind and double checked, from memory, all the gear he carefully packed onto his inflatable craft. Satisfied he was ready, he relaxed and his thoughts turned to Jae-sun and Mari. Even after eight years, the memories of the prison camp were still crisp in his mind, but somehow the pain of the camp was blurred as the love held for Jae-sun buoyed his heart, his very being.

Gun-ho smiled as he remembered the time when he was eight and Jae-sun tried to explain to him what ice cream tasted like. He'd never tasted ice cream at the camp; such an item would never be sent there.

Jae-sun told Gun-ho to close his eyes and call to mind his mother holding him on her lap, her arms wrapped securely around him, gently stroking his hair with her fingers, humming a lullaby. Once there, Jae-sun told him to imagine that feeling . . .

That is what ice cream tastes like.

The first time he tasted ice cream was just a few days after arriving at Esther Bay. His mother, mother Leetia, was clearing the table after dinner, and she causally asked, "Anyone got room for ice cream?"

He tensed up at her question, instantly calling to mind the description Jae-sun had painted. Gun-ho answered, "Yes, please."

Gun-ho looked at the bowl of vanilla ice cream mother Leetia placed in front of him. He slowly picked up the spoon and dipped, putting the spoon in his mouth and emptying it onto his tongue. He closed his eyes and took in the sensation—*wonderful*. Memories of his birth mother holding him in her arms flooded his mind.

Tears welled in his eyes.

*   *   *

Someone knocked on the door of Gun-ho's berth.

He shook the sleep from his mind.

"Seaman Jackson, it's time to prep for departure."

Gun-ho looked at his watch and realized he'd been sleeping for eight hours. He dressed in his wetsuit and made a final check of all his gear and weapons.

At exactly 2300, his team opened the hatch of the chamber where his inflatable was prepped and ready to go. Gun-ho boarded the inflatable, the hatch was closed, and he checked radio contact.

Slowly the submarine surfaced, and the deck doors opened with hydraulic rams.

Gun-ho looked up as the platform began to rise.

Once the doors above became completely vertical, they descended, leaving the side of the opening in the deck clear. As the platform reached the level of the deck, the chamber beneath him was flooded with seawater.

Gun-ho keyed the mike on his headset and informed the bridge that he was clear.

The submarine began to slowly descend. As the sub slipped beneath the surface, the seawater sloshed over the deck and floated Gun-ho's inflatable off the platform.

This is it! Here I come, Jae-sun!

He pointed his boat toward the GPS setting, happy for three-foot seas with rain and wind blowing mist off the tips of the waves—perfectly yucky weather to approach the North Korean coast undetected.

Gun-ho would be in position to submerge his inflatable in two hours tops.

Chapter Forty-five

That's all we Have

Mari counted the containers of dried food she'd stashed, just enough to barely sustain Jae-sun, Au-Jung, and herself for four days, counting today. Mari exhaled, trying to maintain a positive attitude.

As Jae-sun approached, she couldn't hide her anxiety.

He hugged her. "How much is left?"

"We have enough for four days, barely. That's all we have."

Jae-sun didn't reply; he just patted Mari's back and shuffled away.

"Jae-sun, what is the date?"

Jae-sun turned.

"It is the sixth, March sixth."

"Well, Jae-sun, at least we'll have a bit of food to celebrate my birthday."

"That's right, Mari. We'll treat it as a feast—twenty years old." He turned to walk back to the kitchen.

"Jae-sun, Gun-ho has been gone almost eight years—is he coming back?"

Jae-sun turned to face her straight on. "Mari, it is impossible for me to know for sure, but I hold hope that he will. I have faith that we will be sustained. I do pray it is soon." He turned and walked through the kitchen door.

Chapter Forty-six

Execution

Gun-ho arrived near the mouth of the river at 0100. It was so dark he couldn't see the shore, but he knew he was in the right position based on his GPS. His depth finder indicated ten meters of water.

Gun-ho put on his scuba tanks and slowly submerged the boat.

On the bottom, he unlatched his underwater vehicle from the floor of the boat and energized the electric propulsion system. The vehicle's display screen lit up in red. Gun-ho had already programmed the vehicle's GPS, the coordinates of the point he'd chosen to come ashore. The screen indicated the destination was exactly 1.2 miles from his current location.

He advanced the throttle.

Pre-programmed to maintain a position two feet from the bottom, the machine advanced slowly, its onboard sonar searching the forward path for obstacles.

Gun-ho couldn't see—he had to trust the technology.

At 0215, Gun-ho arrived. He anchored his vehicle and removed his tanks, surfacing for a breath, then submerging to retrieve his pack and a bag which were attached to the vehicle.

Moving toward the shore on the river bottom, about five feet from the vehicle, he breached the surface for another breath, then crouched down, remaining concealed in the river.

In two feet of water, Gun-ho stood and quietly placed his pack and bag on the shore. Donning his night-vision equipment, he scanned the steep bank for the best path to climb to the ridgetop. He put his pack on his back, picked up his bag, and slowly made his way through deep grass to thick vegetation growing on the slope.

The climb up the steep riverbank was about eighty meters. The vegetation reminded him of thick alder growing on the slopes above his home in Esther Bay.

Moving very slowly and carefully, Gun-ho made the top of the bank at 0400, and encountered a fence about fifteen meters ahead. The thick vegetation had been cleared between the bramble at the top of the bank and the fence. Gun-ho remained concealed on the edge and decided to sleep until dawn.

*   *   *

At 1415, Admiral Johnson called the president.

President Trump took the call. "Whatta ya got, Bill?"

"Good afternoon, Mister President, sir. Seaman Jackson is concealed and still, waiting for daylight to assess his circumstances. I will keep you posted, sir."

"Very good. Thank you, Bill."

*   *   *

At 0630, Gun-ho checked his surroundings with his binoculars. About 200 meters to his left, a road led to a guarded gate. The building stood about a half-mile directly ahead. To his right, the fence continued as far as he could see.

The end of the launch facility had big sliding-type doors. He couldn't see the far end of the building, which according to the satellite photos, also had a large door. Gun-ho planned to fly the transmitter drone to the roof and all ten camera-drones through the near door when it opened. His control range was just at a mile, so he should be able to fly them through the building and land them in the rafters. When all were operational, the entire facility could be surveilled.

At 0830 the door opened about two feet—for air flow, Gun-ho assumed.

He decided to begin placing his drones. He unpacked his controller and one of his camera drones.

He used the controller to turn the camera drone on and let it hover two feet above the ground, five feet toward the fence, out of the bramble.

He checked his image quality and flew the drone up and over the fence, then moved it 200 meters toward the building and let it hover again.

He quickly checked left and right.

All clear, he continued flying the drone toward the massive launch facility. Two decorative columns marked the end of the lane where it emptied onto a concrete apron, about ninety meters from the nearest corner. Gun-ho hovered his drone just over the right-side column, looking toward the door.

Just outside the door stood a group of men smoking.

Gun-ho landed his drone on top of the column, and from that position watched the men on his controller screen. A few minutes later the men walked back through the doors.

Gun-ho lifted his drone off the column and ducked through the open door near the top. He checked out the style of rafter—massive bar-joist trusses, probably six feet high. They spanned fifty feet from the west outside wall to a column line, then sixty feet across the center to another column line, then another fifty feet to the east outside wall.

Gun-ho parked his first drone in the middle of the center truss, thirty feet in from the door, looking straight down at the door opening. From that vantage, the drone would see everything that entered the building.

Gun-ho placed camera drones back to back on the center truss every 90 feet between the two door drones, one on each end. He checked the vantage of each with his controller. He had great coverage of the entire facility.

Gun-ho switched his controller to the transmission drone's frequency and hovered it for a few seconds. He pushed it forward, up and over the fence, then down to the launch facility.

He assessed the best place to anchor the transmission drone. The flat roof had an exhaust hood approximately every fifty feet. Each looked like it used natural convection to exhaust the building. Good. The lack of electrical motors meant fewer maintenance visits—less chance his drone would be detected in the months ahead.

Gun-ho flew the drone down to the fifth hood and hovered next to the metal flashing under the edge of the bonnet, then stuck to it with an onboard magnet three inches above the roof so rainwater would not affect it.

He deployed the antenna and slipped the drone into operational mode. Gun-ho allowed all the camera drones to send a few pictures to the memory of the transmission drone, then initiated the first transmission burst up to the satellite.

The next transmission would be in 24 hours.

*   *   *

"Good evening, Mister President," said Admiral Johnson on the phone. "Our boy has placed all his drones and initiated the first burst of data up to the satellite. We have forty perfect images from inside the facility, Mister President."

"That's great, Bill. Can we get him out safe?"

"That's the plan, sir."

"Good deal. Keep me posted, Bill."

*   *   *

Gun-ho glanced at his watch: 1030. In six hours he had accomplished most of his goal. He resisted the notion of calling it a day, lying low, then heading down to the prison camp, because Hans was depending on him to get that bomb on the truck heading inland.

Gun-ho decided to put the GPS bomb in his small backpack, then make his way west 200 meters through the vegetation on the steep slope to a point adjacent to the drive lane just outside the gate. The truck should arrive at the gate in about ten hours.

Gun-ho made his way through the dense vegetation. The road ran parallel to the top of the steep riverbank, then turned toward the gate, a distance of fifty feet. Gun-ho found a somewhat level perch to wait on, just below the brow of the bank at the apex of the turn. He hoped to hide himself on the truck's trailer when it stopped at the gate. He set his watch for 1800, hydrated, and settled in to rest until evening.

At 1750, Gun-ho turned off his watch's vibrate alarm, then stood with his eyes just above the brow of the bank. He was concealed in the foliage, able to look between leaves and branches down the road for approaching headlights.

At 2140, his patience was rewarded. Headlights approached the gate. As they drew closer, he counted three vehicles. The first flat-bed truck made the corner and stopped at the gate. The second truck stopped behind the first. Last came a large semi-type truck with the flat deck trailer that he'd seen on the satellite photos.

Gun-ho waited to see if the guard would come back to inspect the load. The driver said something through the window as the guard stepped over to the gate and began to pull it open.

Gun-ho emerged from the dense fringe, crossed the grass, and slipped behind the truck. The trailer was loaded with what looked like missile parts. He jumped up on the trailer and hid himself in the space where the round missile barrels came together. It was a small area, from the trailer deck maybe two feet high at the highest and two feet wide. Gun-ho lay between, with his head facing the rear.

The guard pulled the gate closed after the convoy moved through.

When he and the gate were separated by five-hundred yards, Gun-ho emerged from his hiding place, ready to disembark before reaching the lighted apron.

As the convoy approached the columns, the trucks slowed to maybe five miles per hour.

Gun-ho hopped off, caught his balance, then slipped over behind the right-side column.

The procession pulled onto the apron and came to a stop.

From the shadows, Gun-ho watched and waited.

The sliding doors opened, and the convoy entered.

Now all Gun-ho could do was wait.

At 0120 on March 7th, trucks approached from the far end of the facility. They lined up twenty feet from the edge of the apron and stopped 75 feet short of the column he was using for cover.

One of the drivers told his comrades he was going to go in and sleep before they headed back. The others agreed, but one of the men reminded them they needed to be on the road by 0630. They all wandered off toward the man-door adjacent to the big sliding doors, leaving the trucks unattended.

Gun-ho watched for ten minutes, then emerged from the shadows. The apron was lighted with wall pack lights; there were no pole lights.

Gun-ho moved through the dark field beyond the apron until his path to the trucks was obscured by the trucks themselves.

The first truck had boxed supplies covered by a canvas. The second truck looked like it was loaded with acetylene. That would be a nice enhancement to his gift.

He removed the GPS bomb from his pack and turned the device on. The batteries would keep the GPS and the triggering device energized for three days. He programmed a twenty-minute delay from the time the truck reached the GPS location until the device detonated, leaving plenty of time for the truck to make it inside the inland facility.

Gun-ho was working on attaching the bomb to the frame when footsteps came toward the trucks. He remained still as he watched the person walk briskly up to the passenger door, open it, and stretch as if to reach for something. The person stepped back and closed the door.

Gun-ho heard a match strike and smelled the distinct aroma of tobacco smoke invading the still late-night air. After standing there for enough time to take a few drags, the man headed back toward the launch facility.

When the man-door closed, Gun-ho breathed again and finished securing his device. He eased back to the shadows on the gate side of the column. Now he had to figure a way to get back through the gate.

Gun-ho checked his watch: 0210. The cover of darkness would be fading in about three hours. Inside the fence he had no other cover; the one-half mile buffer between the fence and the launch facility was a wide-open field. With no cover along the roadway leading from the gate to the facility, he had to get back to the vegetation growing on the steep slope of the riverbank.

Gun-ho headed back up the slight grade in the roadway toward the gatehouse. One hundred meters from the gate, Gun-ho left the roadway on the opposite side and crept thirty meters into the field to get a better view of the front of the gatehouse, and hopefully of the guard. One guard sat in the gatehouse with a kerosene lantern. Satellite images of North Korea showed it very dark at night. They didn't use their limited resources for outside lighting at night, a good thing in this situation. The lantern didn't even cast enough light to illuminate the swing post for the pole gate across the roadway from the gatehouse.

Gun-ho moved closer to the fence until he was directly in line across from the gatehouse, but thirty meters down, shrouded in darkness.

After thirty minutes, the brightness of the lantern began to wane. The guard took down the lantern and set it on a ledge behind him to pump more air pressure into the fuel tank.

With the guard's back turned, Gun-ho silently covered the thirty meters to the gate swing post, ducked under the pole, and disappeared into darkness up the roadway on the outside of the fence. Twenty meters away, he turned and watched the guard rehang his lantern.

Gun-ho crossed the road and slipped into the cover of vegetation on the riverbank—so far so good.

Gun-ho made his way back along the bank to his original position, collected his pack, and descended the bank. At the bottom, where the vegetation gives way to tall grass out to the river's bank, Gun-ho stopped and checked the time: 0445. It would be light within two hours. He'd have to wait at the toe of the steep bank until nightfall.

He couldn't risk travelling up the coast in his inflatable during daylight.

*   *   *

President Trump was seated at his briefing table, enjoying a cup of coffee, waiting for the briefing to start. Once everyone convened, a spokesman for the CIA started the meeting.

"First off, Mr. President, sir, last night at about eight o' clock a major explosion occurred at North Korea's Kim Sung-Il test facility, which is built partially into a mountain. The chatter indicates some sort of an accident. It looks like the facility completely collapsed."

President Trump cast a knowing glance at General McMasters. "That's really something. Thank you. What's next?"

Chapter Forty-seven

Channeling MacArthur

At 2200 on March 7th, Gun-ho moved through darkness from the toe of the slope across the deep grass to the edge of the river, then stepped into the water where he'd come ashore. He took his pack down to his underwater vehicle and reattached it on the rack.

Gun-ho surfaced for a breath, then retrieved his tanks. Ready, he submerged, energized his vehicle, and initiated the preprogrammed command to return to the inflatable.

The underwater vehicle's onboard computer was programmed to set the vehicle on its docking station, which was attached to the floor of the inflatable. As the vehicle maneuvered itself and settled on the docking station, Gun-ho simply reached down through the inky darkness and latched the vehicle down. He moved to the stern and reinflated the boat's air chambers, and it slowly rose to the surface.

Sitting in the boat was like being in a full bathtub. Gun-ho opened the bilge drainplug and started the motor. The forward motion siphoned the water. He pointed the boat eastward to put a little distance between himself and the shore.

Soon enough, he'd head south.

Using his GPS, Gun-ho moved two miles offshore, then turned his inflatable southward. No one could hear him this far out. The night sky was broken overcast with moonlight shining through here and there. The sea was slow-rolling three-foot waves with wide swales.

Gun-ho put his craft on step and spent as much time as he could between the crests, while maintaining his distance from shore. At fifteen knots, he'd need about an hour and a half to travel the twenty-five miles to the point he'd approach the shore.

At 0100 on March 8th, Gun-ho turned southward, now well *en route*. Now with the president's mission accomplished, he dared to let himself transition from hope to anticipation.

He held the tiller steady on his southern tact. He planned to approach the shore at a point just south of the prison gate. He'd hike through the sand mounds the half-mile from the beach to the road that approached the gate. He needed to get near the road before daylight, then remain hunkered down in the scrub brush until 0330 the following morning.

At 0215, two miles north and two miles east of where he wanted to come ashore, he stayed on a southerly tact until he was far enough south, then turned directly west to a point near the shore.

When his depth finder indicated ten meters of water, Gun-ho slipped on his tanks and deflated his boat again. Settled on the bottom, he anchored the inflatable, grabbed his gear, and started for the shore.

As he reached the surf, he slipped off his fins and put on his night-vision equipment. He quickly covered the width of the beach to reach the sanctuary of the dunes. He slipped off his tanks and hid them well; he'd not likely come back for them. He took off his wetsuit and dressed in his black field gear, holstered his pistol, checked his blade in its scabbard, and checked and loaded his suppressed rifle. He loaded his small pack with bottled water and protein bars in case Jae-sun and Mari needed them, then set off toward the road.

Gun-ho weaved through the sand mounds with the help of his night-vision gear. After ten minutes of hiking carefully, he could see the tiny glow of a candle in the gatehouse for the prison camp.

Gun-ho's heart pounded in anticipation, but he called on Jae-sun's wisdom—patience was in order. He only had 22 more hours to wait.

He pulled the crucifix from under his shirt and held it in his hand. In the darkness, he brought it to his lips and thought, *soon enough, I'll return it to Jae-sun.*

It was almost dawn.

Gun-ho moved to his left into a patch of scrub pine trees, concealing himself in the boughs. He positioned himself where he could see the gatehouse and the administration building beyond. After daylight, he'd study the area aggressively from his hide.

At 0745 the sun peeked over the horizon. At 0830 Gun-ho took a first look at the gate through his binoculars. Beyond the gatehouse he spied the end wall of the barracks through which he'd escaped. The truck—the same truck—was parked at the end of the building. Seeing it made him sad, but he channeled that into determination. Before, he was powerless and desperate.

Now he was powerful and dangerous.

At 0930, Gun-ho was watching the front of the administration building when a man walked into view—an old man, a prisoner carrying a bucket. He walked toward the hog pen between the gatehouse and the administration building.

Gun-ho's heartbeat quickened.

He shifted to his left for a better view.

It was him! It was Jae-sun!

Jae-sun stood at the rail of the hog pen and scanned the horizon toward the sea.

Gun-ho knew Jae-sun was looking for him—*had* been looking for him, every day, for all these years. He whispered to himself, "Just a few more hours, Jae-sun—just a few more hours."

At 1800, Gun-ho watched the guard change through his binoculars. He needed to get some rest. He needed to get going at 0325, and that would be the beginning of a very long day. Gun-ho found a comfortable position on the ground, completely concealed in the trees. He felt for Jae-sun's crucifix, then drifted to sleep.

Gun-ho awoke to the sound of wind rustling the boughs of his hide. He glanced at his watch: 0240. He turned off his vibrate alarm and stretched the sleep from his limbs. He ate a little food, hydrated, and picked up his binoculars. From seventy yards, he sized up the guard on night duty. The man's face was illuminated by the candle to his left. He looked to be a young man, about the same age as Gun-ho—but the guard was an obstacle. Gun-ho felt sympathy for him; these would be his last moments on Earth.

At 0325, Gun-ho positioned himself forty yards from the gate-house, directly in front of the window. Gun-ho found his target through the night-vision scope mounted on his suppressed rifle.

All his training, discipline, and determination coalesced in that moment and the moments to follow.

The unfortunate guard died instantly when the bullet entered his skull a half-inch above the bridge of his nose.

Gun-ho stepped onto the road and quietly opened the gate. He silently covered the ground between the gate and the end wall of the barracks.

Gun-ho looked across the prison yard at the guard tower just south of the administration building.

A lit cigarette glowed orange in the open-sided tower.

He grabbed the corner of the barracks with his left hand and stead-ied the rifle over his left forearm. On the guard's next drag, Gun-ho found his target.

He stepped back, reached into the truck, and put the key in his pocket.

Gun-ho worked his way northward along the front of the barracks buildings to the north end of the camp. Just east of the latrine trench stood the other guard tower.

Gun-ho paused at the north end of the last barracks building and listened.

The barracks door opened fifteen meters behind him.

A man walked toward the latrine trench. When he coughed twice, a spotlight flipped on and illuminated the yard around the trench.

Gun-ho stayed out of sight of the tower by remaining on the front side of the barracks, but he could see the prisoner at the trench being watched by the guard.

When the prisoner finished his business and turned back toward the barracks door, the guard flipped the light off.

As soon as Gun-ho heard the barracks door close again, he stood at the corner, took a rest on his left forearm, found his target in his scope, and sent another soul to his maker.

Gun-ho crossed the prison yard and stepped up onto the board-walk in front of the guard's barracks. He slowly opened the door into the hall and turned left toward the barracks door.

The interior door to the sleeping room was ajar.

Gun-ho watched the door and listened. Someone sneezed inside the guard's indoor latrine, adjacent to the sleeping room.

Gun-ho made the decision to move.

He retrieved a gas canister from his pack, set the delay for three minutes, and set it on the floor just inside the sleeping room, then retreated to a dark corner of the hall.

Two minutes later, one of the guards emerged from the latrine and walked into the sleeping room, then closed the door. The gas would release silently, and everyone in that room would sleep for approximately nine hours.

Gun-ho glanced at his watch: 0353.

He exited back onto the boardwalk. He listened and scanned the area, then moved toward the kitchen's receiving-dock door. As he reached the steps, someone in the kitchen screamed!

He moved quickly across the receiving area and raced into the kitchen just as Jae-sun yelled, "Leave her alone!"

Jae-sun flew backwards, backhanded by Mari's assailant.

Mari cowered on the floor, trying to protect herself from blows delivered by a crop.

The guard swung wildly at her. "I'll teach you to steal food, you whore! I'll teach you!"

Major Lee!

Jae-sun found his footing and reached for anything to use as a weapon. He saw motion and turned to lock eyes with Gun-ho.

As Jae-sun recognized him, his knees buckled.

Gun-ho covered the distance to Major Lee and grabbed his arm before he could swing again.

Gun-ho felt Lee's fear.

He spun him around and grabbed Lee by the neck, then held him to the wall. "Remember me, Major? *You* gave me this scar."

Mari scampered to Jae-sun's side.

Ae-jung held close to Jae-sun. "Who *is* that?"

"That is Gun-ho!"

The big man with massive shoulders dressed in black and armed to the teeth looked nothing like the little Gun-ho who escaped all those years ago, but here he was!

Mari whispered, "He returned for us!"

Gun-ho held the major up close to his face and locked eyes. Satisfied the man knew by whose hand he would die, Gun-ho crushed his windpipe with his vise-like grip.

Gun-ho lay the major's body down and turned just as Mari jumped into his arms and hugged him. "You came for us! You really came for us!"

"Happy birthday, sister."

"You too, brother!"

Jae-sun joined the embrace, tears streaming down his face. He turned and motioned Ae-jung to his side. "Gun-ho, this is Ae-jung. She's with us."

Gun-ho embraced them all. "Jae-sun, I found Bill Johnson and gave him your crucifix. He gave it back to me to bring to you. He'll be waiting for us offshore."

Jae-sun's eyes continued to flow as he received his gift, his treasured gift.

"We can't linger—" Gun-ho warned, "we have a ride to catch."

"What are we going to do?" Jae-sun asked.

Handing each a bottle of water, Gun-ho said, "We are taking the truck to the port and stowing away on a garbage scow. We need to move so we still have the cover of darkness."

Jae-sun said, "Gun-ho, Colonel Ji is a prisoner here now. I'd like to bring him with us."

Mari looked at Gun-ho to see how he'd react.

"I'd like to hear that story," Gun-ho answered, "but later. Let's get the colonel and get out of here. Jae-sun, lead the way."

*   *   *

The intrepid group arrived at the little port at 0450. The garbage scow was moored next to a boat ramp. Gun-ho pulled the truck down the ramp to the edge of the water and got everyone onto the dock, then put the truck in neutral and watched as it submerged in the black water. The tide was coming in. By daylight there'd be no sign of the truck at the port.

The gangway to the scow was down, left by the crew as they disembarked. Gun-ho and the others quietly walked up onto the deck. Gun-ho looked around and decided they'd hide in a storage room near the bow and under the bridge. He signaled Admiral Johnson that they had made it onto the scow.

Now they would wait.

*   *   *

Admiral Johnson's helicopter touched down on the deck of the *USS Ronald Reagan* at 0900 on the morning of March 9th. The ship was positioned thirty nautical miles from the shore of North Korea, due east of the prison camp—a clear calm day with a flat ocean.

The Admiral weighed the risks and decided to assemble Jae-sun's wife and Seaman Jackson's folks on the vessel. After a quick briefing, they prayed that the Admiral's optimism would be rewarded.

The Admiral and his guests were set up in the officers' mess. Commander Jones would keep the admiral, and thus his guests, apprised of progress throughout the morning.

At 0922, the commander called down to the admiral to report that the garbage scow was underway, just exiting the port, heading into the Sea of Japan.

*   *   *

Gun-ho had a view to the top of the gangway, albeit at an angle, from a porthole on the starboard side of the storage room.

At 0845, four men climbed the stairs, then raised the gangway and secured it to the side of the scow—four to deal with. Two ascended the stairs to the bridge; two probably went to the engine room.

At 0905, the ship's diesel engine started. The vibration of the idling engine indicated they were about to be underway. Having been briefed with satellite photos, Gun-ho knew the scow typically would travel seven miles due east to drop its cargo. He decided to intervene at four miles. He estimated that they were making about four knots. The ocean was calm; they were making good time.

At 0950, Gun-ho turned to Mari. "I'm going to need your help, Mari. Once we get control of the bridge, you'll need to keep the boat on course while I find the other two crew. Are you okay with that?"

Mari nodded. The storage-room door swung toward the port side of the boat. Gun-ho cracked the door and exited toward the starboard rail. He held it to let Mari slide out, then carefully closed the door. Gun-ho peeked around the corner of the storage room toward the stern. Seeing no one, he moved along the wall to the base of the stairs leading to the bridge.

Gun-ho turned to Mari. "Stay close."

Pistol at the ready, Gun-ho moved up the stairs with Mari right behind. The door to the bridge faced the stern, and it was open.

Just as Gun-ho entered the bridge, the captain turned. The business end of a pistol is not what he expected. He immediately raised his hands in submission. His 2nd mate sat on a chair, dozing. Gun-ho directed the captain to the handrail on the back wall of the bridge and cuffed his wrists to it. He tapped the sleeping 2nd mate on the toe, and cuffed him to the rail as well.

Gun-ho moved the boat's course very slightly to the south and showed Mari how to keep her on course. "I'll be right back."

Gun-ho looked out the back of the bridge, down onto the deck. Seeing no one, he descended the stairs, stepped five feet toward the stern, and cautiously peered over the rail, down into the stairwell that led to the lower deck.

Gun-ho heard two men talking, then saw the top of one man's head as he began to ascend the stairs.

Gun-ho slipped under the stairway to the bridge and let the unsuspecting crewmen arrive on the main deck. Gun-ho stepped out from under the stairs and confronted the men.

One of the men raised his hands, the other bolted to go back down the stairs.

Gun-ho fired his weapon and ricocheted the bullet off the deck just in front of the fleeing man. "The next one will hit you."

The man froze and turned with his hands in the air.

"Good choice."

He directed them to the post holding up the deck on the aft side of the bridge. He cuffed them to the post, then climbed the stairs back to the bridge.

"How are we doing, Mari?"

"Right on course."

Gun-ho checked their position: seven nautical miles from shore, five to go to international water. They were making four knots. They'd reach safety in approximately one hour.

"Shall I go check on Jae-sun and the others?"

"Sure. Don't be surprised by the two guys tied to the post down there." He walked to the top of the stairs and pointed down at the two crewmen secured to the portside post of the bridge deck.

Mari nodded and descended the stairs.

*   *   *

One of the observers of the North Korean coast guard called his commander.

"Sir, the scow that leaves the port each week is one mile beyond its approved limit, and still appears to be under power, heading toward international water."

The commander thought a moment. "Do we have a patrol close?"

"Yes, sir, we have a patrol ten miles northwest of the scow."

"Send the patrol to intercept the scow and figure out what is going on."

"Yes, sir!"

*   *   *

From the bridge of the *USS Ronald Reagan*, the radar man was monitoring the progress of the scow.

"Commander Jones, the scow is exactly one mile from international water. Two North Korean coast guard patrols are coming up fast, three miles behind the scow and gaining."

"Are the submarines in place?"

"Yes, sir. They are in place and ready."

"Good. Okay, guys, move ahead at ten knots. Send the destroyers up at twenty knots."

*   *   *

Gun-ho checked his GPS; they were approximately a half-mile from international water. He looked ahead and didn't see any friendly ships—not yet, anyway. Gun-ho walked out onto the deck behind the bridge and glassed the sea.

"Crap!"

Two miles back, two patrol boats were coming up fast from the northwest. They had to be North Korean patrols.

Gun-ho walked back to the helm and checked the GPS: 500 yards to go—not that the North Koreans would stop at the line.

Gun-ho scanned the sea ahead.

The sail of one submarine was coming toward them a hundred yards to his left, the sail of another a hundred yards to his right. The scow would slip right between them in seconds.

He turned to the door and looked behind. The two patrol boats were a half-mile out.

Gun-ho walked back to the helm. The two subs were completely surfaced, both with cannon out. They moved between the stern of the scow and the approaching North Korean patrols.

Two destroyers approached, one on his left, one on his right. They looked on course to back up the subs.

He stepped out the back again. The North Koreans were stopped, the subs between the scow and the North Koreans. They were no doubt on the radio asking what to do. On the horizon ahead, a huge ship appeared—an aircraft carrier. He squawked the carrier and looked behind again. The destroyers blocked the path of the North Koreans.

They made it!

Gun-ho brought the scow to a stop and killed the diesel engine.

A cruiser pulled up to the scow and tied on. Ten marines boarded the scow and took the North Korean crew into custody.

Gun-ho and his group boarded the cruiser. The cruiser paralleled the carrier, and the carrier crew lowered the gangway.

Geon Jae-sun climbed the steps to the deck of the carrier and was greeted by his wife and his friend, Admiral Bill Johnson.

Gun-ho arrived on the deck last, just after Mari. From the top step, he watched Jae-sun's greeting and smiled broadly.

Then Gun-ho's folks appeared from behind the throng. Gun-ho's heart skipped as he walked around the crowd and hugged his mom and dad. He turned to invite Mari forward. "Mom, this is Mari."

Leetia drew her hands up over her mouth. "Happy Birthday!" She opened her arms, inviting a hug.

Mari accepted. Gun-ho clasped his dad's right hand in his own.

The two warriors embraced.

Chapter Forty-eight

The Last Laugh

On Monday morning, June 19th, Geon Jae-sun went on the air for the first time:

"Gooood morning, ladies and gentlemen. This is Geon Jae-sun, speaking to you *live* from the studios of K-F-O-X. This is the premier broadcast of my new radio show. If you recognize my name, you'll know I've been gone for a while—a good long while. But now I'm back, and do I have news to share with you, boy do I . . .

Fresh Ink Group

Independent Multi-media Publisher

Fresh Ink Group / Push Pull Press

ॐ

Hardcovers
Softcovers
All Ebook Platforms
Audiobooks
Worldwide Distribution

ॐ

Indie Author Services
Book Development, Editing, Proofing
Graphic/Cover Design
Video/Trailer Production
Website Creation
Social Media Management
Writing Contests
Writers' Blogs
Podcasts

ॐ

Authors
Editors
Artists
Experts
Professionals

ॐ

FreshInkGroup.com
info@FreshInkGroup.com
Twitter: @FreshInkGroup
Facebook.com/FreshInkGroup
LinkedIn: Fresh Ink Group

Saturation Dive Team Officer-in-Charge (OIC) Mac McDowell faces his greatest challenge yet, leading the team into a critical Cold War mission. With a security clearance above Top Secret, Mac and his off-the-books deep-water espionage group must gather Russian intel to avert world war. Join nuclear-submariner Mac as he extreme-dives to a thousand feet, battles giant squids, and proves what brave men can achieve under real pressure, the kind that will steal your air and crush the life out of you. *Operation Ivy Bells: A Mac McDowell Mission* updates the popular bestseller by Robert G. Williscroft, a lifelong adventurer who blends his own experiences with real events to craft a military thriller that will take your breath away.

Fresh Ink Group

Four Seasons Series
Larry Landgraf